CANDACE, THE UNIVERSE, AND EVERYTHING

ALSO BY SHERRI L. SMITH

Lucy the Giant

Sparrow

Hot, Sour, Salty, Sweet

Flygirl

The Toymaker's Apprentice

Orleans

Pasadena

The Blossom and the Firefly

Pearl: A Graphic Novel, art by Christine Norrie

What Is the Civil Rights Movement?

What Was the Harlem Renaissance?

What Was Reconstruction?

Who Were the Tuskegee Airmen?

WITH ELIZABETH WEIN

American Wings: Chicago's Pioneering Black Aviators and the Race for Equality in the Sky

CANDACE, THE UNIVERSE, AND EVERYTHING

SHERRI L. SMITH

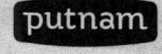

G. P. Putnam's Sons

G. P. PUTNAM'S SONS
An imprint of Penguin Random House LLC
1745 Broadway, New York, New York 10019

First published in the United States of America by G. P. Putnam's Sons,
an imprint of Penguin Random House LLC, 2025

Copyright © 2025 by Sherri L. Smith

Penguin Random House values and supports copyright.
Copyright fuels creativity, encourages diverse voices, promotes free speech, and creates a vibrant culture. Thank you for buying an authorized edition of this book and for complying with copyright laws by not reproducing, scanning, or distributing any part of it in any form without permission. You are supporting writers and allowing Penguin Random House to continue to publish books for every reader. Please note that no part of this book may be used or reproduced in any manner for the purpose of training artificial intelligence technologies or systems.

G. P. Putnam's Sons is a registered trademark of Penguin Random House LLC.
The Penguin colophon is a registered trademark of Penguin Books Limited.

Visit us online at PenguinRandomHouse.com.

Library of Congress Cataloging-in-Publication Data
Names: Smith, Sherri L., author.
Title: Candace, the universe, and everything / Sherri L. Smith.
Description: New York: G. P. Putnam's Sons, 2025. | Audience term: Preteens |
Summary: "Thirteen-year-old Candace discovers a portal in her locker that connects her across time and space with two other women who also had the same locker as girls, and the three go on to investigate the origins of the portal"—Provided by publisher.
Identifiers: LCCN 2024050980 (print) | LCCN 2024050981 (ebook) |
ISBN 9781524737931 (hardcover) | ISBN 9781524737948 (epub)
Subjects: CYAC: Portals—Fiction. | Space and time—Fiction. | Schools—Fiction. | African Americans—Fiction. | LCGFT: Portal fantasy fiction. | Novels.
Classification: LCC PZ7.S65932 Can 2025 (print) | LCC PZ7.S65932 (ebook) | DDC [Fic]—dc23
LC record available at https://lccn.loc.gov/2024050980
LC ebook record available at https://lccn.loc.gov/2024050981

ISBN 9781524737931
1 3 5 7 9 10 8 6 4 2

Printed in the United States of America

BVG

Design by Kathryn Li
Text set in Velino Ultra

This book is a work of fiction. Any references to historical events, real people, or real places are used fictitiously. Other names, characters, places, and events are products of the author's imagination, and any resemblance to actual events or places or persons, living or dead, is entirely coincidental.

The publisher does not have any control over and does not assume any responsibility for author or third-party websites or their content.

The authorized representative in the EU for product safety and compliance is Penguin Random House Ireland, Morrison Chambers, 32 Nassau Street, Dublin D02 YH68, Ireland, https://eu-contact.penguin.ie.

*To invisible women and
unpossible doorways everywhere.*

Prologue

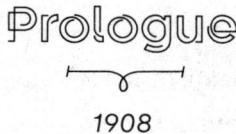

1908

EVERY THURSDAY, ELIZABETH SIMPSON STOOD ON THE sidewalk in the same spot on her way to bringing her father his lunch, skirts carefully lifted away from the mess of automobiles and horse-drawn carriages in the streets. Unmarried at nearly thirty years of age, this lunch duty was her mother's way of making her "useful," rather than daydreaming in the city parks. Not that Elizabeth was daydreaming. She was thinking. Observing. But she could do that on the way to deliver her father's lunch, too.

This Thursday, Armitage Avenue was bustling with traffic in the road and on the sidewalk. After a few close calls, Elizabeth stepped onto the grassy verge that marked the beginning of the new elementary school campus. Her father's lunch pail banged against the side of her trim jacket as she lifted her binoculars to her eyes once again.

Walden Elementary School wasn't technically a whites-only institution. But you would not find any colored students there, thanks to zoning laws and other, less documented geographies. Otherwise, she'd have walked right across that lawn and past the main school building to what she really wanted to see—the area marked off to the north and slowly rising. She trained her binoculars on the blue sky above the growing foundation.

"No need for those," a male voice said. Elizabeth felt the warmth of a body near her left shoulder. She lowered her binoculars.

"Pardon?" He was tall, broad shouldered, skin like mahogany. He tipped his cap to her. A working man's hat.

"Miss, forgive my saying so, but every Thursday I see you walk by this spot and stand here with those glasses to your face. Except most days I'm standing over there." He indicated the far side of the field where the construction workers were laying the building foundation. "And while I'm sure it's just my imagination, it seems like you've been looking at me. So I thought I'd wait here today and introduce myself. Ellis Monroe, formerly of Louisiana, currently working construction for the new school." He swept his cap off, revealing a head full of dark, soft, close-cropped curls when he bowed.

Elizabeth straightened and took a step back. "Well, Mr. Monroe, I am sorry to disappoint you. I am not interested in the labors of men. I am a bird-watcher."

She held out her binoculars. After a moment's hesitation, he took them.

"Where am I looking?" he asked. Elizabeth smiled, although the man could not see it. That he was interested pleased her.

"Northeast of the cornerstone," she said. "About twenty-three feet up."

Ellis Monroe moved the glasses with the precision of a land surveyor, which, it turned out, was one of his jobs. "All I see is blue sky, miss," he said apologetically.

"Keep watching," she said. They stood together for a full five minutes, the man not complaining once.

"I'm afraid my lunch break will be over soon," he said, still keeping his eyes on the spot.

"And I'm far too late delivering this lunch pail," she agreed. "My father is a mason in the stone yards past Halsted." She reached for the glasses. Reluctantly, he gave them to her.

"Never knew bird-watching's like fishing. Lots of waiting and hoping," he said. He gave her a look. A warm look. One that she found herself returning. "But I'm a patient man. Maybe we can try again tomorrow."

She did not know whether to take offense or allow the blush that rushed to her cheeks to fluster her. "Good day, Mr. Monroe."

"Good day, miss," he said. She hadn't given him her name, and he did not push his luck by asking.

The next time Elizabeth saw Ellis Monroe, the first story of the school had risen from the ground and the framing was beginning on the second. Soon her birding spot would be on the inside of the building. It was in this state of disappointment that she spotted him striding toward her, a roll of dark papers in his hand.

"I haven't seen you around," he said by way of greeting.

"There are other birds to watch, other roads to walk," she replied. The fact was, she'd been afraid to see Ellis Monroe again. He had seemed so warm, so familiar, it had alarmed her. Elizabeth had planned on spending the rest of her life tending her parents into their old age. A spinster. Not someone who grew flustered at the attentions of a handsome man.

Instead she had come on weekends, when the construction crews were at rest, and watched the strange spot in the sky.

"What's that, Mr. Monroe?" she asked. He held up the roll of papers.

"Blueprints, miss. You see, I've been watching that spot you showed me, northeast of the cornerstone, twenty-three feet up? And I've seen your bird."

Elizabeth's stomach did a little flip.

"I've seen it swoop in and out of God's creation, like a—"

"Like a window in the sky," she said. He smiled.

"That's exactly right. Like a window in the sky."

She returned his grin. Then he remembered the blueprints.

"'There are more things in heaven and earth, Horatio, than are dreamt of in your philosophy,'" he quoted Shakespeare as he unrolled the sheaf before her. "It seems we are about to entomb one of the wonders of the universe."

The blueprints showed clearly where the second-floor corridor would seal the strange window away for good.

"I was afraid this was the case," Elizabeth admitted.

"But it doesn't have to be," he replied.

"What do you mean?"

"I mean, I'm the draftsman for the architect. And I've moved a few fixtures around. Nothing to harm the structure of the school, but . . ." He showed her a second sheet, this one a closer view of the north hallway interior. "They plan on lining the hallways with cupboards for students to store their coats and books inside. No dragging them around on book straps like we used to do, if we were lucky enough to go to school."

Which, clearly, he had been.

"Would you tell me your name, miss?" he asked suddenly.

"Elizabeth. Elizabeth Simpson," she said, surprised. "My people came up from Mississippi," she added, recalling that his were from Louisiana.

"Miss Elizabeth Simpson, formerly of Mississippi, I would very much like to give you a piece of the sky." And then he showed her a certain locker, tenth in the row on the far side of the hallway. "Number 235. It will fit around your window in the sky."

"So the birds can still pass through from wherever they come from," she realized aloud.

"So the birds can still pass through."

They held each other's gaze for a long moment. And Elizabeth Simpson never did become a spinster, but a wife and a mother and a bird-watcher and a science enthusiast. And in time, a grandmother called Meemaw by her granddaughter, Loretta Young. And this story, the story of her life, would be the first of many stories shared over Loretta's crib and on Elizabeth's knee, about locker 235, the window in the sky.

On Thursdays, the sky windows opened and the birds of unordinary colouring escaped their invisible world. Dorianna placed a ladder in the woods, climbed to the sixty-first rung, and pressed her eye to the peephole there. What wonders she saw I shall endeavor to recount, for she told me herself what miracles came to pass in that land beyond the sky.

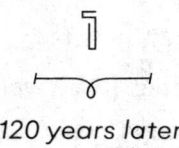

120 years later

"CANDACE!"

Candace Wells nearly dropped her phone trying to shove it into her pocket. Totally *not* glooming over photos of her best friend and her next-best friend having fun camping without her.

"Nadiiiiiine!" Candace screamed back, swinging her best friend into a hug. Sure, she'd seen Becca's pics from when she and Deen went to the movies together, and the mall. And that was totally fine, Candace supposed, even if they hadn't invited her. But an actual camping trip? She'd just pretend she didn't know about any of it. She'd fall back on what she was supposed to know about Nadine's last weeks of summer vacation. "How was—were—the Philippines?"

"I don't know the grammar!" Deen bounced as they spun around. Similar back-to-school reunion dances were happening up and down the hallway. "But the trip was great! My lola cooks even better than my mom! Candy Cane! Look at your hair! Is it . . . ?"

Candace broke into a grin. "DPS, Goldengrove Unleaving!"

They both squealed. The Dyed Poets' Society box had promised "lyrical locks" with their poetry-themed colors. Candace's new look was a teeny-weeny Afro in a rich golden yellow that made her brown skin look warm and sunny.

"Cool," Sergio said. Sergio had surprised everyone and delighted several of them with a growth spurt over the summer. His spiky black hair only added to his height. And apparently, he'd been working out, if you were into that kind of thing. Candace caught the look on Deen's face. Oh, she was definitely into that kind of thing.

Deen blushed.

"Nacho cheese hair," Nate crowed. Nate was Sergio's reverse shadow—white, with dirty-blond hair, slender, and a half foot shorter. He looked like a clothes hanger holding a plaid flannel shirt over a faded black tee and jeans, even in the August heat.

"Ignore him," Deen said, rolling her eyes. "It's gorgeous. I was going to go for the Baudelaire, but it was just too many colors and I ran out of time."

Right. Because of the glamping trip with her brother, Mac. And Becca.

"No worries," Candace said. "We can do it this weekend. And I'll wait for our This Is Us drawing, so it can be in full color." Every year on the first day of school, Candace drew a This Is Us picture. She had a whole book of them, starting in kindergarten, in which she and Deen had grown from little stick-figure doodles into full figure drawings, now that Candace knew more about shading and proportions. They had joked it could be a flip-book about growing up.

"Oh. I can't," Deen said. "I've got church and then I've got blah blah blah. Blah blah blah."

Which, to be fair, was probably not what Deen was actually saying, but it's what Candace heard. She and Deen always hung out on the weekends. Summer was a bit different because of family vacations, but this wasn't summer. This was This Is Us time.

"Church is Sunday morning," she said.

"True," Deen said. "But—"

"Unless you go camping," Candace muttered, and turned to her new locker, number 235. She began fumbling with the combination.

"Oh, Cans, you saw . . . It's not what it looks like," Deen said.

"Fun? It looked like fun. But if you don't want to hang out, just say so."

Now was when Deen was supposed to apologize and they'd work things out. When she'd say, *Of course! Come to church with my family! We'll make a day of it!* like they used to when it was just the two of them. But the longer Deen stayed quiet, the harder Candace stared at her locker.

"Hey, girlfriend!" Becca appeared on the scene. She was wearing the same shoes as Deen. Even the laces matched.

"Candace . . ." Deen said.

But Candace wasn't listening. She could feel tears stinging her eyes. Her face was hot. She unlatched her locker.

And it exploded.

Okay, not exploded, but basically exploded. The door flew open and banged against the neighboring locker. And something, some . . . *thing* . . . burst out of the locker like those joke cans of soup with spring snakes inside.

Candace threw her arms up and screamed. The thing screamed too. It was black and white, and she was hoping it wouldn't be red all over, because if it was, it would mean her face was being scratched by talons and she would be horribly scarred for life all because she was in the eighth grade and had a monster in her locker.

Candace wheeled backward and landed on the ground with hard thump. Sergio, Nate, and the other kids were shrieking and shouting, laughing, pointing.

And then a tall Black kid opened the hallway window. And the bird flew away.

"Happens more than you'd think," he said, and reached down a hand to help Candace up. "Birds in the school. Lockers, not so much. Are you okay . . . Candace, right?"

"Right," Candace croaked, letting him pull her to her feet. "Thanks . . . Mitchell?" He was from the other eighth-grade class, the one that ran parallel with Candace's own, but with a different teacher in a different room. Walden had two of every grade, K through eight. Everyone knew everyone, but only kind of, because of it.

"Yeah!" Mitchell said, looking pleased that she knew his name. He dropped her hand. "No problem."

Mitchell swung the window shut and ducked into his classroom. The bird was long gone. She hoped she hadn't hurt it with all the arm waving and terror.

"What's the ruckus?"

Mr. Jones, Candace's new teacher, stuck his head out into the hallway.

"There was a bird in my locker," Candace explained. She was still kind of shaken. Mr. Jones noticed.

"How about you take a moment to get yourself together. Join us when you're ready."

"When I'm . . . what?"

Mr. Jones pointed at her head. She reached up and felt feathers in her new 'do. Oh, great.

"I'll grab you a hall pass. You can go to the office and ask the janitor to sanitize your locker."

"I bet it pooped in there," Becca said helpfully. Nate snorted. Sergio grinned.

"Are you okay?" Deen asked.

"Yeah." Candace chuckled nervously. "I'm fine. It just startled me."

The bell rang and the boys fled. Becca tucked her arm through Deen's.

"Remember those birds over your brother's tent?" she said, laughing as if whatever she was talking about was the funniest thing in the world.

"See you in there," Deen said over her shoulder. And then Candace was alone.

She pulled her phone from her back pocket. By some miracle, it wasn't cracked or broken by her fall. Then she reported the bird to the front office and was rewarded with a canister of industrial disinfecting wipes and a pair of rubber gloves.

"Either that, or wait until after school," the office admin lady said. "Budget cuts."

Candace trudged back up the stairs with her cleaning supplies. Why had she thought eighth grade would be so great? Kindergarten—now, that was great. If she were still in kindergarten, she wouldn't even have a stinking locker, or a cell phone to show her pictures of her friends having fun without her. Instead, she'd have a wooden cubby and a hook in the classroom, and Mrs. Davis or the class aide would clean up any bird poop or other mess that came her way.

Eighth grade meant so much more responsibility.

It stank.

Candace banged her hand against the locker door to check for more bird monsters. Nothing. She stepped onto the rim of the locker to peer into the top cubby. Darkness. And a faint scent of . . . Doritos and pop?

Cringing just a tiny bit, she reached a rubber-gloved hand into the abyss . . .

And yelped. Something was in there. And it wasn't bird poop.

She took a deep breath and reached back inside, patting around like a cat under a bathroom door, and hit something. She dragged it forward into the light.

It was a notebook.

A regular composition-style notebook, kind of retro-looking, with a purple cover and a strip of black tape on the spine. In the white box that said SUBJECT on the front, someone had written in purple ink: *What You Need to Know. For Girls Like Me.*

Inside, the first page was a handwritten table of contents with entries like

Body Stuff
Death Stuff
Hair Stuff
Homework
Friends

Candace's mom had told her about body stuff and death and hair. Everyone had something to say about homework. But friends?

She flipped to the Friends section.

And there, in fat bold letters, were the words *These People Are <u>Not</u> Your Friends.*

The *Not* had been underlined twice.

Whoa.

It felt like a sign.

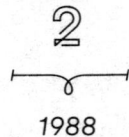

1988

"SHE KNEW YOU'D GROW UP, RIGHT?"

Tracey Auburn wanted to bury her face in her locker. If she could just get it open. She spun the combination lock dial over and over, but she was still holding on to the book tucked under one arm, and her vision was blurred by unwanted tears. She hated crying, hated the way being upset made her feel sweaty, made her hair frizz even though she'd pressed and curled it extra carefully that morning. The way internal emotions leaked out, all salty and snotty. For the last two years, she'd worked hard to keep that from happening.

Her best friend, Dia Andres, hadn't even noticed.

Dia looked like the cover model for *Seventeen* magazine's back-to-school issue—a tweed blazer, vest, and pleated miniskirt, popped white collar with a giant brooch at the throat, Trapper Keeper binder in the crook of her arm, her dad's old leather satchel slung over the other. She leaned against her own locker, number 234, on the second floor of Walden Elementary, and folded her arms superiorly.

"I'm just saying, if I died and left my daughter gifts like your mom did, I'd make sure they were age-appropriate, not childish, you know? Like, we're in eighth grade! She should have given you *Flowers in the Attic* or a subscription to *Seventeen*, or something by Judy Blume."

Tracey stopped fumbling. She and Dia were wearing the same white shirt, the same sweater-vest, only Tracey had on stretch pants with her penny loafers. Which made everything just that much worse, like she was a copy that couldn't get it right.

"Shut up, Dia! *Your* mom wouldn't let *you* read *Flowers in the Attic*. Why would mine? She chose these books for *me*! So just shut up about it already."

Dia scowled at her, nose wrinkling, freckles dancing on her olive skin. "What's your damage?" she asked. "We agreed this was *our* year. We're supposed to shine. Hard to do with you toting a musty old children's book around."

Tracey wanted to kick Dia in the shins. Not that she'd ever do it. But sometimes her best friend really bugged her. Everything had to be about Dia. It had to be Dia's way. But what about Tracey's way?

Okay, so maybe Tracey didn't have much of a way, but she did have this, her mother's birthday gifts. That was the thing about knowing you were going to die: You could plan ahead. When her mom got sick and knew she wasn't getting better, she had planned gifts for the next eleven birthdays, all the way up until Tracey turned twenty-one and graduated college.

At first it had been terribly sad. No gift could replace her mom. Then it was sort of exciting, as Tracey realized her mother still loved her no matter how far apart they were in time and space. And sometimes it was a little eerie. Like, how had her mother known she'd want hair scrunchies to tame her hair when she turned eleven, and a charm necklace with her name written in gold cursive at twelve? She wore one of the scrunchies now, her dark brown natural hair pressed and gathered on the side of her head into a once-smooth ponytail that was now frizzing with anxiety.

After her birthday dinner last night, her father had given her his usual sad Mom-present smile, and slid the package across the table to her, a big rectangle with an uneven feel along the sides when she ran her hands over it. That was the best way to open a Mom present, slowly, anticipating the gift, appreciating the moment.

Tracey had untied the ribbon and set it aside—she was a fan of purple. That much, at least, hadn't changed. And then she'd peeled away the tape, tearing the paper just a bit, which made her cringe. Her mom had picked this paper out. She wanted to save it forever.

And then the present was revealed. Presents, really. A set of hardcover books, the kind bound in cloth, which made them look old-timey. She read the spines. Each said *Skylark* in golden ink, with the numbers one through five etched beneath the word. She ran her fingers across the cloth, rough but also sort of smooth. The books made up the colors of the rainbow, red, orange, yellow, green, and blue. They stopped before purple.

"Your mom bought these for you when she found out she was pregnant," her dad said. "Anything folks said was great for kids, she ran out and got." He laughed. "You had three years' worth of clothing before you were even born. And these books, waiting for you to be old enough to read them. When she got . . ."

Her dad cleared his throat. "Well, I guess I forgot all about them, but she remembered. They're collectibles now. She wanted me to give them to you when you could take care of them properly."

Tracey had smiled and picked up the first book, the red one. "*Window in the Sky*," she read from the cover, "by G. Edward Macey. Shouldn't this one be sky blue?" She'd sniffed the book, the way her mom used to. It smelled warm and dusty and actually kind of gross, but it was a book. It smelled bookish. "I love it," she'd said.

And she did. So much that she'd read it in bed last night, and on the walk to school, and all the way up to her locker, where Dia had taken one look at the cover and opened her big fat mouth.

Said big fat mouth was now trembling with annoyance, as if Dia had so many angry things to say that she couldn't get them all out at once.

Which, for some reason that probably wasn't very nice, made Tracey feel better.

She stopped fumbling, opened the lock, and unhitched her locker door. Opening it would be kind of like shutting the door in Dia's face, which she really wanted to do right now.

"Tracey—" Dia began.

Tracey opened the locker and hung up her backpack, ignoring the dank smell that sometimes wafted from the top cubby.

"Tracey!" Dia exclaimed. "You're such a child!"

Tracey unzipped her backpack. She pulled out school stuff—her Trapper Keeper, her purple notebook with her purple pom-pom pen stuck between the pages, her English book—and shoved some of it into the upper cubby. Heat was rising in her face. She was going to full-on cry, or scream, or *show her feelings* if she didn't hurry up and get out of there. She shuffled through her bag and pulled out what she needed for the first half of the day.

She grabbed her school books. Her palms were sweating, like she was crying through her hands. She untucked her chin and added *Window in the Sky* to the pile in her arms.

"Tracey," Dia said. "Bird!"

Something black, white, and beaky shot through the air toward Tracey's face. She screamed. Ducked. And it flew into her locker. Into the top cubby. With her stuff.

"Dude!" Jason Kemp shouted from the locker across the hallway. "A bird just totally dive-bombed Auburn! It's probably, like, crapping in her locker right now." Jason Kemp was kind of a jerk. And he was loud. Everyone in the hallway stopped gathering their books and turned to stare.

Tracey closed her eyes and counted ten slow breaths. When she opened them, Dia was still there. And so was Jason.

"Are you okay?" Dia asked.

"That bird totally attacked you!" Jason crowed. "Right at your face!" He peered into the darkness of the upper cubby. "Must've flown out when we were . . . I'd get a new locker, man. That was wild. Get it? A wild bird?" He belched into the locker. It echoed, spreading a faint scent of Mr. Pibb and Doritos.

"Later." He dropped his skateboard with a clatter, hopped on, and rolled away to class.

"Gross," Dia said.

Tracey clutched her books to her chest. She'd seen the bird fly over her head. Black feathers. Striped wings.

It couldn't be.

She looked down at the novel on top of the stack in her arms. *Window in the Sky*. A book about a magical place. With talking magpies. That looked just like that.

"Earth to Tracey," Dia said.

Tracey blinked. This was the real world. The bird was just a bird. Sparrows and things got into the building all of the time.

"We're going to be late," Dia said.

"I . . . I need my pen."

Dia took off, shaking her head. Tracey banged on the underside of the cubby shelf. If the bird was still there, wouldn't that scare it back out again?

Nothing moved.

Cringing, she reached into the upper cubby of her locker, hoping the bird really *was* gone.

It was.

And so was her pen. And her purple notebook.

Wait—had she unpacked them, or left them at home?

Tracey stepped up onto the lip of her locker's threshold and peered into the cubbyhole. Something was back there.

She pulled it into the light.

It was a pen. Not *her* pen, but a fountain pen. Purple, old-fashioned, fat barreled. Like the ancestor to her purple pom-pom pen. The class bell rang.

Tracey glanced up and down the hallway. She was alone.

She peered into the darkness of her locker and whispered, "Hello?"

But no one answered back. And she was late for class. She looked at the pen again. It looked almost new. It would have to do.

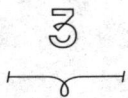

CANDACE STARED AT THE WORDS ON THE PAGE IN FRONT of her. *These People Are <u>Not</u> Your Friends.*

It was like the notebook *knew*.

It knew that Deen had ditched her for Becca and that Candace had had to ask her *mom* to help with her hair instead.

It knew that Becca was replacing Candace as Deen's best friend, even though Candace and Deen had been "Candace and Deen" since kindergarten, and *Becca* had only been part of "Candace and Deen and Becca" since fifth grade.

So at lunch, when Candace found Becca and Deen giggling together on the way to the cafeteria, and heard Deen whisper, "Sergioooo," Candace grinned and said, "What are we laughing at?"

"Oh, you won't get it," Becca replied. "That camping trip was so *balk*!" *Balk*, Candace presumed, was a new best friend term they would let her in on. But Becca just grinned at Deen, gave Candace a shrug, and said, "I guess you had to be there."

I'm here now, Candace thought, but then decided she didn't have to be. Instead, she took the purple notebook and herself outside, where she ate her sandwich morosely on the Walden Elementary playground with her back up against a maple sapling, and opened up the notebook.

A little bird landed in front of her expectantly, so she dusted the crumbs of her PB&J off her lap and onto the grass.

"Hope you don't have a peanut allergy," she said.

The bird pecked the grass and didn't die.

It stood there for so long, Candace decided to draw it. Candace loved to draw.

She opened the purple notebook. The second half seemed empty of advice. She flipped to the last page and began a quick sketch. But as she drew, the image morphed from the little chickadee in front of her to the terrifying black-and-white bird that had flown out of her locker and scared the bejeezus out of her. She drew the bejeezus moment. It was pretty realistic. Enough to make her heart race. She snapped a picture of it with her phone and saved it in her "Not Bad" digital sketchbook, which until now was mostly full of pics of her annual This Is Us portraits of her and Deen, along with the least-wonky drawings of her family and things that didn't move, like shoes and landscapes.

She finished in time to see the real bird fly away.

"You and everyone else!" she called after the bird, and signed her drawing with her signature, *Candace!* Then she flipped to the Friends section of the notebook again.

These People Are Not Your Friends.

Candace's stomach twisted again. A purple arrow was drawn in the bottom right-hand corner. She turned the page and read:

Everything is not okay, is it?

No, it was not.

Do you have a sinking feeling in your stomach?

She did. That funny feeling hadn't gone away with the

PB&J. And it *did* feel kind of like sinking, like the first drop on a roller coaster, but one that never ended.

Do you feel like your friends don't have your back?

"Huh," Candace murmured. That Mitchell kid had helped her up from the floor this morning, not Deen or Becca. And she had definitely had to clean her locker on her own.

Are you feeling left out, left behind?

"Yes," Candace whispered.

Do you want to know why?

"Also yes, please," Candace said. Another purple arrow. She turned the page.

These people are not your friends. Even if they used to be. That's life. Everything changes.

Candace stared at the page for a long time. It wasn't like the notebook was talking to her or anything. But . . . it was like the notebook was totally talking to her or something. Which was ridiculous. Most likely.

She followed the arrow to the next page.

So what can you do?
1. Identify the Problem.
2. Examine a Course of Action.
3. Attack!

Wow. It was way more aggro than Candace had expected. Besides, how was she supposed to identify the problem? It was either Becca or Deen . . . or Candace herself . . . right?

She turned the page.

Identifying the Problem.

The heading had a double underline beneath the words. Ah. Super useful.

This is the easy part. Problems are archetypes, symbols that appear again and again and again, like history repeating itself. After sixth grade, the subsets tend to be as follows:
1. *Queen Bees*
2. *Bad Boys*
3. *Sponges*
4. *False Alarm Clocks*
5. *Rope Bridges*
6. *Proximity Pals*
7. *Packs*

Queen Bees: If your group has a center, they are the Queen Bee. The rest are drones. Don't want to be a drone? Consider becoming a Solitary Bee, without a hive. (Lone Wolf sounds better ... Think about that.)

Becca was obviously a Queen Bee. Which was why being left out stung so much.

Bad Boys: These are people we're attracted to because they are bad. Rule breakers. Risk takers. Parents and teachers hate Bad Boys. (See Jason Kemp. He even smells bad.)

Did Candace know any Bad Boys? Was Sergio a Bad Boy? Mitchell wasn't. Right?

Sponges: These are your friends who like all the things you like, as long as you liked them first. This includes music, food, and crushes. Spill your guts, and the Sponge soaks it up. And suddenly what you like, they love. It's their whole life! And you look like a dabbler. (Have I been a Sponge? Is Dia my Queen Bee?)
False Alarm Clocks: Do you have a dream or something you hope will happen? Well, don't tell a False Alarm Clock. FACs tell you to wake up and stop dreaming, or that your dreams aren't worthwhile. Probably because they don't have any dreams of their own. (See Practically Everyone.)
Rope Bridges: These are the people who are supposed to get you through hard times. But sometimes they just flip on you, and down you go. (See *Temple of Doom*. See Dia, again.)

It was information overload. Who wrote it? And where did it come from?

Candace flipped to the front of the notebook again, and there it was, written on the inside cover: *Tracey Auburn, Fall '88*.

As in 1988. Or 1888—but that seemed unlikely. They both did, really. How had no one found it, or cleaned out the locker, in forty years?

But then again, here she was getting the inside scoop on the year ahead. Let Becca try to keep up with that! She kept reading.

Proximity Pals: aka "class friends." You meet them on the first day of class and act like friends, but it never goes beyond the classroom doorway.

Oof. That was harsh, Candace thought. But also . . . Merida Sayers, from the other eighth-grade class. She was super nice. They'd taken an after-school art class together last year. Was she even still at Walden?

Packs: Friends, like gum, or pop, come in packs. Do you have a group of five friends? Six? Take another look. Who in your group hangs out together when the others aren't around? That's right, a six-pack is usually made up of two-packs. A five-pack is two two-packs and a spare. Are you a spare? Would you like to be? (See Solitary Bee/Lone Wolf.)

Candace and Deen had been a two-pack once upon a time. Becca had been the spare.
Candace's stomach clenched. She was the spare now.
The end of lunch warning bell rang. Candace headed back to her locker, wondering if there was some sort of test to find your true pack. But the next page of the notebook was blank, and the page after that.
She opened her locker, checking for birds, and dumped the notebook in the top cubby with a sigh. It looked like Tracey Auburn's purple notebook didn't have all the answers after all.

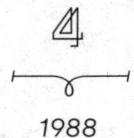

1988

TRACEY FRETTED ALL THROUGH THE PLEDGE OF Allegiance and English and history. Not just about Dia, or her own frizzing hair, but also her missing purple notebook. It was a secret. Like a diary. But she'd brought it to school because she had things to say. Not very nice things. Not the kinds of things you said out loud.

Like how Dia wasn't a very good friend.

Or how the worst part about Dia was that she was probably right. Tracey was thirteen now. Not a little kid.

If her mom had really wanted to help her out, instead of fantasy books, she should have given Tracey a bunch of advice. Like how to grow up. How to be a teenage girl. How to figure out who people really are, and how your best friends can hurt you. How even the people who claimed to love you could make you feel bad.

Because the truth was, Tracey felt bad. A lot.

The truth was, she missed her mom.

And she was angry. Angry that she had to be the kid without a mom, the kid whose dad had to take her shopping for a training bra and deodorant, had to help her buy lady products. The kid who had to turn to magazines to learn about shaving her legs and what to do about cramps and pimples and taming her hair. Not a lot of magazines said what to do with Black hair.

And she was angry that Dia didn't get that, and that Tracey didn't know how to make her understand.

So she'd written it all down in her secret purple notebook to give to her own daughter one day. Just in case she wasn't there to tell it all herself.

Tracey's stomach shriveled. Maybe it was just hunger, but she'd written some pretty mean things in her notebook, and now it was gone. Anyone might have it.

The bell rang for lunch. Tracey raced back to her locker. She dialed the lock, opened the door, and ducked—but no birds flew out. Then she went through her backpack one more time.

Her hair was a mess now. Sweaty palms and a sweaty scalp, and she was frizz city.

She climbed onto the rim of the locker again and reached into the cubbyhole—bird or no bird, she needed to find her notebook. Had Dia taken it? Maybe in the fuss about the bird?

And then her fingers touched something, way back, so far back it made her armpit ache to reach for it. There. She dragged it with the tips of her fingers, then her whole hand.

And breathed such a sigh of relief that it prickled through her whole body.

Her notebook! Safe and sound.

But where was her purple pom-pom pen?

Outside, Tracey let the breeze soothe her worrying. She carried her lunch bag and her notebook and the new old fountain pen behind a tree on the playground. Plopping to the ground, she wiped her hands on her mint-green stretch pants and unloosed her ponytail. She smoothed it as best she could, retied it, and braided the end so that it would keep some sort of shape now that the curl had frizzed out.

Dia knew how to do French braids.

Tracey ate her PB&J quickly, washing it down with a carton of fruit-flavored drink, then opened her notebook. She'd write something about her terrible morning. Dia. The bird. The ridiculous thought that the bird had something to do with *Window in the Sky*. About how she'd just turned thirteen and was pretty sure she wasn't good at it.

She flipped open the notebook to the Friends section, past the glossary of types, until she found a blank page. It stared back at her. She had a new entry to add: *Sometimes you lose people. They go away and they never come back. And there's nothing you can do about it. You just have to be okay with that. Even when you're not.*

She'd been writing about Dia, but rereading the entry, she realized it applied to her mom, too. Had her mom also been her friend? Tracey flipped away from the entry, biting her bottom lip. The twinge of pain echoed lower in her gut. Her mom had been her first best friend.

Laughter drifted across the blacktop. Tracey looked up. There was Dia with two other girls, gossiping and giggling over a magazine. Probably *Seventeen*. Totally age-appropriate. Not childish. Not like Tracey.

Tracey scowled and scratched the pen angrily across the new page. The breeze picked up, rippling the pages, flipping them faster than she could stop them. She slammed a hand onto the last page, before the book could skid away.

And there, underneath her palm, was the bird.

Not an actual bird.

A drawing of a bird.

The bird. The one from her locker. In full black-and-white glory.

It was beautiful. And terrible. And *unpossible*.

And it was signed *Candace!*

Tracey frowned. Who the heck was Candace?

5

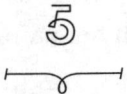

THE REST OF CANDACE'S DAY WAS SORT OF WHATEVER. Mr. Jones had everyone brainstorm science fair projects. "Maybe you can study birds that live in lockers," he joked. Candace didn't think it was funny.

After science, Candace dumped her stuff in said locker—no birds this time—and went to gym class. She got a stinging burn on her leg from an especially hard throw while playing dodgeball, which was a form of torture as far as she was concerned. And then, finally, it was time to go home.

She was hoping tomorrow would be a reset. She would come to school, be happy and friendly to Deen and Becca, and they would eat lunch together again. And she'd show them that bird drawing she'd done. (Maybe she *should* do birds for her science project.) She might even give the drawing to Deen, like a placeholder, a joke version of This Is Us. She could draw herself and Deen, terrified. They'd laugh, and things would go back to normal.

Candace fished around in her locker for Tracey Auburn's notebook. She hadn't meant to throw it so far back. Climbing onto the lip of the locker, she lunged and snagged it with her fingertips, drew it into the light. She flipped toward the last page—and stopped.

There was new writing in the notebook. In the Friends section. This time it wasn't in purple. The ink was black, and it was . . . different. Like the same handwriting, but a different kind of pen, with wider, flowing ink.

Sometimes you lose people. They go away and they never come back. And there's nothing you can do about it. You just have to be okay with that. Even when you're not.

Something fell inside of Candace, like a little spark falling away into the dark. A shudder ran through her brain. Was she going to lose Deenie? Could she change that? Hoping for answers, she turned the page.

FREAKING DIA ANDRES! GET LOST!

What?

"Who the heck is Dia Andres?" Candace asked the book. And who'd been inside her locker?

This was just too weird. She looked up and down the hallway, but no one was watching her like this was a prank. Just forget it, she decided, and thumbed to the back of the notebook. She'd take her bird drawing and then throw the notebook in the trash. Dia Andres, Tracey Auburn. Whatever.

But the bird drawing was not there. Where it should have been, there was only a soft tatter of paper stuck in the spine. Someone had torn it out.

Candace looked around the hallway again. Still no one was

pointing and laughing. Plus, she *had* locked and unlocked the locker. No one could have gotten in except maybe a teacher, but why would they? Kids whose lockers got searched usually knew, because they were in trouble.

Candace stared into her locker. Something was going on. She had no idea. But maybe Tracey Auburn did.

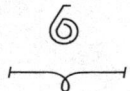

"CANDACE! HOW WAS THE BIG DAY?" HER MOM WANTED to know when she picked Candace up after school. Candace pulled out her earbuds.

"What?"

"Don't 'what' me. I asked how your big day was. How'd the hair go over?"

"Fine." Candace really didn't want to talk about it. She put her earbuds back in. But her mother's mouth was still moving. "Sorry?"

"I said, what color did Deen choose?"

"She didn't."

"What?" Her mom turned around in the driver's seat. "That's . . . odd. You guys do everything together."

"Did," Candace said. Obviously, this wasn't going to go away. She sighed and put her earbuds down. "She and Becca went camping with Mac instead, and they don't even like camping." Neither did Candace, really, but that wasn't the point.

"I'm sorry, hon. There must have been a reason."

Yeah, like not wanting to be friends anymore. "Mom, how do you know if you are proximity pals or, like, just temporary?"

"Good question." Her mom pulled into the left lane. "Time

will tell, usually. People grow apart, or they grow closer together. Is that what you think this is?"

"I don't know."

"Do you want it to be?"

"I don't know."

Her mom's phone beeped. "Hold on, honey, I've got to take this call for work." Her mom tapped her earpiece. "Janice! Yes, I was thinking we could—"

Candace put her earbuds back in.

Ever since her mom's promotion, it was like this. Too busy to talk. Which normally was fine. What was there to talk about, anyway?

―H―

"Mom, how do you look up obituaries?" Candace called into the living room later that night, where her mother was actually watching the evening news, like she didn't have a computer or something. Candace had her laptop out on her bed, ready to hunt down Tracey Auburn.

"Local papers," her mom called back. "The *New York Times* website, if they're famous . . . or TMZ." Her mom appeared in her bedroom doorway. "Commercial break. Who died?"

"Oh, no one we know." Candace pulled out her earbuds. "I found a notebook at school that looks like it belonged to someone who went there back in 1988. I just want to know what happened to her."

Her mom plopped down onto the bed. She loved a mystery. "What makes you think she's dead?"

Candace popped the bubble she'd been blowing. "I don't know. I mean, 1988, right?"

She had said the wrong thing. She could tell by the way her mother's eyebrows moved inward. And then her mother crossed her arms, which was a bad sign.

"How old do you think I am?"

"I don't know. Forty-three?"

Her mom scowled. "Surprisingly accurate. But I was alive in '88, the actual twentieth century? If she was in eighth grade then, she's probably only a few years older than me, and likely very much alive."

"But—" Candace said.

"But . . ." Her mom held up a finger. "You can check the school's alumni newsletter. They usually list deaths of alums there."

"I—" Candace said. Her mom lifted another finger. Candace closed her mouth.

"Or you can just google her and see if she ever left Chicago. Commercial's over," she said, and left. Like you couldn't just pause TV.

"Okay. Thanks, Mom."

A few finger strokes later proved her mom a genius.

Tracey Auburn was very much alive. And she was still in Chicago.

A professor at an actual university.

With an actual email address.

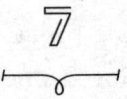

Dear Professor Auburn,

    My name is Candace Wells. I am in the eighth grade at Walden Elementary, which used to be your old school.
    I think I found your purple notebook in my locker. Would you like it back? Please respond.

Sincerely,
Candace Wells

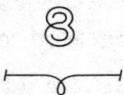

"WHAT ARE WE DOING HERE AGAIN?" CANDACE'S MOM pulled into the parking lot of City College and hung up her phone. It was the Wednesday after Labor Day, and Candace was nervous.

"Just dropping something off. That notebook? I found in my locker?" Candace said. Her palms were sweating. It wasn't a lie or anything. But it was sort of an ambush. The first week of school had rolled by with no response from Tracey Auburn, so after the holiday, Candace had decided to take it straight to her office. Without telling her. Which, to be fair, she would have done if Professor Auburn had written her back.

Her mom undid her seat belt. "Right. The ghost. Well, let's get this over with so you can go back to being a normal kid."

"Hey!" Candace said, dragging her backpack toward her. "This is normal! And you don't have to come. I'll be quick."

Her mom ignored her, and soon they were walking through a metal detector and following the guard's directions to Tracey Auburn's office on the second floor of the English department.

The closer she got, the more Candace's heart pounded until it filled her ears. The purple notebook in her bag. The woman she was about to meet. It all added up to something that made Becca and Deen seem insignificant. Like maybe this was some kind of hidden-camera TV show. Or maybe, just maybe, real space-time continuum stuff. Either would be pretty cool.

"Here we go," her mom said, reading the plaque on the door, PROF. TRACEY AUBURN, MA. She was reaching up a hand to knock when her phone rang. "Shoot. Honey, I've got to take this. I'll be right here. Don't take too long."

A piece of paper was taped to the door with some sort of class code on it that Candace couldn't decipher. Candace knocked, heart pounding louder than her fist.

"Enter," said a husky female voice.

Candace opened the door, and there she was. An attractive older Black woman sitting at a big old oak desk. The real live adult Tracey Auburn.

"Um . . ." Candace stood in the doorway, clutching her bag. The woman behind the desk looked up.

"Hi. Come on in," she said, as if she had been expecting Candace.

The woman turned back to her computer screen. Candace edged her way inside. She felt dizzy. Not actually dizzy, but a weird sense of mental vertigo, like reality and unreality had just been superimposed in her brain. She sat down. The chair was real at least, hardwood, straight-backed, and severely uncomfortable.

"So, hi!" the woman said again, looking up from her monitor. She gave Candace a practiced smile. Brown eyes, brown skin, dark brown relaxed hair. She looked like a talk show host in her gray blazer, tasteful rose-colored blouse, and thin gold necklace. "You're thinking about taking Comp 102?"

"Are you—" Candace started and stopped. How could she explain it?

The woman frowned. "You're awfully young."

"What?"

The woman reared back. "You're not one of my students."

"Oh, no," Candace said. "I go to Walden Elementary?"

The woman picked up a beautiful old purple pen, the kind with a nib instead of a ballpoint, and put it down again. She closed the cap with a snap. "Huh. Let me guess. Are you asking for money? Is that what they're doing these days, sending kids to do their dirty work?"

Candace pinched herself through her coat. "Are you Tracey Auburn who went to Walden back in 1988?"

"Sorry, kid, I'm not giving money. I'm a college professor. An *adjunct*," Tracey said, like that was a word Candace should know, and not a very good one. "I went to public school for a reason. You tell them I'll give when I see them bring back the school library."

"I'm not here for money," Candace said. "My name is Candace Wells? I emailed you? About this?" She pulled the notebook—Tracey's notebook—out of her backpack and held it up. "'What You Need to Know. For Girls Like Me'?"

Candace once saw a nature documentary about the melting glaciers in Alaska. Sometimes a glacier breaks off a baby glacier. It's called calving. A whole icy chunk just snaps and shears off, leaving a smooth cliff face behind with a big groan.

Tracey Auburn's face calved. Confusion, fear, surprise, joy, all sort of jammed up in the place between her forehead and her eyes, and then . . . dropped. Leaving a smooth blankness behind.

And then she said, "I'm sorry, but office hours are for students. Enrolled college students. Have a nice day."

"But I thought—"

"Yes?" The woman gave Candace an expectant look that said questions would not be welcome. Candace tried desperately to formulate one anyway.

"Professor?"

They both turned to see a pimply-faced guy in a seriously bold striped shirt smiling apologetically. "We have a four o'clock."

"Yes, we do, Eric. Come in." Professor Auburn turned to Candace. "As I said, enrolled college students. Please shut the door on your way out."

"Wait! Do you at least have my bird pic—" Candace managed to say before she found herself back in the hallway, Eric the legit college student shutting the door in her face. And then her mother, still on her call, appeared, smiling, and steered her toward the stairs.

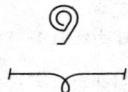

TRACEY STARED INTO SPACE. WAS SHE SWEATING? SHE was starting to sweat. She blinked and tried to focus on her student, Eric, who was in mid-plea.

"So if I could get an extension, I'd really appreciate it . . ."

Tracey nodded to indicate she was listening, but instead of opening his file, she opened her email.

"It's just that I've been really overwhelmed . . ."

There. Candace Wells. *I think found your purple notebook in my locker.*

"Professor?" Eric asked. Tracey blinked. How long had she been ignoring him?

"Um . . . sorry, Eric. There are no extensions. But you still have two days."

Eric's face fell, but Tracey wasn't even pretending to pay attention anymore. Her purple notebook. The missing purple notebook. The one she'd thought had been stolen. The one she'd been so terrified Dia would find . . .

"Are you ignoring me?" Eric asked.

"No!" she said. But she was. Tracey spun in her chair. Behind her, on the credenza, was a framed drawing. "You should probably get going. Every minute counts."

Eric clutched his bag to his chest and scrambled out of his chair.

"The library's open until ten p.m.!" she called after him.

She picked up the picture frame. It was old. At least forty years. The drawing inside was a bit faded by time. She peered at the signature. *Candace!*

"Unpossible," she said.

Everyone knows there are doorways in the earth, caverns, tunnels, even the cellar beneath your own house. But just as surely as there are doorways down below, there are windows in the sky. Dorianna had been through doorways her whole young life. But this window was the first.

"SERIOUSLY?" CANDACE MUTTERED.

"What?" Cerise had the locker next to Candace's. They weren't exactly friends, but she was nice. Unlike the person strutting toward them.

"That," Candace said.

"Curled up and dyed, fools!" Becca sauntered down the hallway, adoring sixth and seventh graders gawping as she glided by with Deen on her heels. While Candace was being kicked out of Tracey Auburn's office, Becca had undergone a transformation. Baudelaire's Mille Feux from Dyed Poets' Society had turned her long dark hair into a veritable bonfire of color. Her newly layered locks, dipped in shades of auburn, burgundy, pale blond, and deep gold, put Cerise's pink-tipped natural blond shag to shame.

"Becs, that's awesome," Sergio said, appearing out of nowhere.

"Way awesome," Nate echoed.

They were right. It looked amazing. *Becca* looked amazing. Who managed that on a Wednesday night? It had taken Candace two days to do a single shade.

Cerise followed Candace's flickering gaze. "Huh. Somebody dropped a load of cash for that," she commented, and zipped up her backpack. "Later, Wells."

"She *paid* someone?" Candace gasped. She'd used all of her own allowance just to buy the do-it-yourself stuff.

"Yep," Cerise said, walking backward into the crowd. "Super popular at my mom's salon. For, you know, rich people."

Candace involuntarily cupped a hand to the back of her head, as if she could hold her hair on, or change it somehow. Because she wanted to change it now. To make it not just surprising, but better. And also, was Becca rich? Or just bad with money, like her mom said about people who bought more than they could afford.

"Looks great!" she said as Becca strolled past her. "You too, Deen."

Deen had at least kept one promise and dyed her hair, too. But she'd gone with Homer's Wine-Dark Sea, even though she'd said *she* wanted the Baudelaire. And worse, she'd skipped the bleach, so what little color there was looked more like a whisper than a shout.

"You like it? I think it's kind of . . . understated," Deen fretted. "It looks better in sunlight. Full sunlight."

"It suits you," Becca said.

"Aw, thanks!" Deen cooed.

"Great," Candace said, just to have something to say. Then she got really interested in her locker because her fists were clenching, and that hurt because she was holding her house keys.

Becca wasn't just a Queen Bee, she was also a Sponge. And Deen was just letting Becca sponge all over her. Which sounded gross, and it *was* gross, in a different way.

Candace swallowed hard and got busy rushing to class so she wouldn't say anything she'd regret.

One thing was abundantly clear: These people really were not her friends.

⁓H⁓

When Mr. Jones announced the end of the day, Candace loitered in the back of the classroom, looking at the row of paperbacks in the free lending library. The last thing she wanted was to talk to Deen or Becca. Or worse, not talk to either of them as they headed off together in their new little twindom. So she lingered, and ended up finding a book on wildlife drawing.

From his desk, Mr. Jones looked over his glasses and said, "I used to be quite the artist back in the day myself. Comic books. Superheroes. Monsters... I loved drawing monsters."

Which was kind of hard to imagine, really. Mr. Jones was just so... normal.

He cleared his throat—and the dreamy look from his face—and stood up, straightening his glasses. "There's another book on perspective over there if you're interested."

She was.

"If you're serious about doing birds for your project, you can actually tie your science and art together," he added, taking the book from the shelf. "Look at statistics for bird populations, consider the science of migration, and since I see you doodling every day, look at this!" He flipped the book open to a page entitled "The Golden Ratio." It had a photograph of a nautilus shell with a diagram over it of a rectangle with smaller rectangles and squares marking different places on the spiral. "This is a mathematical equation called a Fibonacci sequence. It appears all over the place in nature. Like cauliflower, seashells, even people. Read up on it. It will help you get your proportions right. Ask Ms. Parker in your next art class. She'll help you out."

Ms. Parker was the school's art teacher, only she taught every grade and sort of floated around the school. Candace's next art class wouldn't be for a week. She thanked Mr. Jones and took both books with her.

The halls were almost empty when Candace reached her locker and reorganized her backpack with homework for the next day. The purple notebook was still right where she'd shoved it in the back of her bag after the embarrassing trip to Tracey Auburn's office. She scowled at it, and at her locker. Then, on a whim, she felt around the top shelf cubbyhole. Nothing. No birds had come back. No new surprises had appeared. Notebooks didn't actually time travel. Lockers were just stinky metal boxes shoved into the walls of miserable institutions.

Candace shuffled down the stairs and out the front doorway. School was just school. Candace wasn't lucky or clever or special. She was just—

She checked herself. Downward spirals like this usually meant one thing. She was getting her period. Just like every other unremarkable teenage girl. All she wanted now was potato chips and a chocolate bar. Even her cravings were cliché.

"Excuse me."

"What?" Candace snapped. She wasn't in the mood to chase down a stray kickball or talk to a dog walker or—

"Kid."

"What?" Candace turned around.

It was Tracey Auburn. Here. Outside Walden Elementary. With a briefcase over her shoulder. And a framed illustration in her hand.

"Did you draw this?" she asked. She held the picture up.

It was the Bejeezus Bird Attack.

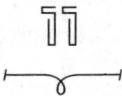

11

CANDACE'S PHONE BEEPED.

Her mom texting. **Stuck in a meeting. 30 minutes late.**

K. I'll be on the playground.

That was one good thing about elementary school—you could always sit on the swings.

Which was a funny look for Tracey Auburn, but she went with it anyway. She sat with her nice shoes on the ground, manicured hands wrapped around her swing's chains.

"This is so weird," Professor Auburn said. Which, of course, applied to the whole situation. But then she added, "This used to be a park. Like a little green field. They just paved it over, like in the song."

Candace didn't know any songs about playgrounds. Not that she was thinking of one. *She* only had eyes for the thing in her lap. Her drawing, with her little signature in the corner.

It looked older, as if it hadn't been sketched fresh just a week ago. A little faded and crumpled. Torn at one edge. She'd forgotten how well the plumage had turned out, fractured like broken glass mosaicked back together again with the white streak still visible, but incomplete. She really should have torn it out of the notebook the day she drew it. But that was back when notebooks didn't travel through time.

"Why is it framed?" Candace asked.

"Because it's a bird of unordinary colouring." Professor Auburn looked intently at Candace as she said it.

"A what?"

Professor Auburn frowned and said it again, slowly, like she was teaching Candace a new phrase in a foreign language. "A bird. Of unordinary. Colouring."

A kickball sailed passed them. They both watched it arc away and bounce against the side of the school. A fourth grader ran to fetch it.

"Right. But what's that?" Candace asked.

"Ungh!" Professor Auburn kicked in her heels and leaned back in her swing. Candace winced.

"Is this a test? That I absolutely failed, or something?"

When she swung forward again, the professor looked different. Her whole body seemed looser. Younger. "I thought you were pranking me the other day. But then I remembered the drawing and... Well, it's a pretty elaborate prank. But you're telling me you've never heard of a bird of unordinary colouring?"

"It's not a prank," Candace said. Even though she'd thought the same thing.

"*Window in the Sky*?" Professor Auburn continued. "The Skylark books? God, what do you kids even read today?"

"Graphic novels and the internet," Candace said. "*Skylark*... Wasn't that a movie, like, a million years ago?"

Professor Auburn's eyes narrowed. "There *was* a movie, but it wasn't Skylark. It was trash. They just used the name to sell tickets, but changed the entire story. I hate it when they do that. Just so some little white kid in Peoria feels seen."

"Whoa. Professor Auburn, you're a fangirl?"

"Fanwoman," Professor Auburn grumbled. But there was a tiny little smile fighting with the right side of her face. And she began to swing. "And please, call me Tracey.

"Anyway." She reset the conversation. "I do happen to love those books. And when this picture showed up in my notebook back in '88, a.k.a. 'a million years ago,' I kept it. I thought someone was breaking into my locker. Like this kid Jason Kemp. Wonder what happened to him. At any rate, he was also there when . . ."

"When what?"

"When . . . the other thing happened." Professor Auburn—Tracey—trailed off, remembering. "Did I dream that part? That can't be . . ."

"What part?" Candace asked.

"A bird that looked like this . . . flew into my locker in eighth grade." She paused and took back the drawing. "I must have dreamt it . . ." Her hands were trembling, the framed drawing quaking slightly in her grasp.

Candace's whole body ignited like a live wire, electricity arcing from every fingertip. "It flew out of my locker last week!" she said.

"What? The same bird?" Tracey's voice was now shaking like her hands.

"Different decade," Candace confirmed.

Tracey leaned against the swing chain and said, "Unpossible."

Which must have meant she was really surprised, too, because that wasn't even a word.

The Garden of Uneaten Things had grown smaller, which should never happen for things that have not been eaten.

"But that's unpossible!" Steedy neighed.

"You mean *im*possible," Dorianna said.

"No, not at all! Many things are possible for imps. That's what 'impossible' means. Devilishly tricky little creatures, imps. They get up to all kinds of astonishing things. But '*un*possible' means the complete absence of possibility.

"It's simply not possible for all of the Uneaten Things to disappear entirely. If that were true, this garden wouldn't exist at all."

The garden *did* exist, even Dorianna could see that. Just not as much as it apparently had before.

"What makes the unpossible possible?" she asked. But Steedy shook his head. He didn't know.

12

TRACEY AND CANDACE STOOD AT THE TOP OF THE second-floor staircase of Walden Elementary.

"This is all so surreal."

"I bet," Candace said. "I never want to come back here when I'm your age," she added.

Candace spun the dial on the locker while Tracey scanned the row. "They're . . . What is this color, beige? They were orange when I went here."

Candace popped open her locker door. A smell wafted out, only this time it was less like nacho chips and more like the mouth of a cave. The air felt different. "It's got something to do with the top shelf," she explained. Candace took off her backpack and pulled out the notebook. Tracey made a whooshing sound with her breath.

"Can I see that?"

"It's yours," Candace said.

Taking the purple notebook from Candace, she shook her head. "I've been at this school, looking at this view, with this book before," she said in a list-making sort of way that sounded like she was trying to convince herself. "Whoa. Déjà vu."

"You said that already," Candace said.

Tracey frowned. "Wait, did you just quote . . . What's that from?"

"I have no idea. My mom says it. I think it's from the eighties, so I'm speaking your pop cultural language to make you feel more comfortable."

"Funny, kid," Tracey muttered. She paused a moment, smoothing her hand over the cover, then flipped the notebook open to the first page. "How is this even possible? I thought I'd lost this. I was so afraid Dia had found it, or that creep Jason Kemp." She shook herself and closed the book. "What happens next?"

"I guess I'll write something in it and put it on the shelf, and we'll see what happens?" Candace pulled a pen from her backpack.

"Do you think I'll just suddenly have a new memory?" Tracey asked. "Or will, I don't know, will we have jet packs or something? Time paradoxes in movies are always so *big*. I hope we're not breaking the time line."

Candace laughed. "You really *are* a sci-fi nerd. I don't think it's that deep. I mean, we've done it already, so if we broke the world, I guess it's already broken."

"Oh, it's broken all right, but I don't think *we* had anything to do with *that*," Tracey said wryly.

"Well, don't look. I'll write something, and we can see if you remember it." She scribbled *This is Candace* on the notebook's new last page. "Should I say anything encouraging, like, 'you'll be a great professor someday'?"

Tracey blanched. "No! We . . . don't want to mess with the future, right?"

"Good point." Candace closed the notebook and put it on the top shelf. She shoved it as far back as she could and shut the locker door.

"How long does it usually take?" Tracey asked.

"I don't know. I mean, I didn't know it was happening at first, and then it could be a while before I looked again." She glanced at her watch. "Plus now it's after school, so maybe she's gone home. I mean, maybe you've gone home. If time runs the same in each . . . time." She suddenly felt squirmy. "Maybe we should just check it now."

Tracey looked squirmy, too. "It's not even been a minute. Let's give it ten minutes," she decided.

They waited. The last few kids jumped down the stairwell. The school seemed to sag, empty but for a few tired teachers and staff.

For the first time, Candace noticed the curve in the ceiling of the hallway, "coved" it was called, like a little chapel, but long and straight and dotted with LED lights. And then the lights shut down, and the sun through the classrooms was the only source.

"It's pretty when it's empty, in a way," Tracey offered. Candace had just been thinking the same thing.

Tracey glanced at her watch. "Time."

"Do you feel anything? Any new memories?"

"Nope."

Candace opened the locker and dragged the notebook down. She flipped to the last page and took a deep breath. "Whoa."

On the last page, in elegant purple script, someone had written:

Loretta Spencer. 123 Robinson Lane, McHenry, Illinois. I'll be waiting.

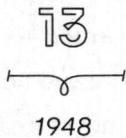

1948

"SO YOU FINALLY GOT IT, HUH?"

Loretta Young looked up from her field notes and into a pair of dark brown eyes in even darker brown skin. She smoothed her dress, flipped her notebook closed, and capped her purple fountain pen. Her last year of elementary school was just beginning, and so were her observations.

"Excuse me?" she said.

"That locker," the boy watching her said. "I've seen you looking at it for forever, like the last lollipop in the candy store, and now it's yours."

Loretta grinned.

"That's right. I sweet-talked Mrs. O'Donnell in the front office into making this one mine."

Loretta always made sure to offer to help out in the office before school started. She ran the mimeograph machine, cranking out copies and delivering them to the different classrooms.

"You'll make a wonderful secretary," Mrs. O'Donnell liked to tell her.

Loretta would say *I hope not* to herself and "Yes, ma'am" out loud with a smile.

Now she smiled up at her new locker, industrial-looking

green powder-coat paint over steel. A small brass plate read 235 over a series of five vents in the door, to allow for airflow.

"But why?" the boy wanted to know. Loretta knew who he was, of course. Steven Horatio Loman. He was in the eighth grade, too, though they'd never really spoken. Loretta knew everyone by name—including their middle names—thanks to her field notes and her special office access.

"I'm a scientist," she said.

Steven looked at the locker and back at Loretta.

"All right, Miss Scientist. What's so special about 235?" he asked.

"Everything," she replied, and held out her hand. "And my name is Loretta."

"Folks call me Stevie." He took her hand and shook it firmly, but not too firmly. His palm was warm and dry.

"A pleasure, Steven." When his eyebrows went up, she added, "I don't want to be like most people."

"All right." Steven leaned against the wall, his long legs making him look like a giraffe. Which gave her an idea.

"Can you help me?" she asked. He straightened up. She tucked her notebook under her arm and riffled through her bookbag. "Do you think you could put this on the top shelf of my locker? It's got to go way in the back, and I don't think I can reach that far."

"Sure, but . . . is that a sack of . . . birdseed?"

"That's right." She thrust it into his free hand and dialed the combination on the locker door for her first look inside.

The part she could see was a bit disappointing. It looked

just like her locker from last year at the other end of the hallway. But the upper cubbyhole. Now, that was interesting.

"Do you smell that?" she asked. A cool, almost cave-like smell drifted from the upper locker.

"Do I want to?" Steven said.

Loretta laughed. It was a big laugh, too big for her frame. Her aunt said it was horsey, but it was also a family trait. Loretta's horsey laugh neighed around the locker and set Steven laughing, too.

"You trying to catch rats or something?" he asked as she took back the little sack of birdseed and poured the contents into a shallow dish she took from her bag.

"Or something," Loretta said. "Here you go."

Steven slid the dish of seeds into the top cubby.

"Push it back as far as it goes," she said.

She opened up her notebook again and jotted a few notes with her fountain pen.

Steven was still there when she finished. "Thank you, Steven."

"Walk you to class?" he asked as the warning bell rang for first period.

"Sure."

He was smiling at her. She smiled back, and—*bloop!* A bird flew out the locker, singing.

"What the—" Steven said as it winged its way down the hall.

But Loretta forgot all about Steven. She was following the bird.

"You dropped your pen," Steven called. With a sigh, he picked it up and put in on the locker shelf for safekeeping.

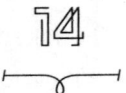

14

"THAT'S UNPOSSIBLE," TRACEY SAID. SHE LOOKED FROM the locker to the notebook. "Did this really just happen?"

"Yes?" Candace wasn't sure why she sounded unsure. She had seen it. Written it. Found Tracey. It was *all* happening. "Should we go? To McHenry, I mean?"

Her brain, no, her whole body felt like a shaken bottle of pop. Fizzy. About to explode.

"Maybe . . ." Tracey's watch beeped. "Gah. I've got to go. Um . . . McHenry. That's somewhere toward Wisconsin. I've got class tomorrow, but Saturday's free. You?"

"Saturday, sure," Candace said. Sure what, though? *Sure, I'm free to take a road trip with a strange adult to an even stranger adult outside the city limits?* "I'll have to ask my mom."

Tracey's face rearranged again. "Right. A mother. You're a kid, and we don't technically know each other. Um . . . can I meet her, maybe? Or I could just go and tell you how it went."

"No way," Candace said. "This is, like, the only cool thing that's ever happened to me. I'm coming. Going. Whatever. I'm coming with. My mom will understand. I'll tell her it's a field trip."

"On a Saturday?" Tracey said dubiously as they headed back down the stairs.

"It's fine. She's got a deadline. I can say I'm with Deen."

Overhead, a bird flew through the closing door into the school. Tracey gawped.

"That was it! A bird of unordinary colouring!" She turned around to go back into the school, but the door had locked behind them. "Darn it! Do you think it's going back to your locker?"

"I hope not. My locker's closed, anyway."

Tracey's watch beeped again. "Look, I have an evening lecture. Can I drop you off at home or something?"

"No, my mom's picking me up. You could meet her now . . ."

A look Candace recognized flickered across Tracey's face. Panic. "I think I need a minute. But soon, yeah?"

Candace's stomach fell. "Sure . . . but, Tracey?"

"Yeah, kid?"

"Thanks for believing in me."

"I believe *you*, not *in* you, Candace. You're not the Easter bunny. But thank you for finding me. I'll see you Saturday. Email me the address—after you talk to your parents." Tracey hurried away across the park to her car.

"Wait, you forgot your—" Candace looked at the notebook in her hands. "I guess I'll keep it for you," she muttered.

"Who was that?" someone said behind her. Candace jumped. It was Deen.

"Hey! I mean . . . Heyyy . . . Why are you here so late?"

"Looking for you! We need to talk," Deen said.

"What? Okay, yeah," Candace agreed. "I've missed you—"

"Are you mad at me?" Deen asked. She looked like she'd been crying and then had splashed cold water on her face, making her cheeks match her red eyes. The effect was alarming. Why did people do that? Was the extra water supposed to camouflage tears?

"What? What happened?" Candace asked. She reached out for her friend, but Deen leaned away.

"Answer the question. You're avoiding me and not talking to me—are you mad at me?"

Candace shrugged, dropping her eyes. "I don't know," she mumbled.

"Well, you're being really unfair! Asking me to choose between you and Becca?"

"Wait, what?" Candace's spine straightened like a fireman's ladder. "Who said that?"

Deen wavered uncertainly. "Becca? And Sergio?"

"Becca *and* Sergio? Since when do you listen to Sergio?"

Deen blushed, and Candace gasped. "You *like* Sergio, don't you?" It was weird. Obvious, but also weird. And the kind of thing a best friend should tell another best friend.

And then Candace remembered Deen and Becca whispering at lunch. Over Sergio.

"Deen—" she began. And had to stop because maybe, just maybe, this was what it felt like for a heart to break. "Deenie," she began again. "I never asked you to do anything, did I? Except hang out and dye our hair. If that's having to 'choose' between me and Becca, I'd say it's Becca who's asking you to choose between her and me."

Deen looked startled. "What? That's not true! You don't even know what's—" She stopped, blinked. "Becca said—"

"Geez, Deenie! Think for yourself! Becca isn't your brain!"

"And you're not a true friend!" Deen wailed.

"What?"

"I didn't mean that," Deen said quickly.

But Candace couldn't hear her over the sound of a heart that was definitely shattering now. She walked away, trying not to run.

Thankfully, her mother was waiting at the curb. Candace got in, stuffed in her earbuds, and slumped in the back seat.

"Well, hello to you, too," her mother shouted over the sound of angry girl band music.

"Hi," Candace grumbled. She should probably talk to her mom. Her mom would understand. "Sorry. I—"

"Just a sec, hon, have to take this," her mom replied, and tapped her earpiece.

Candace would tell her later. About being friendless and miserable. Oh, and about Tracey Auburn and Loretta Spencer, and why she needed permission to take a road trip with a relative stranger to visit a complete stranger who, from the quick search she did on her phone, didn't have any social media accounts. Honestly, she could be going to McHenry to be murdered. She should tell her mom. Or her dad. Which one of them would be most likely to let her do the thing without worrying she'd be kidnapped or just disappear?

It wouldn't be so bad to just disappear for a while, would it? Maybe the world would fix itself while she was away.

"Explain this to me again," Candace's mother said that night, dishing out bowls of chili mac.

"It's a field trip," Candace said. "Up to McHenry. Research for a thing at school." So far, nothing she'd said was a lie.

"An overnight thing? Why didn't I see a permission slip?"

"Not overnight, but I don't know how long it'll go. But there'll be an actual professor there from City supervising."

"In McHenry? Who else is going?"

Candace dug up a lie. "Becca and Deen and me, some other kids. It's for the science fair."

"Sounds cool. Okay. I'll need a name and contact info. I'll send some pocket money to your phone. Call me when you get there and when you're headed home. I love you. Taste this." Her mother kissed her cheek and thrust a wooden spoon loaded with chili at Candace in one swoop.

"Good. Hot," Candace said. "Love you too."

And that was that. A shiver of shame ran through Candace, but she kissed her mother back.

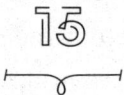

THE NEXT DAY AT SCHOOL WAS AWFUL. LIKE, BROKEN-air-conditioner-in-a-heatwave-lunch-fell-into-the-gutter-surprise-test awful, even though it was a Friday. Candace took her seat in the back of the classroom, the penalty for a last name that started with *W*, which meant she could see Deen and Becca whispering to each other. Mr. Jones's weird seating chart had somehow managed to put them exactly side by side. Last year, the class sat in little clusters, and Candace was closer to friends. She supposed it made sense now, that she was in the back.

Mr. Jones talked about how the class could do STEM or STEAM projects. He seemed to be looking directly at Candace when he said that meant art could count. Then he paced around the aisles announcing the pop quiz on the reading from last week.

Candace might have disappeared from the earth as far as Deen and Becca were concerned. And Sergio and Nate. Sergio kept watching Deen and Becca, which was good for Deen, Candace supposed. But the way Becca was looking back at Sergio didn't seem good for anyone. And Nate just looked annoyed. Which was bad for Nate.

No one looked at Candace. Well, except for the adults at the school. Mrs. Higbee in the front office smiled at her. Mr. Jones saluted her when she thanked him for the new book. And the janitor nodded at her when she was the first one in the hallway after school. The first one out the door and down the stairs, waiting for her mom to pick her up.

And tomorrow was Saturday. The trip to McHenry.

Candace stood a little straighter as Becca and Deen passed her by on the sidewalk, whispering loudly to each other in that we're-ignoring-you-but-you-can't-ignore-us way. From the whispers, they were going to have a sleepover that weekend.

But Candace was going to explore the space-time continuum, so take that.

"Yahtzee," Candace's dad said.

"Pictionary," her mom countered.

Dinner was over, the table cleared. For some sad reason—maybe because they sensed Candace no longer had any friends—her parents had declared Fridays to be Game Night. It seemed like a very white thing to do. The families in ads for board games were never Black. When Candace had pointed this out, her mother had held up a box that said Pictionary—Black History Month Edition. Which had made her laugh enough to agree to play something. But that had been Wednesday night, when the plan was first announced. Now it was Friday, and the world was a flaming bag of dog poo. Plus she had the illicit road trip to McHenry tomorrow with Tracey. And that had her stomach in funny knots that felt different from the friendship knots that had just unraveled in her chest.

"Cans?" her mother prompted.

Candace slumped onto the table. "What's the point?"

"Family time," her father said. "A chance for us to catch up after a hectic week." He looked at her mom as he said it, clearly reciting something she'd told him. She nodded her head slightly, and his face brightened like he'd been given a cookie.

"What's there to catch up on?" Candace said, smearing her cheek against her outstretched arm.

"That's what we'll find out. Over a friendly game of . . . Life?" her mom suggested.

"Black History Edition?" Candace mumbled.

Her mom picked up the box. "No, it's Underrepresented Peoples Edition."

Candace made a sound that could be spelled *p-f-f-t*. "I don't want to play."

Her dad actually looked relieved. "This means I can watch—"

"No, Carl," her mother said sternly. She stacked the game boxes and put them aside. "This means we can just sit together and talk. I'll make cocoa," she added. The cocoa was literally the only thing that kept Candace from slumping out of her chair and onto the floor.

"Candace," her dad said firmly. "Sit up and act like a person with bones."

"I don't want to," Candace said.

"And I don't want to drink cocoa and talk about our feelings, but I am a grown-up, and I will do it! And you, young lady—"

"I'm just a kid—"

"Are a *young adult*. And you will act like one, too. Just make your mother happy, or I *will* make you sad."

Candace turned to look at him. "How?"

Her dad blinked. "What do you mean, how? Everything you have right now is because of your family. I control your food, your clothes, your high-speed-internet access, the roof over your head. Which one of those would you like to go without for a week?"

Candace sat up grumbling. "You'd starve me?"

"Probably not," her dad grumbled back. "Just . . . just let's do this so your mom can stop hassling me."

"What's she so worried about?" Candace pulled her seat in closer to the table and crossed her arms over her chest.

"You, Candace. You've been more frazzled and mopey than usual. I tried to tell her it's because you're thirteen, but she—"

At that moment, her mom returned holding three mugs by their thick ceramic handles.

"You didn't start without me, did you?" she asked. She beamed at them, shoving what looked like icebergs of marshmallow in a chocolatey sea toward each of them. Sitting down, she claimed the third mug for herself and wiggled her bottom in the chair.

"No, not really," Candace's dad said. "We were just talking about the challenges of being thirteen in this day and age."

Candace's mom got a hungry look in her eye. "Oh, do tell. What's going on, Cans?"

Candace sighed and took a fortifying sip of her hot chocolate. It was thick and bittersweet—70 percent dark cocoa was the trick. And a pinch of salt. Soooo good.

"Deen and I are over. Becca's convinced her I'm trying to make her choose between us, which I absolutely am not. But if I were, I'd say choose me because Becca's a sponging Queen Bee and she's totally making eyes at the boy Deen likes, and that's not something I would ever do, and not just because Sergio's a dork, either, you know?"

Candace's dad's eyes had glazed over. They narrowed briefly at the mention of a boy, then glazed again when it was clear Sergio was no threat. Candace's mom, on the other hand, looked like a kid in a candy store.

"Oooh, that's awful! One time, I liked a boy, and I told my friend Maria, and the next time I saw her, she was arm in arm with him flirting up a storm, and I was like, 'I can't even believe you.'"

"Rude!" Candace agreed.

"I tell you, some women, some girls."

Candace's father concentrated on his cocoa. Savoring each sip.

"Well, I say Deen's a smart girl. She'll come around. And if she doesn't, you're better off without her," Candace's mother said. "Right, Carl?"

"Sure," Candace's dad bleated. Candace's mom shoved her chin toward him. He sat up straighter. "Um . . . and how's school?"

"Oh, she's got a field trip to McHenry with a college professor!" her mom announced.

"What's in McHenry?" her dad asked.

"Just a . . . thing for school." Candace covered her lie with another gulp of cocoa.

Her mom frowned. "Tell us more about this 'field trip' without a permission slip. You said you'd be with Deen and Becca. Is that not the case?"

Candace's stomach roiled.

"It's kind of like . . . an alumni thing? That professor, Tracey Auburn—"

"Of the mysterious notebook?" her mom asked.

"Yeah. She actually went to Walden in 1988. We're going to visit another alumni—"

"Alum," her father corrected.

"Alumna if it's a woman," her mother added.

"Alumna," Candace said. "Loretta Spencer. She lives in McHenry. It's like . . ." Candace's brain whirled for an explanation that didn't mention space-time portals or lockers.

"Like a legacy circle!" her mom offered. "That's fantastic. Connecting kids with past graduates so you can see the future. Especially now, right before high school. It's such a pivotal year. And I hear it's working wonders in colleges, especially ones with low numbers of Black students. Knowing the path was blazed before you can really build a solid foundation for your future. I approve!" her mom said with a nod like a judge's gavel.

"When's she picking you up?" her dad asked.

"Ten?" Tracey had texted her at lunchtime.

"Well, ask her to come early so we can meet her," her mom said.

Candace's stomach was doing a weird little sideways shudder, right to left, left to right. What was even happening?

"Invite her to breakfast. I'll make French toast," her dad said. "With bacon!"

Candace smiled tightly. "I'll get my phone."

16

"MOM, DAD, THIS IS PROFESSOR AUBURN, MY . . ." SHOULD she say "friend"?

"Legacy mentor," Tracey said. Candace had given her a heads-up about the cover story. "Tracey Auburn, pleased to meet you." Tracey stepped forward to shake Candace's parents' hands.

"Carl," her father said.

"Cheryl," her mother said.

The four of them stood in the doorway sizing each other up until her dad said, "Well, this bacon's not gonna eat itself!"

A shuffle of coats and comments about the weather, and they made their way to the kitchen table. Candace's dad pulled a casserole dish of hot French toast from the oven, where it had been warming, and an oblong bowl of bacon.

"The good stuff," he said, placing it on the table. "Wife thinks it's a waste of money, but I order this from Tennessee. Best bacon in the world. Thick-cut, hickory-smoked—"

"Rice and Sons?" Tracey asked.

"Rice, no! Denton's!" her dad said, and they were off arguing the virtues and shipping costs of real country pork products from the genuine South.

Candace took a bite of the prized bacon in question and

traded raised eyebrows with her mother. This was going better than expected. When Tracey compared the French toast to her father's own cinnamon-swirled specialty, Candace could swear she saw hearts in her father's eyes.

"See, Candace, appreciate this!" he said, spreading his arms to indicate the table. "Weekends at Café Carl will stick to your ribs and your heart for the rest of your life."

"I know," Candace agreed, patting her stomach. In her jeans pocket, her phone buzzed. She looked at it under the table.

"May I be excused?" she asked. Her mother waved her on and offered Tracey more coffee. Candace headed down the hallway to brush her teeth again and check her phone.

It was Becca.

Group hang at Nate's tonight.

Candace stared. Why the heck was Becca texting *her* of all people? The little ellipsis bubble indicated she was still typing.

You should come. You and Deen need to talk.

The heck they did. And with *Becca* in the mix? Candace brushed her teeth while she composed the perfect response in her mind. She rinsed, grabbed her phone, and wrote back: **Sorry, busy.**

She grabbed a shoulder bag from her bedroom doorknob, preloaded with snacks, a water bottle, her sketchbook, a wallet, and Tracey's purple notebook. She dropped her phone into the bottom, where she'd be less tempted to check it.

"Ready?" her mom asked when she reached the kitchen again.

"Yep."

"Thanks for this, Tracey," her dad said. "We'll do it again."

"I'll bring the bacon," Tracey offered.

"Call me when you get there," Candace's mom said, shoving two twenties into her hand. "Be home by dinnertime."

"I'll take care of her, Mrs. Wells," Tracey assured her.

"Please, call me Cheryl."

And then they were out the door and in Tracey's car, and Tracey said, "That was really nice."

And Candace said nothing at all because bringing a grown woman home to meet her parents had gone far better than bringing home anyone her own age. But the silence felt weird, so she said, "My dad makes some mean French toast."

"Yep." Tracey nodded and started the car.

17

THE ROAD TO MCHENRY WAS NOTHING TO WRITE HOME about. Flat freeway gave way to flat highway, and the tall buildings of Chicago gave way to the flat suburbs, and then fields, and then nothing but leafy trees, dry grass, and blue sky. Candace and Tracey rode with the windows down. The cracked two-lane road seemed to go on forever, past tree-lined gutters and wide golden meadows. Tracey reached for the radio. Candace stopped her.

"Actually, I was wondering . . ."

Tracey glanced at her, eyes mostly on the road ahead. "What are we doing? Me too. I mean, we met through a space-time portal! And this Loretta Spencer has something to do with it. I tried to google her."

"Me too."

"So you know that—"

"She doesn't exist. At least not on Google."

"Weird, right?"

"Yep. But that's not what I was going to ask."

"It wasn't? Huh. That's *all* I've been asking myself since this all started. What am I missing?"

Candace suddenly felt ridiculous. "Never mind. The other thing is more important." She tugged at her short curls with nervous fingers and slipped on her headphones. She thumbed her phone for some music, studiously avoiding the new text from Becca that she was refusing to read. And the one from Sergio.

"Don't bees like hats," Tracey said. Candace pulled one ear free.

"What?"

"I said, don't be like that."

"Oh."

"The universe has thrown us together for some reason, Candace. So what do you want to know?"

"It did, didn't it?" Candace realized aloud. "So maybe the question I'm about to ask is the whole reason this is happening."

Tracey shrugged. "Apparently literally anything's possible."

"Okay. But it's kind of personal."

Tracey's shrug looked a little more tense. "Go ahead. Ask me anything."

"What did Dia do?"

Tracey smiled. "Seriously, kid? Dia? That was so long ago, it doesn't matter. All in the past, all forgotten, et cetera."

"Really?" Candace asked. It seemed unlikely. "You sounded pretty upset. I mean, really upset in the notebook. Does time just make everything go away?"

Two more telephone poles and five trees passed before Tracey said, "Not everything. But a lot of things. Like Dia."

"But . . . when you were my age, she was important to you. Is anything from then still important?"

Tracey slowed as a truck pulling farm equipment appeared on the horizon. The WIDE LOAD sign across the back was the brightest thing for miles.

"Sure. I still love some of the same bands. I still love books. I still write. Sometimes."

"That's cool. I like to draw. Maybe I'll still do it when I'm your age."

"Yeah," Tracey said. It sounded kind of bitter, but maybe that was just how it sounded.

The road sped beneath them.

"Did you know the Underground Railroad used to stop here in McHenry?" Candace asked.

"No, I did not."

"We learned about it in school."

Tracey smiled. "Boy, are things different today. When I was your age, the Railroad was only in the South. Like once you got past the Mason-Dixon Line, it was over."

"But that doesn't make sense. I mean, it brought people north, right?"

"Right." Tracey sighed. "It's funny what we don't question. We should ask more questions."

"So . . ." Candace said, inspired, "what happened to Dia?"

"Not those kinds of questions, kid. I already told you—"

"Not *with* Dia, *to* her. You're a college professor now. What's she do?"

"No idea."

"You never looked her up online?"

"What for? We went our separate ways. The end."

"Oh."

Candace sank deeper into her seat and watched the road disappear underneath them. Maybe she'd be just as blasé about

Deen in forty years. Deen and Becca and Becca and Deen. "I need new friends," she mumbled.

"We all do," Tracey said.

This time when Candace put on her headphones, Tracey let her. A moment later, the car radio came on. People talking about current events or something. Candace turned up her volume a notch and tried to zone out. If this was all over quickly enough, she could be home in time to go to Nate's. Find out what Deen and Becca wanted. Maybe by tomorrow things would be better. Just a conversation, and they'd be friends again.

"Oh! Can we stop for Slurpees?" she said suddenly. She pointed to the 7-Eleven billboard on the side of the road. "I have to pee."

"Sure."

Candace took her time in the little bathroom. She washed her hands and stared at her face in the mirror. One way or another, things were going to change today. She'd have Deen back, or Becca would win, and that would be that. And also, the space-time portal thingy would maybe have a name. That was super important, too. Probably. Deen would flip out when she told her, at least. Candace felt a little lighter at that thought.

Outside, Tracey was sitting on the bumper of her car with a cup of coffee and a Slurpee in her hands. "Didn't know if you wanted cherry or blue raspberry, so I mixed it."

"Awesome," Candace said. "Thank you." The cup was ice-cold. She tugged her sleeves over her hands and accepted it.

They drove and nursed their drinks for a few moments. Then Tracey turned off the radio.

"Look," she said, "my mom died when I was nine."

"Aww! You're an orphan!"

"Please don't make that sound again," Tracey said. "It makes me feel like a puppy video."

"Aww! Oops. Sorry," Candace said. "But puppy videos are cute."

"I am not a puppy video."

"Sorry." Candace blinked. And then gasped. "Oh! *What You Need to Know. For Girls Like Me.* That's why you wrote the notebook, for girls without moms?"

Tracey looked embarrassed. "Yeah. Mine wasn't around to tell me how to grow up, so I started taking notes, I guess. In case I had a kid of my own."

"But..." Candace had so many questions. Did Tracey think she was going to die young, too? Did she actually have kids? The answers were not really, no, and do you want to hear this story or not? Candace wanted to hear this story.

"Anyway," Tracey said insistently, "after the notebook went missing, books saved me. I read a lot of fantasy—something my mom loved—and I started writing it, too. At first it was wish fulfillment, stories where my mom didn't die, or she came back, or it turned out she was, like, an elf or an angel or something. I outgrew the wish fulfillment pretty early on, but not the writing.

"Dia was my best friend. But she didn't get it. She thought we were too old for fantasies. I don't know what happened the day I wrote that in the notebook, but—"

"Ohhh," Candace interrupted. "She was a False Alarm Clock!"

"A what?"

"It's in your notebook. Someone who tells you to wake up and stop dreaming."

Tracey made a noise between a laugh and a sigh. "That's about the size of it. I can't believe I wrote that."

"You were a smart kid," Candace said, making Tracey blush. "So did you stop being friends?" she asked.

"Not until high school. Because it turned out Dia loved writing, too, but what she called 'real writing.' She was going to be a journalist, and I was going to be a best-selling novelist. But 'serious stuff.'" She kept making air quotes with one hand. "Not fantasy, you know?

"Then, senior year, I ran for editor of the school literary magazine. Dia was supposed to start a school newspaper."

Tracey fell silent.

"And? What happened?"

Tracey smiled, but it wasn't a happy smile. "The school said no to the newspaper, so Dia stole the editorial job from me."

"What?" Candace choked on her Slurpee. "What a jerk *and* a Sponge!"

"Totally! And *that's* a term I remember," Tracey said, gripping the steering wheel. "And when I confronted her about it—"

"You actually *said something to* her?" Candace gasped.

"Wouldn't you?" Tracey said.

"Uh . . ." Candace had *kind of* confronted Deen, but not really. And not Becca at all. "Not exactly?" she said.

"I understand. At your age, I was the same. But by my late teens, I guess I'd changed. I called her out on it, and do you know what she said?"

"What?"

"That I wasn't that good a writer. That I should be more *sensible*. Like she hadn't been my best friend for half my life and hadn't understood how important it was to me. Like it was—"

"Time to wake up," Candace said sadly.

"Right. Bye-bye, dreams. And that's what happened with Dia. We went our separate ways, and good riddance."

"Sorry," Candace said after a moment.

"It's not your fault. I'm sorry it's got me so worked up," Tracey replied. "I mean, it's been forty years. Dia freaking Andres . . ."

Tracey's voice was as steady as her driving, but there was the edge of a tear in her eye. Candace sucked down the sweet blue syrup in her cup, wanting to wash away the ashen taste filling her mouth.

"That's messed up," Candace said, her tongue cold and blue. "Ow, ow, ow." She clutched her head.

"Open your mouth. It'll warm up the nerves in the roof, cut the brain freeze."

Candace did as she was told. "That's magic."

"That's science." Tracey smiled, for real this time. Then she turned right. The signal clicked off and on like a metronome. "This is it."

What Candace had taken for a dirt road was actually a long, curving driveway of dark gravel that disappeared behind a row of fir trees a hundred yards ahead. Tracey stopped the car before they reached the trees. She was quiet for a long moment.

"It's funny. When you're a kid, it feels like life is just about to start happening around the next corner. Then you're my age, and I guess you're still looking around corners, waiting for it to start."

Candace slipped her straw in and out of her cup, making a dragging noise like a little trombone. "That's depressing."

Tracey smiled. "Candace. We met through a portal in space and time. This is *it*. The corner is *here*."

They both looked down the driveway in front of them. Tracey reached over and gave Candace's arm a squeeze.

"Ready?"

TREES GAVE WAY TO A SURPRISING HOUSE. A CIRCULAR driveway curved in front of a long, low white single-story home that looked like something out of a sci-fi movie from the '60s. It was made of slabs of some quartz-like material and had full picture windows in odd places, like corners and entire walls.

"It must be one big hallway," Candace guessed, eyeing the long rectangular shape.

"Mies van der Rohe," Tracey said.

"Gesundheit," Candace replied.

"Hardee har. Mies van der Rohe was a Chicago architect."

"I know," Candace said. "You can't grow up in Chicago without knowing about Mies van der Rohe and Frank Lloyd Wright."

Tracey looked impressed. By the house and by Candace. "It's beautiful," she said. She put the car in park and fished around the back seat for her purse.

A white woman in faded jeans, a pale half apron, and a cardigan appeared and knocked on the window. Her graying hair was piled at the crown of her head, held in place by two wooden hair sticks.

"Hello, there! You must be Tracey and Candace," she said, with a little wave. Her accent was musical. "Come in! Come in!

We have tea and coffee at the ready." She wiped her hands on her apron. "Pastries, too!" as if that was added incentive.

It was. Candace's stomach growled. Despite the giant Slurpee she'd just sucked down, or maybe because of it, she felt a little queasy.

The woman clopped across the driveway, revealing red clogs as bright as candied apples. They stood out against the pale symmetry of the house like little flashing emergency lights. Tracey did not follow right away.

"What kind of accent is that?" Candace said.

"Danish?" Tracey guessed.

"Huh," Candace said. "I don't know why, but I was kind of imagining she'd be Black."

"Let's find out."

"If she's Black?" Candace asked, but Tracey was already opening her door.

"If she's Loretta. Hello!" She called out to the white woman, who was now beckoning to them from the doorway. There was something creepy about it. A kind-faced older white lady in the woods offering treats . . .

The weighty weirdness of it all finally hit Candace. And the ridiculousness of worrying over Becca and Deen suddenly crystallized. Candace was in the middle of a legitimate scientific phenomenon (and possibly a fairy tale). Had Neil Armstrong wondered if the other astronauts liked him before he set foot on the moon? Did Hansel worry if Gretel thought he was mean? Maybe worrying over Deen had just been her brain's way of distracting her from this hugely momentous thing she was about to experience.

"Look," Tracey said from outside the car.

In the picture-window hallway house, a woman was watching. She was small, birdlike even, with her hands resting on top of a wooden cane. Pale brown skin, soft gray hair in a permed wave about her shoulders. She wore an elegant outfit of cream slacks, a white blouse, and one of those ruana shawl thingies tossed about her shoulders despite the warm weather.

Tracey waved at her. "I'm guessing that's Loretta Spencer."

She looked like a woman with answers, not child-baking ovens. Candace got out of the car.

⁓H⁓

"I am Lotte," the lady with the candy-apple shoes said. "Here they are, Miss Loretta," she announced, showing Tracey and Candace into the living room, two steps down from the foyer. Entering the room was like sinking into a bowl of cream. Off-white on off-white on off-white, the sofas, walls, and carpets lay restfully on the eyes. The coffee table—rounded, abstract glass on a teak base—held a tray of pastries, just as Lotte had promised. Bookcases of the same teakwood were built into two walls. The whole space matched the woman sitting on the off-white sofa across from them. The teak-colored cane had been discarded, left leaning against the side of the sofa. Loretta Spencer's legs were crossed at the knee, her hands resting on them. She wore a silver-colored ring with a large opaque stone on one finger.

"Forgive me if I do not rise," she said in a voice like seven years of Catholic school. "Take a seat. Coffee?"

Lotte bustled around pouring coffee for the older women, an extra-milky coffee for Candace, and placing small plates of pastries within reach of each of them. "Call if you would like anything else," she said, and left the room. She came back a few moments later with a little carafe of water and glasses, then disappeared into the house.

Loretta Spencer took her coffee with cream and sugar, so that it, too, matched her outfit and the room. Candace wondered what color her house should be, given her marigold hair, torn jeans, and purple jacket.

"Lotte didn't take your coats," Loretta commented.

"She offered. We're just not sure how long we'll be here," Tracey said. "You see—"

"I assumed you were here because you are ready," Loretta interrupted her.

"I'm ready," Candace said.

"For what?" Tracey asked.

"For answers," Candace said. "Right?"

Loretta Spencer gave them both a look. This woman must have been a schoolteacher at some point. It was the sort of look only a teacher could give.

"Humph," Loretta Spencer said. She turned to Tracey. "Tell me, what year were you given locker 235?"

"Back in 1988," Tracey said. She was perched on the edge of the sofa she shared with Candace, like an attentive student. Candace sat a little straighter, her jacket rustling loudly in the quiet room.

"And you, young lady?"

"Last week," she said.

"Eighth grade changes everything," Loretta murmured. Then she put down her coffee cup and did the strangest thing—she whistled. Loud and high, and twittering. And a bird flew into the room.

Not *a* bird. *The* bird.

Lilabet stared at Queen Dorianna's magpie. The queen had promised to send her home, but the directions her bird had given made no sense.

"But I don't understand," she said.

"That's too bad," the magpie replied. Its voice was as melodious as a flute, and as scratchy as a cat. "A thorny situation, all brambly and tangled as a hedgerow."

"But you said the way was simple!" Lilabet exclaimed.

"Oh, it is! But *you* are not. You're all tangled up and brambly, like I said. Perhaps you've got a knot in your brain?"

19

THE BIRD SETTLED ONTO THE ARM OF THE SOFA BESIDE Loretta.

"What the—" Candace gasped.

"Ack!" That was Tracey.

"You've both seen a bird like this, correct?"

"Yeah," Candace said, "but, like, flying out of my locker screeching."

"And into mine. Forty years ago," Tracey added, like she no longer believed the sky was blue.

"Locker number 235. It was my locker, too, once upon a time—1948, to be exact. And before you ask, Ms. Auburn, this particular bird is not eighty years old. At least, I don't think it is. I didn't get that close a look the first time. But he's definitely of the same breed."

"It's a magpie," Candace said, offering up what little she'd learned from the books Mr. Jones had lent her.

"But not a North American magpie," Loretta said. "An *inter-dimensional* magpie. I call it a Jordan."

"A what?" Tracey said.

"Note the plumage, the white stripe common to the average magpie. It's not white here, is it?" She pointed to one of the

Jordan's wings. He obligingly spread both wings out and began to sing, the exact whistle Loretta had used.

And she was right. The white-striped wings weren't white at all. They were . . .

"Invisible?" Candace said. Where white feathers should be, the wings were almost translucent. The whiteness came from the color of the sofa and the wall behind the bird. A faint iridescence, like the oily sheen on a starling's feathers, was the only sign that a strip of Jordan had not completely disappeared.

"I imagine they are quite visible, just not here."

"Not. Here," Tracey said, deadpan. Her eyes widened. "Oh my God," she breathed. "It really *is* a bird of unordinary colouring!"

Loretta gave her a sharp look. Tracey had moved close enough for the bird to peck her eyes out, Candace wanted to say. But saying it might cause the bird to peck Tracey's eyes out, so she held her quivering tongue, remembering the way the thing had dive-bombed her back in August.

"If not here, then where?" Tracey asked.

Loretta shrugged elegantly. (Candace would have to learn how to do that, so her mom wouldn't accuse her of slouching anymore.)

"*There*," Loretta said. Like she'd said "Karen" or "the office." Candace was already missing something. "This world of ours is more porous than we think," Loretta added. "For some of us, anyway." She nodded at the bird.

"You mean, like, the spirit world?" Candace asked, remembering a bad experience with a Ouija board at a sleepover with Becca and Deen last year.

"Child, ghosts don't exist. I'm talking about science! Imagine time and space like a string. It's not linear, it's tangled up in knots. Those knots are crossing places. Locker number 235 is a knot. A forty-year knot. And these birds know how to pass through them to the other side."

Candace made a face. "So Jordan's a time-traveling bird from the past?"

"No! And not 'Jordan.' This is not a pet with a human name. He's *a* Jordan, one of a type. Jordans are birds from the *knot*. I've been bird-watching for more than eighty years now, and these little fellas have no nesting ground that I can find. Granted, there are more places to look, but it seems that they live in the in-between."

Tracey was looking at Loretta now with an expression Candace couldn't place. Frightened? Hopeful? Young? Was that possible, for a middle-aged woman to suddenly look like a ten-year-old kid?

"Why Jordan?" Candace asked. "Don't scientists usually name things after themselves?"

"She means the River Jordan, like in the Bible, yes?" Tracey said.

Loretta nodded. "Look it up, youngblood," she said to Candace. *Youngblood?* Whatever that meant, Candace was not going to look it up. She put on her skeptical face.

"So how do you know all of this?" Candace asked. "I mean, despite the weird bird, how do we know you're not just, like, off your meds? No offense."

That earned Candace another withering look. "Oh, I know my physics, child. I was bright as they come, even back in 1948, for anyone with eyes to notice. But this . . . this was not my discovery, per se. It was my grandmother's."

Tracey blinked. "Your grand . . . When was that?"

"Keep up, girl. This is a forty-year knot!"

Candace did the math. "Your grandmother was a *physicist* in *1908*."

"My grandmother was a Black woman in 1908, so no, technically not a physicist by training. What she was is a birder."

Candace felt the sofa shifting under her like a little boat on a wild sea. "I'm sorry?" She was clearly not as bright as they come, she supposed. Candace wasn't sure if the old lady was nuts or if she should feel sorry for her unbright self.

"A birder. As in 'bird-watcher,'" Loretta said. As if *bird-watcher* wasn't a perfectly clear term to use instead. "Do you know when Walden was built?" Loretta asked.

"The eighteen hundreds?"

"That's when construction started on the old building." Loretta nodded. "But they didn't complete the new wing—where our locker is—until 1908. So, in my grandmother's day, the only thing surrounding the knot was clear blue sky.

"Meemaw loved birds and was known to climb trees to count eggs. She was a member of the Audubon Society later in life. Mail order, of course—colored people were not exactly welcomed. At any rate, she was counting the magpie population and had her eye on this unusual bird. Had a color variation apparently. So she recognized it. And it goes flying twenty feet over her head, and—*bloop!* Disappears in midair. And while she's watching—*bloop!* It's back again, this time with some colorful string in its beak."

Candace laughed. Bloop? Loretta gave her another corrective glare, and she sobered up.

"Sorry. Go on."

And so she did. She told them about her grandparents' love story, and the building of the school they all went to, and the locker, and birds.

"Meemaw kept a journal of her observations of this window in the sky, but like I said, she was a Black woman in 1908, so even if she could have put the science to it, no one was listening to her. Except for her grandbaby. She passed it on to me as stories about a little girl named Dorianna."

Tracey gasped.

"And then one day, she was gone," Loretta continued. "But her stories stayed with me. And the science. And locker 235."

Tracey was sitting on her hands now. She looked like she was going to burst. Candace scootched away from her just a bit.

"Of course, the world had changed by the time I was in college. Enough for an education. Not enough for a job. So I wrote down my grandmother's stories. Added my own touch. Put a man's name on it, and—"

"*Window in the Sky!*" Tracey shouted. "You're G. Edward Macey! I knew it! Macey was a woman! And a Black woman, to boot! I wrote my graduate thesis around it! Hoowee, that's exciting!"

Loretta grinned at her. "Smart girl."

Candace did not feel included in the compliment. "Can someone please fill me in?"

Tracey whirled to face her. "*Window in the Sky*, Candace! Birds of unordinary colouring?"

"Right. That *Skylark* movie?" Candace said. But Tracey had turned back to Loretta.

"She's too young to know the books. I am too, actually. But my mother bought them for me before I was even born, and I adored them!" She turned back to Candace. "It's about a land that can be reached through a window in the sky, and doorways in cuckoo clocks, and this girl who climbs inside with one of the birds as her guide and has all these adventures in the Land of Many Times."

"Like *Doctor Who*," Candace said.

"No! And kind of. Yes."

"Or *The Wizard of Oz*? The guy who wrote that lived in Chicago," Candace added, glad to know something about something at least.

"As I was saying," Loretta said. "When I was old enough, I went to Walden. Took until eighth grade to get assigned to locker 235, but I did it. And I've been studying it, and knots like it, ever since. Meemaw's stories were a sort of code for the science. And she was mostly right. But I couldn't be sure until the two of you connected because—"

"Because it's on a cycle," Candace interrupted. "Every forty years."

"Now you're catching up." Loretta's eyes twinkled in the afternoon light.

"But why didn't you contact me back in the eighties?" Tracey asked.

"I tried. But I wasn't sure what could travel. People can't, for some reason. Maybe it's just the size of the hole."

"But wait," Candace said. "Tracey and I were both in school

when we shared the notebook. But you just wrote us to come here. How did you know you'd live here eighty years later? And how old are you?"

"Ninety-three, little girl, and I didn't know. I wrote that note on Thursday."

"But how?" Candace asked, hoping she wasn't being dense.

"Yeah," Tracey said. "How?"

Loretta took her cane in hand, rose to her feet, and smoothed her trousers.

"Come on, then."

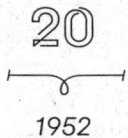

1952

LORETTA AND STEVEN LEFT THE ROAD SOMEWHERE between Crystal Lake and Woodstock. McHenry County was a world away from the skyscrapers of Chicago. High summer grasses, full-headed trees, and the buzz of crickets in the fields—exactly the sort of place to look for birds.

"They call this Pleasant Valley," Steven read from the map. Despite the distance from the road, they could hear the sounds of construction up ahead.

"Well, that won't be good for birding," Loretta said, but her curiosity led her on. "The papers say there's a church group building a summer camp up here for city kids."

Steven paused in the heat and took a sip of water from the canteen slung over his shoulder. He had a small Brownie camera around his neck. Loretta carried her supplies in an old canvas shoulder bag.

"It's pretty country," Steven said. "But when you say kids from the city . . ."

"All kinds of kids," Loretta confirmed. "All colors."

Steven grinned. He looked nervous to Loretta. "Kind of hard to believe we're welcome in the boonies." McHenry was as white as any suburban or rural town outside of Chicago.

Loretta shrugged and began to sing, "This land is your land, this land is my land!"

Steven joined in until they reached the trees, where, by mutual agreement, they fell silent.

"Here," she said, stopping in front of a shrub.

She pulled her observation journal from her shoulder pack and flipped it to where a twig was pressed between the pages. Found in locker 235, along with other detritus, when she volunteered to help her old elementary school staff clean out the lockers at the end of her junior year.

"*Betula pumila*," she said, holding up the twig with its dried leaves the same shape as the green leaf cookies her aunt bought at the local bakery, but shorter, like delicate little fans. "Dwarf birch. Rare in Illinois, the folks at the botanical gardens said. And unheard-of in the city. But you can find a few of them here."

She looked up at the trees, the sky. Somewhere around here was connected to locker 235.

They found a good spot and settled to the ground to watch. One of the nice things about Steven was his patience. He pulled out a tattered copy of *The Illustrated Man* by Ray Bradbury, and let Loretta do her thing.

Half an hour later, she nudged him and pointed with her binoculars. In the tree above them was a magpie. It leapt from a branch and into the air. Loretta followed it with her lenses. There! The same strange not-there coloring on the wings.

"This is it," she whispered.

They followed the bird from a distance and were rewarded with its burst of song.

Another bird sang out from the treetops.

And another.

And another.

Ahead, in a clearing, the sky was full of magpies snatching june bugs out of the air.

Loretta sank to the ground and began taking notes. Steven took a few shots with his camera, but they both knew they would probably be blurry.

An hour later, the birds had disappeared. They had no luck following them this time, though.

Hiking back out to the road, they came across a sign. LOT FOR SALE.

"I'd love to own me a piece of this place," Loretta said with a sigh.

Steven leaned down and pecked her on the cheek. "Here, let's take a picture and make a pact." He posed her by the sign. "College first, then jobs, then we come back out here and buy this whole place up!"

Loretta leaned against it proprietarily and grinned. The shutter snapped.

"Your turn." Loretta took the camera from him, and they switched places. She was adjusting the focus when a sheriff's car appeared down the road. Steven straightened. Loretta stood close to his side.

"Afternoon," the white man in the car said.

"Afternoon, sir." Steven and Loretta nodded in unison.

"That your old Ford up the road a ways?"

"My father's," Steven said. "He let me borrow it for the day."

"For what exactly?"

"Bird-watching," Loretta explained, holding up her notebook.

The sheriff chuckled. "First this camp, now little black birds. Times are a-changing," he said to himself. "Now, what are you taking pictures of this sign for, then? Not a bird in sight."

"Just daydreaming, sir," Loretta said. "Wishing I could buy a place out here."

"Oh, this place is not for sale," the sheriff said.

"But the sign says—"

"Sign's wrong." The man squinted at them in the afternoon sunlight.

"Too bad," Steven said quickly. "You've got a beautiful place out here. We'll just get our car and be on our way."

"You do that," the sheriff said. "And thanks for stopping by."

He followed them slowly the whole walk back to the car. It wasn't until they were close to Crystal Lake that he pulled away, and Steven took a breath.

Loretta patted his leg. "We're fine," she told him. "We're fine."

"If you say so." His laugh was shaky. "Was it worth it, Miss Scientist?"

"Knowledge is always worth the price," she said. And began to hum as they reached the highway. *This land was made for you and me.*

21

LORETTA LED CANDACE AND TRACEY DOWN A LONG hallway. Windows lined one side, looking onto the wide green expanse of the backyard and the deep forest beyond. Candace spotted a doe grazing at the edge of the yard. The wall of windows ended in a vestibule of warm teakwood and subtle lighting before a set of glossy black double doors. Loretta reached into her pocket. Her tan on cream on white outfit, the silver pearls on her wrist, all stood out starkly against the black doors. Her thin hand emerged holding a set of keys looped onto an extendable cord, like a janitor for an unbelievably fancy school. She unlocked the door. It swung open without her needing to touch it. If Candace had a door like that, it would be covered in fingerprints. She edged carefully through after the other women.

The room inside was just as softly impressive as the living room had been. It was an office, a really beautiful one, considering it had no windows. Instead, the teak walls were lined with bookcases on one side, with display cutouts for glass vases or other items. Recessed lighting shone on focal points around the room, highlighting subtle bits of sculpture, making the wood glow. There was a desk in front of the back wall, beneath a framed painting of . . . Candace stared at the painting. It didn't look like anything.

She spun on the cream Berber carpet to take in the living-room-like space to her right. A fireplace, cream-colored sofa, and chairs. It felt like a showroom, but it also felt like Loretta. And it smelled softly of sandalwood, or maybe cream soda. Candace's mouth watered.

Behind her, the door swung shut. The only sound it made was the compression of air as it resealed.

"Airtight?" Tracey asked, noticing it too.

Loretta nodded and shrugged at the same time. Simultaneously noncommittal and forthright. Another thing Candace would have to learn how to do. Tracey frowned. Candace gave her an expectant look, but the older woman just shook her head.

"This is it." Loretta led them to a bookshelf to the right of the desk. Built into it, just above Candace's line of sight, was locker 235. But not *her* locker 235. This one was a weird orange color, and not even the whole locker, but the upper half, sitting there on a shelf as if it were a hotel room safe.

"That's—" Candace said.

"My locker," Tracey finished. They glanced at each other. Candace felt dizzy. Despite the previous conversation, here she was now, standing in this honeyed hush of a room with an elegantly honeyed hush of a mad scientist and a college professor, and they were all not the same person, but each of them was a point person for a mystery of the universe that made her want to vomit all over the beautiful cream Berber rug. Or shoot lasers from her eyes. Because that was the kind of power that something this . . . powerful . . . should give you. Instead, she felt inadequate and her palms were sweaty.

"It's a replica," Loretta said. "With modifications, of course. The size and, well, the contents are a bit different."

"Meaning?" Tracey said.

Loretta reached up and spun the combination, the knob looking oddly appropriate, even misplaced as it was on the small slice of locker.

"This," she said, "is the other side of the knot." She reached in, fished around, biting her tongue in a bizarrely Charlie Brownish way. "There!" She withdrew her hand. In her fist, she was holding a purple pom-pom pen. It was sort of dirty, with bits of leaf and what looked like bits of feather, but it was a pen.

"What the—" Tracey blinked. "I lost that in eighth grade!"

Loretta's mouth twisted into a bemused smile.

"I lost a pen, too. Still hoping it turns up one day." A funny look crossed Tracey's face, but the old woman didn't seem to notice.

"Either way, it's not the direct passage I assumed," Loretta explained. "At the end of my junior year of high school, I found an unusual twig in our locker that came from a plant local to McHenry. Took some years of looking, but I found the knot." She waved at the locker in front of them. "At first, I thought there was a time gap. Maybe the windows align at certain intervals, during which objects can be passed from one side to the other, hence our connection. But I was wrong. It comes down to—"

"Birds!" Candace said, stepping forward to take the pen from Loretta's hand. The silver strands in the purple pom-pom were missing in places, and the pen itself had dents in it. Beak-shaped dents. "Interdimensional magpies!"

Loretta nodded, looking pleased with Candace. "Sometimes they take what comes through the holes. They drop it back later. The notebook is likely too heavy for a bird to carry, but imagine it like a pass-through window at a diner. You put the notebook on the ledge in the kitchen, I can pick it up behind the counter. There's some sort of connection. Which means there's something on the other side. That ledge has to be *somewhere*." She shrugged elegantly again. "At least, that's my hypothesis.

"For a while, I collected everything they deposited here, but there wasn't much rhyme or reason to it. Certainly nothing to identify the origin with any specificity." She pulled a box from a lower shelf and opened it. She was right. It looked like someone had unraveled a purple sweater. There were tangles of yarn and string, a few bits of shiny paper like gum wrappers, and twiggy things—the kind of stuff you'd expect a bird nest or something to be stuffed with. None of it particularly noteworthy. "Turns out it's not every day a bird plucks a rare plant species. But even this junk has its uses. Gum packaging changes over the years. So do the materials for making the rest of this stuff." She poked at the tangles of string. "With enough forensic research, a pattern emerges, and you two are the final proof. This"—she nodded at the locker—"is a forty-year knot."

Tracey stepped up to the locker. She was taller than Candace and Loretta. She looked easily into the dark opening.

"Huh."

"Yes, 'huh,'" Loretta said. "But that's not what I wanted to show you. Now, come and sit by the fire."

Candace followed Tracey to the sofa and picked up a tchotchke from the side table—some sort of interlinked wooden puzzle—and fidgeted with slotting the pieces into their correct place. Loretta took a side chair. She picked up a remote from the glass table and turned the fireplace on. Another click of a button, and a screen lowered from the ceiling above the fireplace. Not a TV screen. A map.

"Let's get down to brass tacks," Loretta said.

Candace shifted on the sofa beside Tracey. "What are those?"

"She means 'business,'" Tracey translated.

"I have no children, no heirs," Loretta said. "I'm a touch shy of one hundred years old, and I have built my house, and my life, around this." She indicated the locker, the knot, the everything. "And there is more to know. I'm afraid my better bird-watching days are over, which is where you youngbloods come in.

"Help me," Loretta said. "Help me complete my map."

She turned on a light that illuminated the screen. Most of the state of Illinois was marked with red and green dots. Dozens of them.

"Every red dot is a sighting of a magpie going into a knot. The green dots are where I've seen magpies coming out. It's possible the pairs closest together mark the entry and exit points of the same knot. But as you can see, it's not an even number. Maybe some exits have no entry, and vice versa. Or maybe they have many more. I would like to find out before I die. Will you help?"

Candace looked at the upright old lady. She seemed like she'd be good for another forty years, but she was in her nineties! She could go any day.

"Sure," said Candace.

"How?" Tracey asked at the same time.

Loretta cut Tracey that schoolteacher look Candace admired and feared. Tracey, also a teacher, cut one back. It was like a wizard duel using nothing but eyebrows.

"I like to know what I'm committing to," Tracey said.

Loretta conceded with her eyebrows. "Fair enough. Bird-watching. We look for sightings, and go check them out."

"Cool, like ghost hunters," Candace said. Becca and Deen would be so jealous if they ever found out. Bunches of people probably went on sneaky secret camping trips, but how many of them got to look for knots in the space-time continuum? Three. The number was exactly three. And she was one of them.

"Oh!" she recalled. "Do you mind if I draw what we find? I have a science project on birds due in two months."

"Keep the knots out of it, and you've got yourself a deal," the old woman said. "The way I see it, these things have stayed hidden from men for so long for a reason. Last thing I want to see is the military or big business get involved."

"They'd use it for cheaper shipping." Tracey laughed.

"Forty-year shipping!" Loretta guffawed. Which was shocking. Her laugh was the only inelegant thing about her, Candace decided.

Tracey's laugh faded. She frowned down at her hands and sighed.

"Okay, I'm in," she said. "As long as it's confined to weekends. I teach," she explained to Loretta. "We're on quarters, and I'm hoping for tenure this year."

"That's wonderful, Tracey," Loretta said. And Candace tuned out while the women chatted about school and money, and about books in which balloons went to the moon. Eventually they were done. Candace and Tracey took a bathroom break, and they exchanged phone numbers.

"See you next weekend," Loretta said as she waved them though the front door.

"Bye!" Candace said.

Her phone was buzzing, telling her the hangout at Nate's was starting. She thumbed it into silence. Hanging out was fine and all that, but next weekend, she and Tracey were going to join Loretta at some place called the Magic Hedge. Just the name had her excited.

"That was so cool," Candace said as they climbed back into the car. The smile on her face felt good.

"We actually just met the author of *Window in the Sky*," Tracey said. "It is amazing, kid. Too bad she's lost her mind."

"What?" Candace yelped. "You think she's . . . ?"

Tracey started the car. "Kid, that woman's not a scientist, she's a writer. It's her job to be inventive."

"But the locker, and your pen, and the bird!"

"A locker, *a* pen, *a* bird. The world is full of strange things, but knots and interdimensional magpies? It's just unpossible."

"*Im*possible," Candace corrected. Tracey scowled. "But you said you'd go to the Magic Hedge. We said we'd help her!"

"And we will. By keeping an old lady company in her later years. You get your science project. I get, I don't know, maybe a journal article about the real G. Edward Macey. Don't look at me like that! I wouldn't do it without her permission, but the world deserves to know. And in the meantime . . . Look. We're doing a nice thing. Not intergalactic science—"

"Interdimensional science," Candace said.

"But a nice thing."

A lump settled into Candace's stomach that didn't feel very nice at all. "Well, I think she's telling the truth," she said.

"You're entitled to that," Tracey replied, pulling onto the main road.

"And you're a real party pooper," Candace said. She folded her arms across her chest for emphasis, but Tracey didn't seem to mind at all.

22

GROUP HANG AT NATE'S.

Candace's phone buzzed the unhelpful reminder three times after they left Loretta's, like a doomsday countdown.

One hour before the party, when they were back in the city. Fifteen minutes before, while she was telling Tracey goodbye. Time!—and here she was at home standing in front of her closet. Wondering if she should go.

"How was it?" Candace's mom appeared in the doorway.

"Good," Candace said. "Loretta Spencer's, like, really old, Mom. She was an eighth grader in 1948! She was alive during World War II!"

"Isn't that something?" her mom said, coming in and sitting down on the edge of Candace's bed.

"She was really impressive. Oh, and she and Tracey are going to help me with my science project," Candace said belatedly. They'd all agreed not to tell her parents about the knots, but she had to have some reason for spending weekends with them.

"That professor and an old lady want to go bird-watching with you?" her mom asked dubiously.

"Weird, huh? But it turns out Loretta—she said I can call her Loretta—is a birder. That's how she put it. And her grandma was a birder, too. So she can help me . . . identify . . . things . . ."

It felt strange telling half-truths to her mother. But there was no way her parents would let her keep hanging out with Tracey and Loretta if she told them why. Like Tracey, they'd say Loretta had dementia and then get a restraining order or something.

"Earth to Candace," her mother said, waving her hands in front of Candace's face. "After a long day of bird talk, are you hungry? We're ordering in Chinese. Moo goo gai pan or moo shu pork?"

Candace dropped down on the bed next to her mom, two different sweaters in her hands.

"Becca says they're hanging out at Nate's tonight."

"Really?" her mom said, perking up.

"I don't know if I should go. I mean, we aren't speaking."

"Then how do you know—"

Candace showed her mom her phone. "Becca texted me."

"Well, you and Deen *do* need to talk," her mother reasoned. "Assuming you want some kind of closure or reconciliation."

Candace didn't want closure or reconciliation. She wanted to punch Becca in her smug face and smack Deen upside the head for thinking Candace was the problem. (Why was she in such a violent mood?) But all she said was "I guess."

"All right. Then how about this," her mom said. "We'll get moo goo gai pan *and* moo shu pork, and I'll keep them in the fridge. Depending on how the night goes, we can midnight feast away our sorrows, or have leftovers tomorrow. Day-old takeout brunch. How's that sound?"

"Congealed," Candace said. "But good." She held up the two sweaters. "Which one says 'peace talks'?"

Her mom squinted, first at the black cable knit, then at the olive-green one. "I'm gonna go with the one that actually has a peace sign on it," she said, pointing to the pink peace symbol on the green sweater.

"Good point," Candace said. "Too obvious, though?"

"Or possibly sarcastic . . ." Her mom stared at the sweater. "Depending on how it goes. But it's not the clothes that make the man, as they say."

Candace took a breath. "My stomach hurts."

"Remember when you were little and ate too much Halloween candy and you were afraid to throw up?"

"Uh . . . yeah? Like every year?"

"Right, so two lessons. One, you never learn. And two, you always felt better afterward. Think of this like that. Whatever happens, this is the hard part."

"The barfing part," Candace said.

"That's my girl." Her mother planted a wet kiss on her forehead and went to order tomorrow's congealed brunch.

—⚘—

Nate lived in a cool house close enough that Candace could walk during the day. Her mom had agreed to pick her up if it ran late.

The house was a brownstone three-story walk-up with a skinny backyard that had a firepit and nice lawn furniture. But unlike the two-story duplex Candace's family shared with a retired accountant in the upstairs unit, Nate's family owned the entire building. The inside of the house reminded Candace of what art galleries look like in the movies, only moodier. The living room was deep yellow, with sculptures in glass cases along the wall. The furniture looked like art, strange shapes and angles. Nate's parents were collectors. They were also drinking wine and eating stinky cheese when she showed up.

"Candy, right?" his mother said, shoving a half-eaten piece of cheese toward the inside of her cheek with the same hand that held her wineglass, her other hand holding open the door.

"Hi, Mrs. Saperstein," Candace said. Her friends' parents never got her name right. Like they had to go for some throwback version of it that they couldn't let go of.

"They're out back roasting frankfurters. Plenty left, if you're hungry."

"I'm fine. Thanks, Mrs. Saperstein. Mr. Saperstein." Candace nodded at Nate's dad as they passed through the kitchen to the back door. Mr. Saperstein was perched on a stool in front of their massive marble kitchen island. His eyes and thumbs were glued to his smartphone.

Candace opened the back door and entered the weird little back stairwell. Three steps down to yet another door and then out into the backyard. Nate said it was for fire safety or something. Tonight, Candace saw it as neutral territory. The minute she opened the second door, she'd be in the line of fire. Or maybe, just maybe, it would all be fine.

She opened the door.

The group hang wasn't exactly cozy. At least twelve kids were crowding Nate's tiny backyard, playing Frisbee despite the obvious dangers of roasting marshmallows and hot dogs over the firepit, not to mention a sticky version of the infamous Chicago wind, the Hawk, blowing just over the top of the ten-foot-high wood plank fence that framed the area. Twelve kids pretending that it was still summer.

No one even saw her come in. Music was playing, but not too loud, since the neighbors were literally on top of the party. Two girls from the other eighth grade, Merida and Stephanie, were there by the chips table. Nate was doing a handstand against the wall, trying to show off for whoever would look his way, which was no one. Sergio and Becca— What? Sergio and Becca were making out! In a papasan chair! In the back corner! Candace knew it—Becca wasn't just a sponging Queen Bee, she was a thief! But worse, Deen knew it, too, and she was *still* with them. Deen "I have a crush on Sergio and shared it with my new bestie Becca" was just sitting there, perched on the arm of a neighboring chair like a lapdog waiting for its owner to finish her people business and get back to walking. It was pathetic, disgusting, and oh-so very wrong. Candace knew she should go to Deen's rescue, but Deen was not looking at her really hard. So maybe she wanted to sit next to her fake best friend while said fake bestie made out with her dream boyfriend. What did Candace care?

"Bird girl!"

Candace froze. Someone had come through the door behind her. It was the boy from the other eighth grade. Tall, lanky, deep brown skin.

"Mitchell!" she exclaimed a bit too loudly. Out of the corner of her eye, she could see Deen and Becca both take an interest. Sergio was leaning in for another kiss, but Becca pushed him away. Candace turned all the way toward her new best friend.

"Actually, I was hoping you'd be here," Mitchell said. Before she could ask why, he added, "Can I get you a pop?" He waved a magnanimous hand toward the cooler being used as a bench next to the firepit. "Or a hot dog?"

"Will you burn me a hot dog? I'll get the drinks," Candace said.

"You're on, pardner. I'll take anything brown or clear." And they went around either side of the firepit to accomplish their missions.

"Excuse me." Candace ousted the girl sitting on the cooler and crouched down, smiling as she rooted for a brown pop—Coke, Diet Coke, Barq's... All she found was Sprite and a bunch of sparkling waters. She settled for two Sprites.

"Candace."

Becca was standing above her, arms crossed over her chest, her multicolor hair tucked under a beanie. Deen stood behind her looking like a victim.

"Hey, Becca." Candace rose slowly. "Thanks for the invite."

"We didn't invite you for a party," Becca snapped. "We invited you—"

"I didn't invite her," Nate said, coming up behind them with Sergio.

"*I* invited her," Becca announced. "She hurt Deenie. She needs to apologize."

"Deen?" Candace looked around Becca to her friend. "Do you want to talk?"

Deen shrugged. "I guess."

"Want me to come with you, Deenie?" Becca took Deen by the hand, her oversized shacket flapping like a little kid in adult clothing.

Fortunately, Deen said no.

"Want a pop?" Candace asked. Deen shuffled in front of Becca. Sergio reeled Becca back into his arms.

"I'll take a water," Deen said.

"Cajun hot dog!" Mitchell appeared, a blackened hot dog on a skewer in front of him like a flag.

"Wow. That's intensely black," Candace said. She took the offered bun and slid the dog off of the skewer. A second hot dog, equally burnt, remained.

"Thought I'd try one, too," Mitchell said. Then he took in the scene. "Oh, my bad. I'll just . . ." He slipped a Sprite out of the crook of Candace's elbow. "Thank you," he whispered, and backed away. On tiptoe.

A laugh built inside Candace. It evaporated when Becca attained escape velocity from Sergio's mouth and reached for Deen's arm again.

"She's obviously not taking this seriously."

Candace took a sloppy bite of her char dog. "C'mon, Deen, let's talk somewhere private," she garbled, and hooked Deen's other arm, dragging her off toward the house.

In the in-between space between the back door and the fire door, they sat on the steps.

"Want a bite?" Candace offered. Deen snapped off a piece of hot dog.

"This is so good," she said.

"Salty." Candace nodded. "A fatty, salty, meaty flavor bomb." She swallowed the last bite. That Mitchell sure could cook. "So . . ." Candace wiped her hands on her pants.

"So," Deen said.

"I thought *you* liked Sergio—"

"Did you know Becca doesn't eat hot dogs?" Deen said. "She says they're nothing but pig snouts and buttholes."

Right. She probably learned that on the secret camping trip. Candace's eyes dropped, along with her stomach. And there was her sweater staring back at her. Peace. Candace took a breath.

"She's probably right," she conceded. "Except for the beef ones. Those are cow noses and cow buttholes."

Deen snorted. Candace had missed that painful nose rip of a laugh. And then Deen was sobbing.

"I do like Sergio! And I think Sergio might have liked me, too, until Becca did that thing she does."

"The hand on the arm and the hair toss?"

"Yeah, that. My hair doesn't toss like that." Her sad bruised-plum-colored hair.

"Mine either," Candace said. Her own two-inch curls flattened, but never tossed.

Deen snorted again, but it was a watery kind of snort. Candace fished around in her pockets for a tissue. She unfolded the three she found and held them to the light to check for snot. One good one left. She handed it to Deen.

"Sergio's an idiot," Candace said.

"Yeah, but Becca's great," Deen said. "I can't blame him."

"*I* can. Want me to blame them both, so you don't have to?"

Deen smiled, a wry little smile. But it melted. "Let's not be mean to Becca, okay?"

"When have I been mean?"

Deen sighed and folded her arms on the top step. She

rested her head. "You were mad about the camping trip and everything."

"Upset, yes. But I'm not mean," Candace said.

"Okay," Deen replied. Which was not the same as agreeing.

"What the heck, Deen?"

"What?"

"That. What's so precious about Becca?"

"Candace! I said don't be mean!"

"Fine! Forget it. I'm gonna get another dog."

Candace headed down the steps and back into the yard. So much for the tearful reunion and best friendship renewal ceremony she'd been hoping for.

"Is everything—" Sergio appeared, looking anxious.

"It's fine."

Candace sidestepped him and yanked another hot dog from an open packet on the picnic table. She stabbed the skewer through it lengthwise and the hot dog split. It fell off the skewer. She stabbed another, and another, until one stayed put. Rescuing the discards, she broke them into smaller pieces and shish-kabobbed them. And then she remembered there was moo shu pork at home, and moo goo gai pan, and people who loved her without it being weirdly accusatory.

And then she remembered she was lying to those people. To her mom and dad. And that two women fifty times her age were taking her birding next Saturday morning and this was now her life.

Her head began to throb. She pushed her way to a spot by the fire, the flames painting everyone's faces red, their hair marigold, like hers. She roasted her hot dogs on the flame and tried to steady her breathing. Steady. Steady. Eat a few burnt offerings. Go home. Eat. Leave. Eat. Leave.

"Your wieners are burning," the girl on the cooler said. Candace pulled them from the fire and blew them out. The parts that weren't completely black had shriveled in the cooling night air and looked like old fingers. She ate a few of them. The others were unsalvageable.

"Don't leave," someone said as she made her way out the back gate and into the alley that ran behind Nate's house. But she was already gone.

"Bird girl!" Mitchell stood in the alley behind her. "You forgot your Sprite."

Candace held up her actual can of Sprite, not the one he was holding.

"Fine, you caught me," he said, jogging up to her. "It was a ploy. Are you okay? That vibe earlier with those girls was . . . real."

"Just drama for no good reason," Candace said.

"Gotcha. Well . . ."

"Thank you for the hot dog. It was really good."

"Thank you for the Sprite," he said.

And they stood there for what felt like really a long time.

23

ON MONDAY MORNING, CANDACE WAS CAREFULLY opening her locker when Mitchell appeared.

"Hey," he said.

"Oh, hey." It was weird seeing a boy a couple of days after figuring out he might like you. And that you liked him, too.

"So," Mitchell said. He ran a hand over his hair. Was he nervous? He looked nervous. That made Candace nervous, but in a smiley way.

"What's up?" she asked.

"Um . . . I tried to follow you online?"

"Yeah? Oh . . . yeah." He had tried, but she hadn't accepted his request. "It's just . . . my feed's mostly, like, bad drawings? It's not . . ."

"I like your drawings," Mitchell said.

"What? How have you . . . ?"

He pointed to her locker. Right. The inside of the door was full of bird drawings now. Candace was maybe a little obsessed, she realized, but knowing Tracey thought her art was good enough to save for forty years had been super inspiring.

"Busted," she said, and pulled out her phone. "Okay, there." She held it up and showed him where she'd accepted his request to friend her.

Mitchell grinned and pulled out his own phone. "How about I get your number, too. Just in case."

Candace was thinking, *In case of what?* But she was also giving him her number and smiling, and it was totally something she and Deen should be squealing about in the girls' bathroom before class, but Deen hadn't so much as looked her way this morning. Candace had been standing there with her mouth open, ready to say hi, to try to start again. But Becca had steered Deen away like she was a celebrity and Candace was her crazed fan.

Which was fine. Because she had a new friend.

The warning bell rang for class. Mitchell backed away toward his classroom and held up his phone. "I'll text you."

Candace was still smiling when she took her seat. Which really seemed to bother Deen and Becca, so it was extra good.

Candace woke up the following Saturday at the butt crack of dawn. Time to go to the Magic Hedge. She pulled on jeans and a fleece, and she shoved her sketchbook into her backpack with a thermos of vanilla-flavored coffee that her mother—who woke up this early just because she liked to—had made for her. Tracey texted to say she was outside.

"Be safe," her mother said.

"I will. It's just birds," Candace said.

Outside, it was super quiet and the September sky was still kind of dark. Tracey's car was idling at the curb. Candace knocked on the window, then waved goodbye to her mom, who was watching from the living room.

"I haven't been awake this early since college," Tracey said by way of greeting.

"I haven't even been to college yet," Candace said with a yawn.

They sat in the car, each sipping the coffee they carried. Then Tracey told her to buckle up, and they pulled away from the curb. On Lake Shore Drive, Candace stared out at the city lights reflecting on the water, and the first blush of sun in the sky. At Montrose, Tracey pulled off the Drive.

The Magic Hedge was pretty unmagical. It was also just a hedge. The long row of bushes were less lush and more brush with autumn, and taller than Candace, but they still screened the spit of land from the road and the noise of the city. Several birders in heavy sweaters, with binoculars around their necks, disappeared into the trees, their eyes trained on the middle distance.

Loretta was sitting in the parking lot like an asphalt queen, in a massive folding chair next to a beautiful gold-colored Jaguar.

"How come she can park here?" Candace whispered to Tracey. They had trekked from the street.

"She's Loretta," Tracey said. She also had a handicapped placard. Lotte waved at them from the driver's seat and lowered her window.

"Going to run errands. I'll pick her up at ten thirty for lunch."

"Okay!" Tracey called back, and returned the wave.

"Who eats lunch at ten thirty?" Candace muttered.

"People who wake up in the dark," Tracey replied as they closed the distance across the lawn to Loretta. A few birders shushed them, as if birds weren't used to people talking. They dropped their voices to church whispers.

"About time," Loretta greeted them. Candace didn't like to think how early she and Lotte had gotten up to make it all the way here from McHenry.

"Good morning to you, too," Tracey said.

"Hi, Miss Loretta," Candace chimed in.

"So, what's the plan?" Tracey asked.

"You two youngbloods go walk. And take these." Loretta thrust a pair of binoculars into Tracey's hands. She nodded at the set hanging from Candace's neck. "You got the best eyes of the three of us. Follow that trail. Everybody else'll be looking at the hedges and the brush and trees. You look between the branches. Knots like a good piece of open sky. You're looking for one or more of our Jordan 'pies."

"Bloop!" Candace said. Loretta smiled.

"That's right."

"What about you?" Candace asked.

"I'm an hour into my bird sit. I'ma stay right here with my blanket and my electric socks and see what comes to me." She waved her own binoculars at the slowly brightening sky above the lake. "I sit in a different spot each time, and wait to see what happens. Take good notes. Accuracy is the difference between science and speculation. We'll meet back here in an hour, then decide what's what."

Candace and Tracey tromped off down the path. The last thing Candace wanted to do was press a set of cold metal binoculars to her face. She pulled her hat lower over her ears.

"Did you hear that?" Tracey asked, her breath puffing clouds in the air. "Miss Loretta's been out here for an hour already. Lotte must encourage it, to get her out of the house."

"Baffling," Candace muttered. Why would anyone want to leave a warm house this early in the morning?

They came to an opening in the path. Just as Loretta had predicted, the other birders were peering into bushes and looking up at the leafless trees. Tracey and Candace stared at the sky and waited.

"This seems kind of useless," Candace said after a few minutes.

"Well..." Tracey said.

Candace swung her backpack off her shoulders and retrieved her thermos. "Want some more coffee?" She added a cupful to Tracey's travel mug, and they continued along the trail.

"Hawk," Candace said, pointing at a bird circling over the trees. The sun was beginning to brush the tips of the treetops.

"Good eye," Tracey said. "I think that's a red-tail."

"You know birds?" Candace asked.

"Nope. Just red-tail hawks. It's a pigeon or a hawk in my book."

"Bird ID'ing is so hard," Candace said. "I've got this app that will tell you what's what, but you have to take a picture, and most birds don't stay still long enough."

Tracey turned in a slow circle, scanning the sky. "I've spent so much of my life dodging birds, it's a new concept trying to pay attention to them."

They moved on, but the tree branches got so tangled, it seemed unlikely they'd find clear sky this way, so they doubled back.

"Can I ask you a question?" Candace asked.

"Sure."

"How long is too long to wait for a boy to text?"

"You mean, for you to text the boy?"

"For me to expect him to text me. Like, when should I just get over it?"

Tracey nodded. "Good question. Depends. Is he super busy? Did he say he would text?" Tracey was super busy, but she was here.

"He asked for my number."

"How long ago?"

"Monday? I went to a thing after you dropped me off, and there was this guy from my school and... well, he seems nice."

"Nice. Is that code for cute these days?"

Candace shrugged, embarrassed. "It's just, at school, he acted like he wanted my number, but here it is, practically a week later, and nothing. Crickets."

Tracey whistled low, earning her a scowl from a passing birder. "Well, it is only Saturday," Tracey said. "Early Saturday, at that."

"I guess."

They had made their way back to the starting point. It wasn't anywhere near ten thirty a.m., but Loretta and Lotte were already waiting for them.

"It is officially too cold to continue," Loretta said.

"But it's just warming up," Candace pointed out. The sun was now spilling a tepid yellow light across the lawn.

"It's coldest just before sunrise."

"Is that true?" Candace whispered to Tracey. Tracey shrugged.

"Let's get breakfast," Loretta said. "There's a diner near here that actually knows what grits are. Follow us." Loretta and Lotte strode back to her Jaguar, Lotte carrying Loretta's gear.

"Grits," Candace repeated. Tracey glanced at her.

"Grits. Southern breakfast fare. Hominy. From corn?"

"I know what they are. 'Hominy' sounds good, like music, or that thing when a word sounds the same but means something different."

"Homonym."

"Right. Like 'grits' could be dirt. Well, dirts."

"Agreed."

Tracey dialed up the heat as they drove, and Candace nodded off in the car. She came to in the diner parking lot and followed everyone inside. Only after a giant hot chocolate and a pecan waffle with hot maple syrup were in front of her did she feel human again. Tracey got eggs Benedict. Loretta got her grits with a ham steak and eggs over medium. Lotte sat at another table doing a crossword puzzle in front of a giant stack of pancakes.

"Are you sure she doesn't want to sit with us?" Candace asked, pouring syrup on her waffle.

"She's fine," Loretta said. "Lotte has zero interest in birding." Which Candace didn't think was the same thing as wanting to sit alone in a restaurant when the people you were with were a booth away, but whatever.

"So you've never searched the Magic Hedge before?" Tracey asked Loretta.

"Oh, I have. Many times. But three sets of eyes are better than one, and birders keep spotting magpies here even though they aren't native to the area. So it seems likely there's a knot around here somewhere."

"You've found a lot of them," Candace said, recalling the map in Loretta's office. "Why are there so many in Illinois?"

"I wish I could tell you." Loretta carved a delicate bite of ham. "I have my suspicions but not enough data yet." Candace folded a not-so-delicate hunk of waffle into her mouth.

"Miss Loretta, Candace here has a question," Tracey said with a grin.

"Mrph!" Candace choked down her food. "What? I don't— Tracey!" She blushed and shook her head. And she couldn't stop the silly smile stretching her cheeks now. Why did embarrassment make her smile?

"Well?" Loretta said.

"Well . . . there's this boy at school. He asked for my number, but he hasn't texted me."

"And he shouldn't!" Loretta said. "He should *call* you. A man's voice is like a love letter. A text is like a wolf whistle on the street."

"Whoa," Candace said. "I like that."

"I do too," Tracey said.

"So, how long should I wait to hear from him?"

"That's not what you're asking. Waiting is the same as not waiting, time is still passing by," Loretta pointed out.

Candace sighed. "You're right."

"What you really want to know is how come he hasn't called you yet," Loretta added.

"I told her it's only been a few—" Tracey began.

"Because he doesn't want to." Loretta folded her napkin. Candace's stomach plummeted.

"Be direct, why don't you," Tracey said.

Loretta laughed. "I am direct, child. I thought you knew that by now. If a boy is interested, he'll let you know. If he's not, he's not. 'A few days' has nothing to do with it." She gave Tracey the side eye. "Even before they invented cellular phones."

Candace thought back to that moment in the alleyway. "So then, what about when a boy acts interested, *says* he's interested, and then he *still* doesn't text or call?"

"I'm single," Tracey said. "If I knew the answer to that, I might still be single, but I'd be rich."

They both looked to Loretta. Who took her sweet time chewing her breakfast and following with a slow sip of coffee.

"Ladies," she said when she was done, "the answer is simple. He's a fool. Knows what he wants but not how to get it. Story as old as the hills. And I say, if that's what happens, be grateful you dodged that bullet. Nothing worse than loving a man who can't treat you like what you're worth. And that is all there is to say about that." She slapped the table. Candace was deeply impressed.

"Thank you, Miss Loretta."

"You're welcome, dear. Now, let's get ourselves home. I'm about due for a nap. I think we all are. Next weekend won't need to be so early."

Candace gave a little cheer. She pulled a folded-up twenty out of her pocket, but Tracey picked up the check. Adult friends were good like that.

And if Mitchell couldn't get it together, who needed him? Not Candace, that was for sure.

24

CANDACE DREW BIRDS. AS THE DAYS GOT A BIT SHORTER, she spent Saturdays bird-watching and Sundays sketching what she saw. No Jordan magpies or interdimensional knots, but plenty of other native Chicago birds and not-so-native ones.

To the west, at the Thatcher Woods Forest Preserve, Candace and Tracey watched flights of blue herons along the Des Plaines River. In Humboldt Park, Loretta pointed out two types of hawks and an actual peregrine falcon. And at Eggers Grove down south, they found about a million sparrows and ducks, and even a yellow-headed blackbird, whose head feathers were exactly the same shade as Candace's Goldengrove hair.

"Don't see them much around here," Loretta said. "Must have gotten lost or blown off course by a storm."

Candace made quick sketches and tried to take photos, but shooting pictures of birds took more skill and a faster camera than her cell phone. The next day, she researched yellow-headed blackbirds online and drew a picture of the bright and dark little creature tossed by a storm, with the Chicago skyline in the background.

"Very cool art," Mr. Jones said. It was the more-than-halfway point to the science fair, and he was reviewing everyone's progress on their projects. In front of the whole class. Which could be useful, getting ideas from everyone. Or humiliating, being judged by your peers. In seventh grade, you only had to present your work once, and only the teachers made comments—not your ex–best friends. At least she got to sit at her desk, instead of standing in front of everyone.

"Cool art," Mr. Jones repeated, holding up the blackbird drawing. "Right, class?"

Candace's heart pounded in her chest, her stomach, her hands and head. Could a heart even do that? It felt like it could. She couldn't look up, couldn't turn to see the faces staring at her little bird drawing. She was storm-tossed. She was going to be sick.

"But," Mr. Jones said, "where is the science? How might biology or ecology come into play in this piece? Any ideas, class?"

"It's a storm, right?" Sergio said. "So how about weather patterns?"

"Meteorology," Mr. Jones said, with a nod. "Good idea. Anyone else?"

Candace took notes as the class chimed in. "Climate change?" someone offered.

"Right! Is it getting more dangerous or difficult to migrate as weather patterns change?" Mr. Jones said with another encouraging nod.

Nate called her project birdbrained, but he insisted he meant bird navigational techniques, how birds figure out where to travel. Candace's cheeks burned, but she wrote it all down, and mumbled her thanks to everyone.

Then it was Sergio's turn to talk about his rocket experiment, which Nate called a space case. Nate was planning to reenact Pompeii with a baking soda volcano. And then Deen and Becca got up and presented their research to date into hair coloring. Not genetics, like Mr. Jones suggested, but actual hair dye. They planned to take pictures of their hair under microscopes to see how the structure changed as their overpriced dye jobs faded.

"Or you could consider factoring in other things like shampoo and conditioner. There's a lot at work when it comes to hair follicles," Mr. Jones said. Other students chimed in with questions about the type of hair dye, whether or not the hair was bleached, and if it was safe to dye hair at all. Candace kept silent. She felt like her marigold hair, newly redyed last weekend, was shining like a spotlight on her head. But then Nate called the project harebrained, and Candace had to stifle a snort. But, because *harebrained* is spelled like a rabbit and not like *hair*, Nate wasn't able to walk it back, and Mr. Jones made him apologize.

Ms. Parker loomed over Candace's sketch pad.

"Where did you learn to draw feathers like that?" she asked.

"Um . . . online videos? And . . . feathers?" Candace said.

"Are you asking or telling me?" Ms. Parker asked. She was a lean, medium-toned Black woman with soft, straightened hair styled into loose curls that she held back with invisible pins or hair product or sheer willpower. She was that sort of woman—a perfectly straight spine, manicured fingernails. Always in a pencil skirt and blouse. Nothing about her said "art teacher." More like "gallery owner," Candace always thought. Ms. Parker was all business.

"Telling," Candace mumbled. She hated this part of class, when the teacher went around and looked at everybody's work. But this was worse, because she wasn't just looking at Candace's bird sketches, she was *considering* them.

"Mr. Jones told me you had some skills, but mostly raw talent," she said after a moment. "I see he is right. Videos are useful, but will only get you so far." She pulled a small notepad from her skirt pocket. How she had kept a notepad there without causing a bulge in her trim figure, Candace could only guess. She jotted something down and handed it to Candace.

"The Hall of Birds?" Candace said, reading the note.

"The Field Museum. Live subjects are great for quick sketches. That can help you capture motion. But if you want to go in depth, science-fair-project depth, you need something that stands still." Ms. Parker tapped the paper with a French-tipped fingernail. "The Hall of Birds."

"Thank you," Candace said. She was grinning. She stopped herself. She'd been to the Field Museum before, of course. Back in fifth grade, they'd called it "the Dead Zoo" because all of the wildlife was stuffed and mounted. And really, she wasn't excited about that. But Loretta had texted to say rain was expected all weekend, and their birding trip was canceled. (Lotte drew the line at letting Loretta sit in the rain.) Now maybe they could bird indoors—even if those birds were only taxidermy. She would invite them after school.

The bigger reason for her grin was because Mr. Jones had told Ms. Parker she could draw, and Ms. Parker had agreed. Even better, she'd practically said so in front of Deen and Becca. Sure, they had love triangles and camping trips and salon-styled hair, but Candace had raw talent.

At the end of the week, when other kids were making plans for their Halloween costumes, Candace was not. And even though her parents had approved the museum trip with Tracey and Loretta, the lack of Halloweening weighed on her. Usually, she'd go trick-or-treating with Deen and Becca, with Sergio and Nate tagging along. But they still weren't exactly talking, except when school made it necessary, and Becca had apparently decided that she and Sergio were too old for dressing up. As if you could ever be too old for awesome costumes and free candy.

"You got a costume yet?" Mitchell asked when she was at her locker, packing up for the weekend.

"Nope." Despite her lack of friends, she didn't exactly want to talk to Mitchell either. He still hadn't texted her, but every day at school he acted like that didn't matter. Like school friends weren't totally different from outside-of-school friends. Talking to each other at school was practically mandatory. A text, on the other hand, would have been next-level. Candace missed having next-level friends.

"Me either," Mitchell said, oblivious to the entire subtext of their nontexting conversation. "My mom used to make my costume, but this year she's too busy. We usually go to my cousins' house and have a big dinner, then take all the little kids out."

"Cool," Candace said, zipping up her backpack. It wasn't like he was inviting her or anything. She took a breath, aware that she was being grumpy. "I'm going to the Field Museum this weekend," she said. *Want to come?* she did not say. The question stuck in her throat and sort of croaked out like a weird duck call instead.

"What was that?" Mitchell asked.

"Uh . . . nothing." Candace closed her locker and her mouth. Maybe she was birdbrained after all.

"Whoa."

Even though Candace had been to the Field Museum before, it made a big impression each time. For one thing, the building itself looked like an ancient Greek temple, with wide steps leading up to a massive stone building with rows and rows of columns holding up the entrance, and small ones all along each side. Then there was the main hallway, a soaring white room lined by more columns and archways, dominated by a massive, rust-colored dinosaur skeleton—Máximo the Titanosaur, which stood more than two stories tall.

Beside Candace, Loretta chuckled. "This place has changed a lot since my day. Back then, the biggest thing in this hall was those two elephants," she said, pointing to a dais with two taxidermied bull elephants, one charging the other with its trunk raised in what looked to Candace like a bellow of fear or pain. "Never understood why they had to be fighting, though."

"Somebody probably thought it looked cool," Tracey commented.

"They probably looked cooler in the wild," Candace said. The expression on the charging elephant looked sad to her. It was depressing. Maybe the Dead Zoo wasn't such a great idea after all.

"Let's not lollygag, youngblood," Loretta said, and led the way past Máximo to the Hall of Birds.

According to the museum guide, the hall held over a thousand species. And unlike those earlier field trips when Candace's class rushed through the exhibits in a whirl of jokes, whispers, and shushes from the teacher, this time, every single object meant something.

It meant the shape of a bird's wings, and how it varied from one species to another. It meant the color of the plumage, and what shades Candace could hope to capture with her pencils and markers. It meant learning about habitats, and populations, and a million other things.

Tracey and Loretta held back, allowing Candace to wade through the flood of information. There were displays on migration patterns, magnetic line navigation, the science of flight, and the role of birds in maintaining the ecosystem, including how they helped spread seeds with their poop. There were seabirds and land birds and flightless birds on display, stuffed and mounted as if in mid-flight. The Dead Zoo was awful, in a way, but also amazing. Most of these birds had died before Candace was born, she told herself. And she would never have gotten the chance to see any of them up close in the wild.

"Science is kind of sketchy," she said over grilled cheese sandwiches and cups of soup in the museum café. "I mean, it's cool to see, but someone killed all those birds. That can't be right."

"You're talking about ethics," Loretta said. "When does the evil men do in the name of knowledge outweigh the good? That's the tipping point, and a lot of people have argued over where it is for all sorts of scientific endeavors. Is it right to test on animals, for instance?"

"No!" Candace said vehemently.

"But what if it leads to a cure for cancer in humans?" Tracey asked.

"Still . . . no? Who says humans are more valuable than lab animals?"

Tracey sighed. "The law, for one, and some religions. Lots of people do." Tracey bit her lip, and Candace wondered if it was cancer that had taken Tracey's mom.

"But that doesn't make it right," Candace said.

"No, that doesn't make it ethical," Loretta replied. "Right and wrong are very simple concepts. Ethics weighs the value of each thing, and tries to come out on the side of the greater good."

Candace suddenly felt terrible. An eighth-grade science project wasn't exactly the greater good. "According to who?" she asked.

"Whom," Loretta corrected her, then smiled. "And that, my child, is ethics."

"Maybe that's what my project could be about," she said a while later, as they descended the stairs to the parking lot. "Finding that balance. Mr. Jones says birds are affected by stuff like the weather and things humans do. But we wouldn't know that if we didn't study birds. And maybe in studying them, we can find a way to help?"

The wheels were turning in her head. On the drive home, they passed the Lincoln Park Zoo, a living zoo instead of a dead one, with animals kept in cages for study, for entertainment, and also for maintaining the populations of endangered creatures.

Kind of like grade school. Only kids weren't endangered, and in school, the kids did the studying. And wasn't Tracey's purple notebook like a field guide, studying animals in an enclosed environment?

It was only that night, as she flipped through her notes and sketches, that Candace realized the Field Museum, for all of its specimens, was missing one thing. There hadn't been a single Jordan magpie on display anywhere.

It was a rare bird, indeed.

The heat was on in the small gym where the science fair was being held. It was a weird one, falling on Halloween, so most of the kids were in some sort of costume. Candace went as a birder. She wore a sunhat, with binoculars around her neck. Pretty accurate, if also last-minute. Not that anyone got it. Deen wore an orange jack-o'-lantern T-shirt over black leggings. Mr. Jones came as a vampire, with fake blood dripping from the corner of his mouth and an oversized pair of fangs that he had to keep taking out in order to give feedback on the projects. Becca, true to her word, was not in a costume. Except she was wearing a seashell headband and a sea-green dress, so clearly, she was everyday-cosplaying a mermaid. Sergio hadn't gotten the memo. He was in his usual T-shirt and jeans.

Nate, on the other hand, was dressed in a bedsheet toga over his jeans, with a golden laurel leaf crown. He made a big deal out of "igniting" his volcano and flooding the miniature Pompeii he'd created out of action figures and plastic blocks at the base.

It was actually kind of cool. Candace's project was less demonstrative. When the judges came by—Mr. Jones, the assistant principal, and a student's father who apparently worked in a lab—she pointed her way through three posters' worth of illustrations of the sorts of birds, like the golden-haired blackbird, that were beginning to show up in Chicago out of season. She'd learned that while most birders just watched, some were the sorts of scientists who captured, tagged, and released birds. This was one way of tracking populations, but it also raised questions of ethics, like how did it change the life of a bird to have a metal tag on its leg or a tracker in its wing? Could other birds tell if one had been captured by humans? Would it change the way they treated that bird?

"Lots of good questions," Mr. Jones said when she was done. "Now I have one for you. If you discovered you could reincarnate a human being with lightning, would you?"

Candace blinked. "What?"

"Reincarnate," the parent judge said. "It means 'bring back to life.'"

Candace knew that. "I know that . . . sir. But it . . ." She looked at Mr. Jones, who was giving her encouraging eyebrow wiggles. "It wouldn't be . . . ethical," she concluded. "I mean, what if it went wrong?"

"Yes!" Mr. Jones crowed. "Future scientists of America! Just because you can do something, doesn't mean you should. A-plus, Miss Wells!"

"Really?" Candace said.

"On the monster quiz, yes," he replied. "On the project, the judges will have to tally their results."

"Did they Frankenstein you, or werewolf you?" Cerise asked from her project across the table, describing the Andromeda Galaxy. "Mr. Jones is asking monster-movie questions for Halloween."

"What did you get?" Candace asked.

"*Creature from the Black Lagoon.* Some old movie about a monster in the water. He wanted to know if it should be left in the wild or brought back to study in a lab."

"What did you say?" Candace asked.

"I said I can't swim."

They both laughed, and waited for the judges to finish their rounds.

Candace eyed her display and felt a twinge of sadness. The science fair had been her excuse to go birding with Tracey and Loretta. They had even helped her with the display. Now that it was done, she'd probably have to give up birding. Or find another excuse to continue it.

That night, when she came home with a green ribbon of merit for her project (it turned out the grade was only about participation), her mother gave her a hug, and her dad gave her an extra scoop of garlic mashed potatoes at dinner. She texted a picture of the ribbon to Tracey and Loretta, who flooded her with clapping emojis and a blue ribbon icon, which was great.

"Mom," Candace said as she headed to bed. "Is it okay if I keep hanging out with Tracey and Loretta? Even though the fair is over?"

Her mother looked up at her from the sofa, where she and Candace's dad were watching some late-night talk show. "Sure, honey. As long as you're having fun, I think it's nice."

"Thanks, Mom." Candace kissed both of her parents good night and went to bed only feeling slightly guilty that she hadn't told them the whole truth about hunting for knots in the sky.

25

NOVEMBER CAME ON COLD AND QUICK. CANDACE'S bird-watching weekends were getting harder to look forward to, even if she did like spending time with Tracey and Loretta. They'd gone to a few other wetland areas and nature preserves, but they hadn't seen a single Jordan magpie yet, and Loretta was starting to look pretty down about it.

But even with the science fair behind her, Candace continued to learn a lot about birds and bird-watching, and her drawings were getting better all the time. She drew sketches during the bird walks, and then worked in greater detail when she got back home.

"Did you know John James Audubon might have been part Black?" she asked her mom one day. She'd been reading up on the National Audubon Society, which had been protecting and observing birds since the late 1800s. Some Audubon folks had been on a bird walk in the same park as Candace and her ladies that morning.

"But back when Loretta started bird-watching, they weren't so 'keen on integration.'" She put down her colored pencils to use air quotes around Loretta's words.

"And here I was thinking you were just looking at birds,"

her mother said. "History is a complicated place, Candace. You'll learn a lot from Miss Loretta, I bet."

Candace could only agree.

She'd learned not to worry about Mitchell's lack of texting. And he still said hi to her in the hallways, so that was good, if confusing. And she'd learned that, despite having had one her whole life, she could carry on without a best friend. At least for a while. But seeing Deen and Becca and Sergio in various combinations, with Nate tagging along, still smarted.

Even so, she was mostly doing fine all the way up to Thanksgiving week, when Mitchell swung by her locker and said, "Anything fun for Thanksgiving?"

And Candace's delusions of fineness collapsed.

Thanksgiving was a Deen-and-Candace tradition. They'd cuddle up in pajamas on Wednesday night and watch *A Charlie Brown Thanksgiving* and make themselves sick on popcorn with jelly beans and toast, like the kids in the cartoon. And then they'd sleep in until whichever of their mothers was present woke them up and took one home so they could have turkey with their own families.

"No," Candace said. "Well, my aunt and uncle are coming to town. If that's what you call fun."

"That's what I call family," Mitchell said. "Can they cook?"

"Yeah. So can my mom and dad."

"Sounds good to me," Mitchell said. "My mom always buys a precooked meal at the place down the street."

"Nothing homemade?" Candace asked.

"Well, we heat it up. But it's more like 'made at home' than the other way around."

The warning bell rang for class. Mitchell backed away toward his classroom and held up his phone. "I'll call you. Maybe we can hang out."

"Cool," she said. But it was more than cool. Not just "I'll text you," but an "I'll call you" and a "hang out"! Hooray!

And then school was over and her mom and dad went into high gear prepping Thanksgiving dinner. They watched all of the Indiana Jones movies on Wednesday night, and all of the Star Wars original trilogy Thursday afternoon.

Aunt Sylvia and Uncle Will, her mom's brother, showed up for Thanksgiving dinner, having driven in from Ohio. ("Traffic is a dream Thanksgiving morning!" Uncle Will declared.) They stuffed themselves silly with the usual fixings, plus her mother's gumbo and her aunt's macaroni and cheese. Aunt Sylvia was Chinese, but she'd grown up in Mississippi. Her soul food was as good as anyone's. Then, while her mom and aunt plotted holiday shopping, she sat next to her dad and Uncle Will as *they* watched all of the Lord of the Rings original trilogy Thursday night into Friday morning. Candace mostly watched her phone.

On Black Friday, after her mom and aunt came back from the sales, they played Black History trivia games. "People forget we have February *and* the day after Thanksgiving," her mother had pointed out. A day when prices were low enough to almost make up for the disparity in pay Black people—especially women—experienced, she said. But just for the one day, Aunt Sylvia had added. She had picked up the Asian American–Pacific Islander Edition trivia game on sale that morning.

"If you come for Memorial Day, we can break it out for AAPI Month," Uncle Will said.

Candace woke up before sunrise on the Saturday after Thanksgiving and stared at the ceiling in the dark. The holiday had come and gone without popcorn, jelly beans, or her and Deen's annual screening of *A Charlie Brown Thanksgiving*. Not even a text saying "Happy Thanksgiving." A tradition of six years down the toilet, just like that. And then there was Mitchell. Would he really call her this time? She'd stared at her phone all week, willing it to buzz. But it hadn't. And now it was time to go birding again. Was it weird that she was actually looking forward to the distraction?

She dressed blearily, pulling on leggings, then jeans, long-sleeve shirt, sweatshirt, coat, and scarf. Gloves. She shoved her sketchbook into her backpack with some snacks and a thermos of coffee, and then undid all the clothes to pee one last time before Tracey texted to say she was outside.

"Have fun," her mother said, folding leftover stuffing into the waffle iron. Uncle Will was still snoring away in the guest room/office, but Aunt Sylvia was eyeing her over a cup of coffee.

"Mrph," Candace said, then kissed her mother's cheek goodbye and gave a side hug to her aunt.

"You just let her roam the city all hours?" she heard Aunt Sylvia ask as she headed out the door.

"She's not *roaming*. It's a legacy circle . . ."

Outside, everything looked brittle. The black road was

frosted gray at the edges. Her nose hairs crackled and froze. Tracey's sedan smoked on the side of the road like a bull building up a head of angry steam from the wrong end. The door cracked when she opened it and got in. Even the seats were stiff and unyielding.

"I'm only doing this for the science," Tracey said by way of greeting.

"Me too," Candace replied. After the science fair ended, she found she was still thinking about everything she'd learned. Including the mysterious Jordan magpie that even the Field collection had never heard of. It was a true mystery, which was kind of exciting, but maybe not at the freezing-before-dawn level.

It had been Loretta's idea to go back to the Magic Hedge in the middle of a cold snap. Her theory was that knots might be easier to spot with the leaves off the trees.

They drove into the frigid city. On Lake Shore Drive, Candace stared out at the frozen waves along the beach, dirty gray caps dusted in white. It must have snowed a little during the night.

Tracey parked even farther from the water than usual.

"We'll walk the rest of the way to stay warm, and keep that from happening to my car," she said, pointing at the few unfortunate vehicles that had parked too close to the lake and were now coated in a thin layer of ice. Their owners would have to chisel them out or wait for the spring thaw.

The Magic Hedge hadn't gotten any more magical since their first visit, but it was still surprisingly busy considering the location on the frozen nose tip of the city, the hour, and the holiday. Today, the birders wore hefty parkas and milled about with their binoculars and cameras peeking out of their coats like baby kangaroos of black metal and glass.

Loretta was sitting in her folding throne, a puffy comforter around her legs. Her electric socks must have been working overtime. "Thirty minutes, youngbloods. It's too cold to tarry today," she announced.

"Good morning to you too," Tracey said.

"Happy Thanksgiving," Candace chimed in.

"Thank you, child," Loretta said, but her mouth had pulled down into a little sad line. Tracey didn't seem to notice. "Thirty minutes, then we'll go get somewhere warm."

"Don't freeze to death while we're gone," Tracey muttered, and she tromped off down the path. Candace followed, dreaming of electric socks. Her nose was frozen, her jaw juddering like it was trying to keep warm with or without her help.

"Let me rewrap your scarf," Tracey said. They paused and for a few frozen moments Candace went scarfless. And then, miracle of miracles, Tracey looped and swooped, and she was as warm as she had ever been at six thirty in the morning in November in Chicago. Which was to say, not very warm, but at least now air passed through her scarf before entering her nose. Her nose hairs wouldn't freeze.

"Thank you!" Candace said, without shuddering quite so much. She peered over her scarf at her gloves. "Did you have a good Thanksgiving?" Candace asked. Tracey shrugged.

"Pretty good. My grocery store makes a decent turkey breast to go. I made an apple pie. Should have brought you some, or I'll just eat it all."

"You had Thanksgiving alone?" Candace asked. "Aww!"

"What?" Tracey said. "You had a houseful of people, I suppose? Cousins and aunts and uncles and the rest?"

"No cousins. Jamie stayed at college. But my aunt and uncle drove up from Ohio."

"Sounds nice."

"It was good." They paused and watched their breath clouding the sky. Candace wondered if she'd miss the knot because of the steam they were creating. "So you're an only child, too?" she asked.

"Yep. Just me and my dad for a long time."

"So . . . is your dad . . . not around anymore?"

"He's around," Tracey said. "Retired to Florida for the deep-sea fishing. I see him in the summer."

They trudged along, the grass crunching like peanut brittle under their feet. A few hawks circled overhead, but the sky remained empty of bloops or birds of unordinary colouring.

"I feel bad for Miss Loretta," Candace said as the clock ticked toward their meeting time. "We've been at this for weeks, and nada. At least I got a green ribbon out of it."

Tracey stopped in the middle of the path. "Candace, I thought you understood. This might not be a thing, you know. Knots and mysterious birds. It might just be an old lady looking for company."

"Company?" Candace spread her arms around at the brambles and trees. "To meet up and send us off into the middle of nowhere? How is that company? We could just . . . I don't know, meet for brunch! This has to be real. Otherwise, explain the notebook and our bird drawing and the missing wing feathers, and no Jordans at the museum, and all of that stuff."

Tracey opened her mouth, but nothing came out. Candace kept walking.

"If you can't explain it, then this is the explanation," she called back over her shoulder.

"Fine," Tracey said, jogging to catch up.

"Fine, what? You agree?"

"I do. About brunch."

They made their way back to Loretta and drove to the same diner as before, technically too early for brunch, but welcome just the same. Lotte took her usual solo booth. Loretta pulled out her observation notes and scowled.

"Used to be I'd see at least one Jordan a month out here. And now not a single sighting. Maybe it's all the traffic."

"Or the cold weather," Candace said.

"Magpies don't migrate," Loretta said. "At least not your garden-variety magpie, that is." She marked an X through the Magic Hedge on her map. "If there's a knot around here, maybe I was mistaken. It must not be in the hedge itself."

Tracey was staring hard at her coffee cup. "About that. These knots. Could we see one of the other ones you've found in the wild?" she asked. She'd somehow already cleaned her plate and was signaling for more coffee.

"Oooh! Could we?" Candace tried to cover her mouth and had to catch a piece of half-chewed waffle. Loretta frowned.

"Not a bad idea," she conceded. "There's one out west in

Batavia, a bit closer for me and not too far for you. Supposed to rain next week, so how about the weekend after next?"

"Candace?" Tracey said.

Candace swallowed. "I'll ask." She wiped her mouth and hand, and pulled out her phone to text home.

It wasn't even noon when Tracey dropped her off. Candace felt like she'd lived a whole extra day when normally she'd still be in her pajamas. No wonder her mom liked getting up early. But then maybe every day was just extra exhausting.

Inside, her dad was watching a James Bond marathon and ironing his work shirts.

"There she is!" he said when Candace came through the door.

"Hi." She shucked herself free of her coat and hat and carefully wrapped her arms around her dad's middle, pressing her cheek to his back. "Where is everybody?"

"Where do you think? Out shopping, even Will. We might go to the movies tonight. They head out early tomorrow."

"I'm sorry I wasn't here to spend more time with them," Candace said.

"You'd just have been carrying bags while your mother and aunt spent all their money."

It was true, a Thanksgiving ritual that Candace actually enjoyed. Deen would always come along, and they would window-shop and make Christmas wish lists and gossip in the food court at the mall. At least, until this year.

"How was it?" Her dad brought her back to the present, Deenless holiday weekend.

"Cold. We saw some hawks."

"That's something."

"Yeah. I'm going to go draw them. It was too cold to take my gloves off before."

"Did you eat?"

"Waffles!" She went to the kitchen and put the kettle on for tea. "Want some? Tea, not waffles."

"No, thanks. Oh, you got a phone call, by the way."

Candace stuck her head out of the kitchen doorway. "No." She held up her phone.

Her dad laughed. "No, I mean a landline phone call. Someone actually called the house. I thought it was a prank."

Candace's heart did a little jump. Had Mitchell called her home number? "Who was it?"

"Deenie."

26

CANDACE'S HEAD POUNDED AS ALL THE BLOOD RUSHED to her ears.

"Can you believe that?" Candace's dad said. "I haven't talked to Deenie on the phone since you all got cell phones back in sixth grade."

Her stomach was jumping now instead of her heart.

"What did she want?"

"Didn't say. I told her you'd call her back."

"Oh. Okay. Thanks."

Deen had called her. *Called* her. Like, on the phone. Not a text. What was it Loretta had said—a call is a love letter, a text is a passing shout? Did that only count for dating, or could this mean Deen still wanted to be her friend?

Candace went into her bedroom and shut the door. She pulled out her phone and opened a new text, then stopped. It had to be a phone call, to show Deen that she was willing, too. That she missed her and that Thanksgiving hadn't been the same without her.

In the kitchen, the kettle began to wail. Candace dropped her phone and raced to turn it off. *Just make the tea,* she told herself, *and by the time you're done, you'll know what to say.* She chose tulsi tea with ginger, because it was supposed to help reduce stress and the ginger gave it a little bite. She chose her favorite mug, shaped like a flower-covered VW van, and filled it almost to the top before carrying it carefully back to her bedroom.

Settling the mug on her side table coaster and herself on the bed, she picked up her phone. Nothing had come to her. Might as well just dial and see what happened. This was a peace talk, but better than last time—a friendship talk. An image flashed through her head of Tracey eating a takeout dinner on the sofa on Thanksgiving. Not that she'd said she had eaten it on the sofa, but it seemed like a lonely thing to do at the holidays. What if Tracey had made up with Dia way back when? Maybe they could have had Thanksgiving together this year, at a real table.

Still, when Candace called back, she dialed Deen's house phone number, just like Deen had done. That way, if it had been some kind of joke or mistake, she could just hang up and there wouldn't be a record of her call. Unless, of course, someone answered.

"Hullo?" someone answered. Shoot! Candace took a breath.

"Hi, Mr. De La Cruz. It's Candace Wells. Happy Thanksgiving."

"To you too. Hold on." She heard him cup his hand over the phone and scream, "Nadiiiiiine! Telephoooone!"

Candace listened to the thump of her own heart and the scuffle of phones being picked up and hung up over the line.

"This is Nadine," Deen said, like she was working in an office or something.

"Deen, it's Candace. My dad said you called."

Candace could hear Deen breathing. "Oh, yeah. Hey, Candace. Happy Thanksgiving."

"To you too."

There was silence. Long enough for Candace to play an entire mental montage of six years of popcorn and jelly beans together.

"So," she said.

"Did your aunt and uncle come out?" Deen asked.

"Yeah. They leave tomorrow."

"Cool."

"Yeah." What was even happening? Candace picked up her tea and took a sip, burning her tongue. "Ah!"

"What?" Deen asked anxiously.

"Nothing. Hot tea. Too hot. So . . . what did you call about?"

Candace could have kicked herself. She shouldn't have asked. The bigger thing to do would have been to invite Deen over. To the movies, maybe, with her family tonight.

"Do you want to go to the—" she started to say.

"I think Becca's breaking up with Sergio," Deen said.

"What?"

"I think Becca's breaking up with Sergio. She just seems really not into him anymore."

"Oh."

"Yeah, it's totally sad."

"Uh-huh."

"And I was wondering . . . Do you think it would be weird if, you know, I asked him out?"

"What?" It was like a soap opera had interrupted their call. "You still want to?" she asked. "After all . . . that?"

"All what? They seemed happy together. It's really sad it's not working out."

"Riiight. But you want to get in on that," Candace pointed out.

"Well, yeah. I mean, I want to be happy, too."

"There are other guys, Deenie."

"Oh, you mean like Mitchell from the other class?"

"No! I mean, yeah, technically, he's another guy, but . . ."

"So it wouldn't bother you if Becca was seeing him?"

Candace almost spilled her tea.

"Is she?"

"No. I'm just . . . I don't know. I'm just saying, if she was and she dumped him, would you still like him, or do you think you could just get over it like that?"

Candace put the mug down gently onto the side table. "Deen, are you telling me that Becca cut in on you and Sergio, and now she's trying to do the same to me?"

Deen sighed heavily into the phone.

"Cans, this isn't about you. It's a hypothetical. God, are you even listening? I still like Sergio! I just don't want to hurt Becca by doing anything, you know? Since you know them, I thought you could give me some advice, that's all. I don't know anything about that other guy."

The conversation had taken a weird turn. An uneasy one.

"I guess . . ." Candace said slowly, "if Sergio is into you, and you're into him, and Becca doesn't care, then . . ."

"You're saying I should ask Becca."

"Um . . . I'm saying you should talk to Ser—"

"Becca might know if he likes me. Huh. I hadn't thought of that. What if that's why she's dumping him?"

"Deen, I think you're jumping to—"

"I wasn't sure at first, but it seemed like he was definitely trying to touch my hand the other night. We kept reaching for the popcorn and jelly beans at the same time. I thought it was accidental at first. Becca must have noticed."

Candace's soul record-scratched loud and clear. "Popcorn and jelly beans?"

"Yeah, they came over to watch the Charlie Brown special. I told them how we used to do it, and they were into it."

"But that was *our* thing."

There was a long pause on the other end of the line.

"Yeah, but . . ."

"But what?"

"Well . . . they did it to cheer me up."

"Because why?" Candace asked.

"Because I was mad at you?"

"Because . . . ?"

"Because you made me feel bad? At Nate's? And you're doing it again, Candace. Honestly, it's like I'm never good enough for you."

"What?" Candace laughed. "I don't even know what's going on anymore. Deen, you're my best friend, you have been for, like, forever. But now it's like you've got Becca on the brain or something. Like you've forgotten me!"

"Forgotten you! With your weird secret old lady friends and your bird-watching and your—"

"Wait, how do you know about that?" It wasn't like they'd been talking or anything.

"Seriously? You keep posting pictures of random fields and diners!"

Candace hadn't realized Deen was still checking up on her

online. Which was kind of nice. She had kept lurking on Deen's feeds, too. But also . . . "That's only on the weekends! And it's not like you're not always posting your stuff! You know what? Just go back to your little love triangle! And if it makes you feel bad, consider that it's your choices that you're feeling bad about, not me pointing them out."

"And I thought I was being nice calling you to wish you a happy Thanksgiving," Deen said.

"You didn't call me for that! Thanksgiving was two days ago! You called to ask me if it was okay to date your new best friend's soon-to-be ex-boyfriend. That is not the same thing."

"Obviously this was a mistake."

"Obviously."

And they both hung up.

"Goodbye!" Candace said to the phone.

"How's Nadine?" Candace's mother asked when she wandered back into the living room a few tearful hours later. Her parents were sitting on the sofa with her aunt and uncle, admiring their haul of affordable sweaters, socks, and Christmas-themed plates.

"Oh, honey, what's wrong?" Her mother was up and beside her in an instant. *See?* Candace thought. *Splashing water on a tear-stained face never fooled anybody.*

Candace sobbed into her mother's arms for a few shuddering moments. A tissue appeared in her mom's hand. Candace mopped her nose.

"Nothing," she lied.

"Oh, baby. It's hard being thirteen." Candace could not help but agree.

"Are we going to the movies?" she asked.

"Do you still want to?" her uncle said kindly.

Candace sniffled. "Yeah."

"All right, then. There's a seven o'clock. Time for a leftovers sandwich before we go."

It was over said sandwiches that Candace's mom remembered her text. "More bird-watching next Saturday?"

"Not until the ninth, and we're driving up to Batavia," Candace said. "Not so early this time, thank Jeebus."

"You had fun today?" Aunt Sylvia asked.

"Yeah! I mean, it was way too cold, but we saw hawks that I can add to my portfolio."

"She started drawing the birds of Chicago for her school science project," her mom said. "And it stuck."

"The Audubon Society actually has a big backyard bird count over the winter break. But I'm trying to find more than just pigeons and sparrows, you know?" Candace said. "One website said you can even find birds from Africa up here at different times of year."

"That's a wrong turn somewhere," Uncle Will said.

"Migratory patterns keep changing," Candace explained. "So I'm hoping to see something interesting one day."

"That's great, hon," Aunt Sylvia said. "And this is with your older lady friends?"

"Legacy mentors," Candace's mom corrected.

"Yeah, Miss Loretta and Tracey," Candace said. "They're not my friends." Candace didn't have any friends. Tracey and

Loretta would never sit on the sofa eating popcorn and jelly beans with her. "It's science," she added.

"Get this," her mom said, "they all shared the same locker at Walden!"

"The same locker?" her uncle said. "I don't think I could tell you where my locker was. Could you?" he asked the other adults. Which was good, because it sent them down a long conversation about lockers and schools and people they knew, which carried on into the car and all the way to the theater, so Candace didn't have a chance to slip up and tell them anything else about knots and interdimensional magpies or how Deen and Aunt Sylvia might have been right, and her real friends were two older ladies she'd met through a window in the sky.

"But it doesn't make sense," Dorianna told the puzzle monkey. "You said if I solved all of the puzzle trees, you would let me go."

All around her, the puzzle trees rose unlocked and at their full height, no longer the magical hedgerow maze she had entered hours ago.

"No, I didn't," the puzzle monkey said.

Dorianna stamped her foot in frustration. "You can't change the rules now," she said.

"I haven't. The rules were 'solve all of the puzzles, and you will go free.'" The monkey sat calmly on its rock and picked invisible nothings from its fur.

"So, I've solved all the trees, but not all of the puzzles," Dorianna realized. "But the only thing left unsolved is *you!*"

"Not every puzzle has a solution," the monkey replied.

27

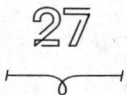

CANDACE HAD GOTTEN VERY GOOD AT DRAWING BIRDS. Mostly it entailed eating lunch alone in the corner of the cafeteria, staring out the window with a sketch pad next to her tray. And ignoring Deen and Becca. And Mitchell, who had smiled and waved at Candace the first day back after Thanksgiving as if he hadn't promised to call and "hang out" over the holiday.

She learned to draw what were called orbital feathers, the tiniest feathers around a bird's eye, from the pigeons that gathered on the windowsill out of the snow. And she read about bird counts and how everyday bird-watchers could help the planet by keeping track of bird populations. And if it didn't exactly fill the hole left by her friends, it was interesting. Sort of.

"Ready?"

Candace spun the combination on her locker and waited for Cerise to get clear. It had become an anti-bird-attack ritual with the two of them. Cerise would get her stuff from her locker first, number 234, and then Candace would stand to one side while she opened hers.

"Go ahead," Cerise said, pulling her parka over her head like a giant puffy shield against bird claws. December had blown in like its usual frosty self, and winter coats made good protection against the Hawk's icy winds, and actual birds.

Candace opened her locker.

"Nope," she said. "All clear." Maybe it would be for another forty years.

"Cool." Cerise pulled her coat on properly.

"Hey, doing anything for Christmas?" Candace asked, unloading and reloading her backpack.

"Wisconsin to see my grandparents."

"Oh. Cool." It wasn't actually. Candace was hoping she'd say she was in town, and maybe they would go see a movie or something and transform their purely locker-based relationship to an actual friendship. One that wasn't about space-time or love triangles, yet totally age-appropriate and nonweird.

"You?" Cerise said.

"We're here. My aunt and uncle usually come, but they're going on a cruise this year. So . . ." She shrugged, aware that the looming holidays with no Deen and Becca and Sergio and Nate were starting to look bleak. "Also, some bird-watching. The Audubon Society does a Christmas Backyard Bird Count? For science," she added, realizing how not-cool that might sound to someone like Cerise.

"Awesome," Cerise said. "Well, have a good one."

And she left.

Candace sighed and put on her coat. She'd spent all of her free time this week in the library, drawing and reading up on birds. Day after tomorrow, they'd head to Batavia to see Loretta's knot. She was excited for it. Which probably really wasn't normal for thirteen.

"Backyard Bird Count!" she muttered self-mockingly. "Ugh. I sound like a loser."

But then again, Cerise didn't know about the knots or the magpies. Not that Candace had seen a knot yet, or another magpie. For all she knew, Tracey was right and Loretta was just a birthday party magician and the wormhole in her locker was a trick.

She stared into the upper cubbyhole, willing a bird to fly out. It did not.

"Pretty elaborate trick," she said, and pulled her books out of her backpack.

Was this what it had been like for Loretta for the past bajillion years? Sounding like a weird bird-watcher when she was supposed to be going to parties or out on dates? Unable to tell her friends how very cool her discovery actually was?

Assuming Loretta had ever had friends. She didn't seem to. But then again, maybe all of her friends were dead.

Suitably depressed, Candace shut her locker door. She had checked an old copy of *Window in the Sky* and a couple of birding books out of the library. She had fully intended to read the Skylark series by the time they drove to Batavia. But most likely, she'd watch the movie. Candace was a disappointment to herself in this respect. But she felt that her honesty made up for it, in a way.

"Ignore her."

That would be Becca. Those were Becca's magic words for *we're walking past you, and you don't matter to us.* Which of course meant that she did.

Candace spun around. "Hey, Nate, Sergio," she said brightly.

"Mitchell!" Mitchell from the other eighth grade appeared from across the hall, but he didn't seem to hear her. Becca smirked at that. And, of course, he had never called her, so it was doubly embarrassing.

"Hey, Candace," Nate said. Sergio was more subdued. He was also carrying Deen's books. Like a chump. Wait, did that mean the switch had happened? Based on the awkward look Sergio gave her, then the books, then her again—yes. Candace raised an eyebrow. And then they were gone into the crowd.

Life was simpler without some people, Candace decided. Maybe it was better, too.

※

"I'm just saying," her mom said. "It would be good for you to hang out with some people your own age, too." Even so, she folded some money into Candace's hand. "You buy lunch this time. Dutch at the most."

"Mom, we're not 'hanging out.' We're doing science. Bird science—"

"Ornithology," her mother said.

"Ornithology, and legacy mentoring stuff. I'm learning a lot," Candace insisted, loading her backpack with Sibley's *Birds of Northern Illinois* foldout guide and two local books specific to Batavia.

"Candy Cane, you said 'bird science.' You're not convincing me."

Candace paused. "So I got the name wrong. Sorry. But Tracey and Miss Loretta are nice, and Becca and Deen are bi—"

She caught her mother's look. "Aren't. And I am trying to make new friends, but they don't call me when they say they will, or they go to Wisconsin or whatever. It's hard. So just, please don't give me a lecture right now, okay?"

Candace's mother studied her face. She drew a deep breath through her nose. "Okay. But maybe we can meet this Miss Loretta sometime. Over the holidays? And have Tracey for breakfast again. Your dad's jonesing for a ham-off."

"A ham what?"

"Rice and Sons versus Denton's." Her mother shook her head. "I don't know, some sort of Southern salt bomb battle. Let's just let them do their thing."

"Okay, I'll ask." Candace shouldered her bag and headed for the door.

"Candace? You tell me if you need anything, okay? If you're unhappy . . . well, you can talk to me."

"I know, Mom." Candace hesitated by the door. "I do have one question."

Her mom brightened. "Shoot."

"Say you meet a boy and he's nice and funny and he says he'll call, but never does. Why does that happen?"

Her mom's face softened. She moved in to kiss Candace on the forehead. "Because boys are clueless like that sometimes."

"When do they get smarter?" Candace asked.

"Some of them grow up. And some grow up just enough," she added, glancing down the hall. In the shower, her dad had just begun to sing. Her mom rolled her eyes. "He never did learn the lyrics to that song."

"I love you, Mom," Candace said, and headed out the door.

Batavia looked like a tourist destination. Cute little buildings with wooden beams in deep colors like mustard and red. There was a windmill on the main road into town. Tracey kept driving past the shops and little restaurants and out onto a wide road that cut through prairieland. Despite the December frost, there was no snow.

"What is that?" Candace asked, pointing to the horizon. Rising up out of the brittle grassland was a cement monolith. It swooped up into the sky like Space Mountain at Disney World, or something space-age like that.

"That's Fermilab," Tracey said.

"What's Fermilab?"

"It's a quantum physics laboratory. They have one of the world's first and largest particle accelerators."

"You mean like an atom smasher? Like that thing in Switzerland that was making all those little black holes?" Candace shuddered. She thought a hall full of dead birds might be unethical. Did scientists have the right to risk tearing the entire *solar system* apart just so they could study what it was made of? Oh, shoot! Was that what they were doing?

"Are we going there?" Candace's voice cracked.

"Relax. The prairies mean there're a lot of birds here. At least that's what the website says. They even do one of those big bird counts at the end of December, but Loretta wanted to avoid the extra crowds."

"Oh." They drove closer to the monolith. "Do you think . . . Are knots little black holes?" Candace asked.

Tracey hesitated. "I'm not a scientist. But it seems to me that black holes are known for indiscriminately sucking in light and anything else that gets too close to the event horizon. The edge," she explained, seeing Candace's look. "What they aren't known for is sucking in and spitting out magpies."

"True," Candace said. It made her feel a little better. But as they got closer to the building, her uneasiness increased. And then they took a turn and moved away from the main facility.

"Whoa, what is *that*?" Candace asked, pointing again.

A giant shuffling behemoth was crossing the road, woolly black-brown fur, shoulders like a dump truck, and glistening, soulful eyes.

"Bison!" Tracey crowed. "Oooh! I've read about these! They brought them in a few decades ago. Cool!"

She slowed the car to watch the bison join a few others on the side of the road. A fence (a woefully inadequate fence, clearly) kept most of them safely off the street. Tracey pulled her phone from the dashboard, where it was doing GPS duty, and snapped a few photos out the window. Candace cracked open her sketchbook and did her best to capture the rolling movement of the animals' massive shoulders.

When the bison moved on, so did they. Loretta and Lotte were waiting for them in a parking lot at the head of a series of trails through the meadows.

"About time," Loretta said.

"Miss Loretta! Did you see the bison?" Tracey exclaimed. She was far too excited about them, Candace thought. But it was kind of nice to see.

"Tracey Auburn, I was here when they first brought those

beasts to this land. Like I said, been doing this a long time. But we're heading this way."

Loretta hefted a walking stick that made her look like a movie wizard, and they struck off down the path. Lotte climbed back into their car and pulled out a bundle of knitting.

"She doesn't want to come with us?" Candace asked. She was developing a soft spot for anyone who looked left behind.

"Believe me, she's glad to be rid of me for a couple of hours," Loretta said over her shoulder. "But it's good of you to ask. She thinks I don't have enough friends."

"So does my mom!" Candace said. "Not that you don't have friends, but that I don't." She glanced at Tracey and Loretta. "My own age, she means." There. She had put it out there, like an offering. Maybe these were her real friends. If so, they'd pick up on it.

"I have friends," Tracey said. "Friends who wonder what the heck I'm doing every weekend tromping around with the two of you." She laughed. "As if tromping around to soccer games with their kids is a bigger prize. No mysteries of the universe to be discovered there."

Loretta threw back her head and brayed that laugh that seemed so unlike the rest of her. Which made Candace and Tracey laugh, too.

"To clarify why we're here, I'll start with a story," Loretta said as they stumped their way across the field. "I used to work here."

"In the lab?" Tracey asked. They all turned to look at the big swooping building in the middle of the field.

"The offices. A long time ago . . ."

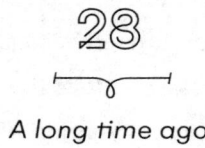

A long time ago

BIRDS CUT BISECTING DIAGONALS THROUGH THE prairie sky, shedding decimals of latitude and longitude with every swoop and sail. The farmers who once lived, planted, harvested, and died here had been lifted off the land by progress in the form of a temple above a reflecting pond, beneath the clear blue sky. A temple to science, where Loretta would have once liked to worship, mounting the wide concrete steps, entering the praying-hands-shaped National Accelerator Laboratory.

She lowered her binoculars. There were a great many birds here, too many for the mechanisms beneath the towering laboratory to frighten away. Though the earth must tremble beneath them.

"You had enough?" Harold asked.

Harold the Second, her mother called him. Loretta had been twice married, both times to men named Harold. But Harold Spencer seemed to be sticking, whereas Harold Mumford had not. Mumford wanted a woman smart enough to understand the world, but not so smart that she wouldn't prefer to see it from the safety of her kitchen window. Mumford liked her stories, her big dreams, as long as they stayed that way. She had left Harold Mumford in a two-bedroom apartment in Nashville thirteen years ago at the age of twenty-two.

Loretta had graduated from Fisk University after studying under her role model and mentor, Carolyn B. Parker—the first female Black American physicist. Professor Parker had been one of the few Black scientists to work on the Manhattan Project, which had led to the creation of the bombs that ended World War II. That war had defined Loretta's young life. It was the reason her father hadn't lived to see her graduate from high school. Why her mother and aunts had banded together to raise their war-orphaned children.

That a Black woman had had a hand in bringing the war to a close had made no small impression on Loretta. That she had done it with *physics* had lit a fire in her. Carolyn Parker was the pair of shoulders she hoped to one day stand on, the hands that would lift her, and her grandmother's discoveries, into the light of day.

But Professor Parker had left during Loretta's sophomore year to get her master's degree in physics from MIT. She'd stayed on to get her PhD. And then she fell ill, and their correspondence grew thin. They had been waiting. Biding their time for the right moment. But, as her mentor had said, academia was not prepared for the likes of them to discover the next frontier.

Loretta had finished her degree under the tutelage of men, some Black, some white, some brown. And Carolyn, as Loretta had come to call her in those final years, died. Leukemia. In all likelihood due to the work she had done on the Manhattan Project.

Loretta often wondered how many of the white scientists on the project had met the same fate.

"I'm ready," Loretta said now to Harold the Second. Harold Spencer had been there when Loretta took the train back to Chicago from Massachusetts in 1960 with her master's degree from MIT tucked into her father's old, soft leather satchel, and an interview at the University of Chicago waiting for her. Harold Spencer had been a train porter, a member of the Brotherhood of Sleeping Car Porters. He was also a rabble rouser, pushing for social change.

They met on the train. And the next day at a lunch counter. And the day after that at the Museum of Science and Industry. Harold Spencer was a patient man. He didn't expect the world, or Loretta, to turn his way anytime soon. They married three years later, once her PhD was complete. And he shed tears just as bitterly as she did when it became clear that the only job she would get in physics in Illinois was as secretary to a man who knew less than she did.

And now here she was, interviewing at NAL, home of the nation's first particle collider. She knew she'd get the job. She'd learned the right balance of showing what she knew without showing too much. Her employer would know she could make him look good without taking up any oxygen for herself. And in return, she could do some spectacular bird-watching on her way to and from the office. If Harold's civil rights activism had taught her one thing, it was that a life's work did not have to be defined by a paycheck.

Here at NAL, the starlings, crows, and blackbirds swooped and swayed like nowhere else. Why would that be?

"Did you know birds navigate through magnetic lines in the earth?" she said to Harold as she climbed back into the car.

"I did. Learn a lot of things riding the rails."

Loretta laughed. Harold liked to pretend he'd been a hobo rather than a working railroad man. He said he liked the wind in his hair, the air of adventure. Truth was, it had been backbreaking work, as had organizing marches and sit-ins and fundraising. Harold was retired now; his youngish wife was not. He was content to follow his hobbies at home while she did "her thing," as he put it.

"Did you know that particle accelerators use powerful magnets to split molecules into pieces?" she asked.

"I believe a gal told me that somewhere along the way." Harold smiled, cruising the car into the parking lot.

"Awful lot of birds," Loretta commented. Harold pulled into a spot.

"Well, I heard they hired a woman scientist out here last year," he said.

"Helen Edwards." Loretta nodded. Neither of them needed to say Helen was white. "*She* doesn't get to have a secretary," she added. Harold smiled.

"Not yet," he said. "All things in good time."

That was the beauty of Harold Spencer. Unlike Harold Mumford, he was an optimist.

Loretta gathered her purse and climbed out of the car.

"Go do your thing, Lo," Harold said. "Get what you came for."

And that's exactly what Loretta did.

Six months later, on a Thursday afternoon, while staring out the window over the photocopier machine, Loretta saw it. The window in the sky. She noted the way the birds avoided it. Except for one bird. A bird of unordinary colouring.

Bloop! It disappeared into the sky.

A moment later, she remembered the copies she was supposed to be making. She gathered them, and the scratch paper left behind by other secretaries. She clipped the discards together, and on her lunch break, she pulled out a pen and began to write.

Herault had been right to carry Lilabet so far through the Maze of Learned Thinkers. For the very top of the Library of Empty Books held a secret, just as Queen Dorianna had implied. Where the stone scribes worked, copying the unseen words in the blank books, Lilabet peered out from the highest balcony in wonder. For hanging above the clouds was a window. A window in the sky.

29

"OH MY GOD," TRACEY SAID. "DORIANNA IS YOUR grandmother! And you're Lilabet!"

"What? Who?" Candace said. She was still reeling from the idea of Loretta working for someone else as a secretary when she seemed more like a person who would have people working for her.

"Youngblood catches on quick," Loretta said. "Well, one of you, anyway."

"Hey!" Candace said, but Tracey was already talking, excitedly waving her hands in the air.

"So, Dorianna goes through the window in the sky and she becomes queen of the land, and she has these birds that tell her the truth about things. Like the Jordan magpies! And in the third book, this girl Lilabet enters the land through a cuckoo clock and she gets trapped in a library. The Library—"

"Of Empty Books," Loretta says with a nod.

Tracey clutched her head, then pointed at Loretta. "And that's you in college and grad school! And Lilabet is traveling with that horse, what's his name—Steedy!"

"Steedy?" Candace said. "A steed named Steedy?"

"After my high school boyfriend, Steven," Loretta said. "Folks called him Stevie. A lovely boy."

Tracey frowned. "Then why'd you make him into a talking horse?"

"Little girls like horses," Loretta said.

"Everyone likes horses," Candace replied. "And unicorns."

"Not everyone," Loretta said. "But yes, Steedy was Stevie."

Tracey gasped. "And then he betrays Lilabet and leaves her in the wrong library, the one with the empty books—"

"You broke up?" Candace said, making a sad face.

"But she finds her way out again with—"

"Another horse named Hairy, like for its hair?" Candace guessed.

Loretta laughed. "No. And yes. With the help of a horse named Herault, the old French for 'herald,' or 'messenger.'"

Tracey squinted. "I always thought that was a reference to Black newspapers and their role in activism." She looked shyly at her shoes in the tall grass. "At least, that was part of my graduate thesis, how the stories paralleled the Civil Rights Movement at the time," she added.

"Good eye, youngblood," Loretta said. "Our lives ran parallel to the movement—mine, Harold's, everyone's. We were all affected. So it was natural to put it in the books, too. But that came later, like you said. Book one was about my grandmother. And number two was about this place."

Tracey looked like she was taking mental notes as Loretta spoke. Candace wondered if she should take notes, too. They had left the marked path and were making their way to a smaller one through the trees.

"How come it's called the Skylark series if the birds are magpies?" Candace wanted to know.

"Candace, read the books!" Tracey exclaimed. "Skylarking is the verb for going through a window in the sky."

"Like going on a lark, youngblood," Loretta added. "A lark is an old word that can mean searching for fun or an adventure."

"So, were you 'skylarking' when you came here?" Candace asked. "Did you know there was a knot?"

"I didn't know, but I suspected. You see, there are a lot of birds around here. It's a protected habitat, and while the varied landscape is certainly welcoming, I have a theory that the particle accelerator beneath us might have something to do with it."

Candace had read a little more about the particle accelerators in the car. She didn't really understand it, but a giant ring, like a racetrack, was built underground here back in the late 1960s. Scientists somehow used giant magnets to speed up little subatomic particles called protons. It had something to do with radiation and X-rays and, basically, science stuff.

"So, it's because of the magnets?" Candace asked.

Loretta smiled. "Oh, youngblood's been reading after all! And you could be right. The particle accelerator uses some powerful magnets. Birds follow magnetic lines in the earth. It's one of the ways they seem to navigate when they fly. So it's possible a giant subterranean magnet is acting like a lighthouse, drawing all those birds, including the Jordans, in."

"Do you think the accelerator could have made the knots?" Candace asked.

"Knots instead of black holes?" Loretta shrugged. "It's possible."

"But the accelerator wasn't around in your grandmother's day," Tracey pointed out.

"No, it wasn't. But time isn't linear, as locker 235 lets us know," Loretta said. Then she shrugged. "These are the big questions. Like the chicken or the egg."

"The chicken," Candace said. "My dad says creationists think God made chickens on the fifth day of creation. But scientists think chickens evolved from dinosaurs. So maybe there was a missing-link chickasaur that had babies with another chickasaur, and those babies would have been the first chickens."

"From an egg," Tracey said.

"But a *chickasaur* egg," Candace replied triumphantly.

"Theropods," Loretta corrected. "That's the right name for your chickasaur. Now, come on, almost there."

She led them down a deer path along the edge of some trees and came to a stop. It was a bright day, the sky was intensely blue, and the sun was at an angle over the trees.

"It's a bit tricky to spot, but I want you to look at the seventh spruce across the field." She pointed with her walking stick at the line of trees that bordered the other side of the meadow. "From the left," she added. Candace counted. "Now follow that tree straight up. It'll look like about ten feet from this angle."

They looked.

"Do you see it?"

Candace stared at the sky. No birds magically appeared. No cosmic spiral of color. Not even a solar-system-sucking black hole. Just a pulsating blue sky, so blue that it almost looked like a cabbage rose of deeper ultraviolet blue pressing against her eyes. Was that . . . ?

"You mean the blue-purple cabbage rose thingy?" she asked.

"That's it! I told you she's got good eyes." Loretta nudged Tracey's shoulder. Tracey stumbled and caught herself.

"Wait," she said. "*That's* a knot? I thought it was just . . . I don't know, too much blue for the human eye?"

"Really?" Candace said.

"Every time you look into a deep sky and see that pulsating bruise of a—what did you call it?" Loretta asked.

"A blue-purple cabbage rose thingy," Candace said.

"It does! It looks like a cabbage rose. How come I never thought of that?"

"Oh." Tracey sounded disappointed. "I thought it would be like a window."

Candace wondered if she thought this meant Loretta really was delusional, or maybe it was her fangirl self that was disappointed.

"It is a window," Loretta said. "But what is a multidimensional window supposed to look like? That!"

She thrust her walking stick toward the knot, and at that exact moment—*bloop!* A bird appeared in the sky. A bird of unordinary colouring.

Tracey turned an unordinary color, too. "Oh my God," she said reverently.

Candace leapt into the air and pumped her fist. "Yes!"

This was really happening.

It. Was. All. Real.

30

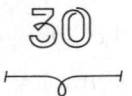

THE WALK BACK TO THE CAR WAS A BIT MORE SOBER, everyone wrestling with their diminutive roles in a massive, unknowable universe. And lunch choices before the drive home.

"I saw a German place," Tracey said.

"It's decent," Loretta agreed.

Candace did as her mother had instructed and put down money to pay for the bill. So did Loretta. And Tracey. Even Lotte—who had agreed to sit with them this time—offered to pay. The waiter sighed when they split the bill four ways, but at least it felt even.

"Oh, by the way," Candace said when the table was cleared. "My mom would love to meet you, Miss Loretta, and my dad wants to have a ham-off with you, Tracey."

Tracey laughed.

"Are you guys free over Christmas?" Candace asked.

"Next Wednesday is my last day until January second," Tracey said. "I'm teaching the winter term."

"Miss Loretta?"

Miss Loretta was frowning. Lotte nudged her. Loretta cut her a dirty look. She patted the table with both hands, like she was calming a horse or something, and said, "It would mean a lot to me if you and your families would join me and Lotte for dinner on Christmas Eve."

Lotte smiled proudly. Candace wondered if it had taken a lot of nudging even before today to get Loretta to ask.

"I'll have to ask my mom," she said. "But it would be fun!"

"It's just me, Loretta, but I'd be honored," Tracey said.

"Yay!" Candace said. No moping around wondering what the dork squad was doing without her. Cerise could have her Wisconsin grandparents. She had Tracey and Loretta. Sure, they were older, and maybe it was all a little strange. But it turned out the whole world was actually pretty strange, which Tracey and Loretta knew. Only, unlike everyone else, they were willing to talk and try to figure it out.

Candace got back into the car feeling lighter. Happier. She had a new set of friends. And it was going to be great.

Candace found her mother on the sofa. Her freshly washed hair dripped from its towel. She looked like she was melting.

"What now?" she asked, reading Candace's face.

"Miss Loretta has invited us over for Christmas Eve dinner. She's got a really cool house. Can we go?"

Candace's mother dropped the phone into the lap of her ratty old purple robe. It was exactly the same color as purple Peeps. A selling point when Candace had gotten it for her for Mother's Day four years ago. Back when Candace really liked Peeps.

"Oh, Cans, your aunt and uncle are coming over."

"I thought they were going on a cruise."

"Norovirus outbreak. And now Jamie's going to be with them."

"Oh." Candace studied her shoes. Jamie was Uncle Will and Aunt Sylvia's youngest son. He was in college in New York somewhere, and hardly ever came to visit Chicago.

"Well . . . what if we all go?"

"Candace, that lady did not sign up to host a whole passel of people for dinner."

"But she has a cook. And Tracey's not bringing anybody, so it'll just be like two families, which was totally on her radar."

"I don't know . . ."

"Please? It would mean a lot to Miss Loretta. A little old lady? In a great big house? And she's got a lady cook servant person. She has Lotte. Lotte makes amazing pastries."

"And we'd be home for Christmas Day?" her mom asked.

"Definitely," Candace said. "Miss Loretta eats lunch at eleven thirty. Dinner will probably be at, like, two or something."

Candace's mother took one of those deep breaths that were like a reset for her whole system. "Okay. Ask if that will be all right. Warn her that Will and Jamie and your father are big eaters, and offer to bring something. Anything. Everything. I don't want her feeding all of us without help."

"Thanks, Mom." Candace sealed the deal with a kiss. "I'll text her now." She hurried off to her room.

"Wait a minute, young lady!" her mother called. "How was Batavia?"

"It was good. We had schnitzel. And don't worry, I paid for my own meal. They wouldn't let me treat."

"Okay," her mother said. "I'm glad you at least offered."

"And we saw buffalo! No—bison. They're basically buffalo. And they're huge!"

She pulled out her sketchbook and showed off her attempt to capture the herd.

"Wow. That's pretty good, Candace. You can kind of smell them on the page." Candace grinned. Her mom flipped to the next drawing.

"That's a pretty flower," she said. "Cabbage rose?"

"Yeah, kind of. Just another thing we saw." Candace took the notebook back. If her mom thought she was being weird, she'd call her out on it, and Candace didn't think she could lie. Then her mom would *really* think she was weird when she told her the truth. She hoped she wasn't being too weird.

"I'm glad to see you happy, baby," her mom said. "Now let me deal with this." She indicated her hair. "And let me know what Miss Loretta has to say. Then I'll go to work on Sylvia."

"Oh, Aunt Sylvia," Candace repeated in the same exasperated way. They both loved Aunt Sylvia, but she could be work sometimes. Especially when plans changed. At least they had a couple of weeks to get her used to the idea.

"Why exactly?" Aunt Sylvia asked again on Christmas Eve.

Fortunately, Uncle Will, Cousin Jamie, and Candace's parents all said, "Get in the car, Sylvia," and then they drove her dad's SUV to McHenry in their Sunday best for a three o'clock dinner.

Candace's dad whistled when he saw the house. It looked incredible, just like Candace hoped it would. The long glass hallway glowed welcomingly in the overcast afternoon light.

Someone had hung oversized wreaths, decked out in white lights and trailing red-and-green-plaid bows, in the center of each window. It looked like a magic candy box.

"What is that?" her dad said. "A Mies van der Rohe?"

"Yep! Well, designed by him. Built later on," Candace said. Loretta had lectured her on accuracy. Candace nudged her cousin sitting next to her in the wayback. "Mies van der Rohe. Famous Chicago architect."

Jamie looked up from his phone. "I *know* who Mies van der Rohe is," he said, and went back to scrolling.

"I love you too, Jamie," Candace said. He laughed, even though he had his earbuds in.

Candace was excited. Too excited, she thought. It was just dinner, and had the potential to be all kinds of awkward. But she also felt a little bit . . . proud? Of Tracey and Loretta. She wanted to show them off. And she wanted her family to like them. If they didn't . . . Well, she didn't want to think about that.

Her dad parked in front of the house, and they all piled out. Her mom and aunt smoothed their long winter skirts—clearly, they had gone shopping together. Both were decked out in high boots, long skirts, and cowl-necked sweaters. Her dad and Uncle Will were in dress slacks and button-down shirts. Her dad wore a pullover sweater, her uncle a cardigan. Jamie was in dark jeans and an even darker sweater. Candace had opted for black boots, black leggings, and an oversized tunic sweater in a dark red, with silver earrings and a green hairband with a bow.

"You look like a Christmas present," Jamie said when she got out. Like that was a bad thing.

Lotte answered the door. She was dressed all in silver, down to her silver clogs and a linen apron.

"Welcome, Candace! And this is your beautiful family?"

"Merry Christmas, Lotte!" Candace made the introductions as they tumbled inside.

"We've got food in the car," Candace's mom said. "Carl, will you and Jamie get the cooler?"

"Oh, you shouldn't have," Lotte said. "But it is always wonderful to have more at the holidays." While the guys unloaded the car and followed Lotte to the kitchen, Candace led her mom and aunt into the sunken living room.

"Whoa!"

There against the back wall was the tallest Christmas tree Candace had ever seen inside of a house. Music was playing; gifts were under the tree. The soft whites and creams of the room looked like snow. It was pure magic.

"This is gorgeous!" Aunt Sylvia said.

"Thank you." Loretta entered the room, using her teak cane instead of the wizard staff from the trip to Batavia. She was dressed all in gray this time, with gold bangles and little gold earrings. "The tree is new. We haven't had one in . . . well, decades, really." She smiled. "Hello, youngblood," she said when Candace moved in for a hug.

"Miss Loretta, this is my mom, Cheryl, and my aunt Sylvia. Everyone else is in the kitchen."

Loretta held out a wiry hand and gripped each woman by the arm. "Welcome to my home. I'm so glad you could come."

The men came in, and introductions were made again. Tracey showed up a few minutes later, her arms full of gifts.

Which reminded Candace of her own gifts. She ran back to the car to get them. It was ice-cold outside, but so warm indoors that she stood for a moment in the driveway, looking up at the afternoon sky. Her cell phone buzzed in her leggings pocket.

"No," she said, her breath clouding the air. Whoever it was could wait. Everyone she cared about was right here.

⌇

Dinner was a major to-do. Loretta's dining room was just as sleek and pale as the rest of the house. Lotte (who did join them for dinner) had set the table with gold candles and plates rimmed in silver and gold. Garlands of holly ran down the center of the table, bringing color to the room. And then, of course, there was the food.

Candace's mom had made gumbo, so that was the first course. Lotte had made an amazing salad—which Candace never thought she'd say about a salad—with fresh pear wedges and pecans and greens and dried cranberries. Candace's dad had brought an entire ham. Lotte and Loretta added an actual roast goose to the table, with chestnut stuffing (which was actually kind of gross) and sausage stuffing (which was not). Tracey did not rise to the ham-off challenge, declaring Christmas dinners a noncompetitive event. Candace's dad threw down the gauntlet for sometime in the New Year, declaring it "Hamageddon."

Halfway through the meal, the conversation turned toward the birding they had been doing. Candace described the way-too-early visits to the Magic Hedge and how she'd learned that birds preferred later, warmer hours, too. But not magpies, which weren't very common in Illinois anyway.

Candace was sitting closest to Jamie, the only one who wasn't up on the birding project, so she pulled out her phone to show him pictures of the drawings she'd done of hawks and cardinals. Her phone buzzed again. She hesitated, stomach clenching.

"You gonna check that?" Jamie asked.

"No." What if it was Deen or Becca looking to ruin her good mood? "Everyone I want to talk to is here," she said. Her smile was a little weak.

"Then give me your phone," Jamie said, reaching for it.

"No! Why?"

"Just give it to me." They wrestled a little over the table until her mother cut her a look. Then they wrestled for it under the table. Jamie had bigger, weirdly strong hands, so he won. He held it in her face to unlock it and then did a series of swipes and taps to the screen.

"Jamie, I swear, if you're reading my texts . . ."

Jamie smiled, eyes on the screen. "Ooooh, why? Got a secret boyfriend or something? A military coupe?" He pronounced the *p*.

"It's coup," Candace said. "Like a mourning dove, coo."

"You'd think with all your book smarts and bird learning, you'd know about this, then." He handed back her phone. He'd installed a new app.

"eBird?"

"You've been using Audubon. eBird is from Cornell. Actual scientists, you know?" Jamie went to Cornell. He believed in "actual" things. "Look." He thumbed through the app and showed her. "Magpie sightings in North America. You can narrow it down, of course."

Of course. Candace's face went hot. She threw her arms around her cousin. "Thank you, Jamie! Look, Miss Loretta! I was using the wrong app!"

It turned out Audubon also used eBird data, just with less access.

Jamie helped the other women download it to their phones and was officially declared the hero of the day. Aunt Sylvia and Uncle Will beamed.

"Worth all that tuition," his father said. "That's a Christmas gift I can believe in!"

Jamie got shy, but he looked pleased.

After dinner, they moved slowly, stuffedly, back into the living room and exchanged gifts. Candace had drawn portraits of Tracey and Loretta from the shoulders up. "Like the *Mona Lisa*," she said. Unlike the *Mona Lisa*, Tracey's featured a bird of unordinary colour flying out from behind her head, and Loretta's background was a bruise-colored cabbage rose. Candace's mom had even helped her find a teak-colored frame so it would fit with the rest of the house. Tracey's was framed to match the bird drawing she'd taken from the purple notebook. Candace had drawn Lotte as a saint with a halo of golden knitting needles around her, a cup of coffee in one hand, and a pastry in the other. The frame was red, like the clogs she'd first seen her wearing.

Loretta and Lotte gave everyone—even Jamie—a pair of hand-knit sleep socks, courtesy of Lotte's labor. "I chose the yarn," Loretta explained. Candace's socks matched her goldenrod hair.

And Tracey surprised everyone with Christmas crackers—

long, shiny cylinders shaped like wrapped candy. "You have to stand in a circle and hold one end, while your neighbor holds the other." They formed a ring in front of the tree, arms crossed in front of their waists, and on the count of three, they all pulled as hard as they could. The crackers broke apart with a series of loud snaps. Everybody jumped and laughed, scrambling to pick up the paper crowns and little toys that fell from each cracker.

They wore the crowns while Aunt Sylvia helped Lotte pour coffee and tea and serve up what everyone declared was the most beautiful bûche de Noël any of them had ever seen. (It was the *first* bûche de Noël Candace had ever seen—a snow-dusted log, complete with red-capped marzipan mushrooms, that was actually a rolled chocolate cake filled with cream and covered in chocolate bark. It. Was. Amazing.)

In short, Christmas Eve was perfect.

While everyone was nibbling the remnants of chocolate on their plates, Candace excused herself to go the bathroom. Which meant pulling her phone out of her pocket so it wouldn't fall into the toilet—something she'd learned to do from horrible experience. Which also meant glancing at the phone and seeing that someone had left a voicemail. Unknown caller. Clearly a misdial. Everyone she knew would have texted.

She settled in for a pee and a listen.

"Hey, Candace—"

Candace yelped and fumbled the phone. She scrambled to rewind the message.

"Hey, Candace, Merry Christmas. Um . . . it's Mitchell. I should have texted. Okay. Bye."

She wiped, washed, dried, and raced back to find everyone

in the living room. "Tracey, guess what! He—" She paused and read the room.

Her parents were leaning into each other, looking startled. Aunt Sylvia looked suspicious. Cousin Jamie was trying not to laugh, and Uncle Will looked confused. Tracey was the only one who didn't look like they were trapped in amber.

"What?" Candace asked. "Could you hear me in the bathroom?"

"Honey," Candace's mom said. "Mrs. Spencer—"

"Loretta," Loretta said.

"Loretta just made a very generous offer. To help put you through college."

"What?"

Her mother's disbelief slowly gave way to delight. Her father looked like someone had taken a weight off of his stomach. Jamie said, "Damn," and gave in to his laughter.

"But why?" Aunt Sylvia said.

"Sylvia!" Uncle Will said.

"Yeah, no, why?" Candace said too. She caught her parents' look. A look that said, *Don't upset the nice rich lady who is going to help us avoid crushing debt, unless you are really uncomfortable with this, in which case we should talk about it when we get home.* It was a really complicated look. "I mean . . . that's really nice of you, Miss Loretta. Really. But you don't have to send me to college for us to be friends or anything."

"Child, that is very kind of you to say. But I'm an old woman with no children, and you're a bright young lady with a future. College is a ways off, and it was just an idea. But it was a good one. I hope you'll accept it."

"I . . ." Candace's stomach felt funny. Like Hamageddon was battling it out inside her guts. Friendship shouldn't come with a price tag or an obligation, or rules like Becca and Deen's ever-changing playbook. And that just started over camping trips and hair dye! What would college do?

"No, thank you," she said, her voice barely a whisper. "I didn't ask for anything. I just wanted to be . . . friends."

"We are friends," Tracey said. "And I think we've all had a big day and a lot to digest." She patted her stomach, but Candace knew what she meant. "If you don't mind, Loretta, I'm going to head home and sleep this off. Maybe we all should. Thank you for a wonderful evening."

Everyone ground into motion then, rising and shuffling around for coats and leftovers and gifts and purses. Somehow Candace found herself alone with Loretta sitting imperiously in her chair by the tree, her hands resting on her cane. Candace felt a tear fall before she could stop it. She wiped it away.

"I'm sorry I upset you," Loretta said. Her voice didn't sound as sorry as her words. "If someone could have helped me the way I—" She took a breath and started over. "Let's just say, life doesn't have to be a struggle for all of us, youngblood. But I guess it is anyway."

"I don't want you to think you have to pay me to be here," Candace said.

Loretta harrumphed and looked away. Were those tears in her eyes, too?

"You're always asking Lotte to join us when we go out. You think I treat her like a servant. Well, she is one, but she's also a companion and a friend. Sometimes I can't tell where one ends and the other begins. Sometimes I can't tell why someone would want to be a friend. What's in it for them?"

"The wonders of the universe?" Candace said. "Windows in the sky."

Loretta smiled at that.

"You know," Candace said, "I've been wondering why my old friends don't want to be friends with me anymore, and you're wondering why your new ones do. Funny, huh?"

"What's funny?" Tracey had come back in, her coat on, her arms full of foil-wrapped ham and other leftovers.

"Oh, Tracey, guess what? That's what I was going to say." She held up her phone. "He called!"

Tracey smiled. "Good. Did he say why it took him so long?"

"No, but he did say merry Christmas."

"When you say 'called,'" Loretta said, "do you mean he texted you, or—"

"A voicemail!" Candace said. "Want to hear his voice?"

Loretta smiled and shook her head. "That's a love letter to you and you alone. Boy might have some sense after all."

"Merry Christmas, Miss Loretta."

"I think you can drop the Miss," Loretta said. "Despite the great difference in age, aren't we . . . friends?"

"Yes!" Candace said, and hugged both of her friends good night.

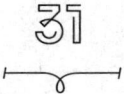

CALL OR TEXT? CALL OR TEXT. CALL OR TEXT. TEXT.

If a call was a love letter—which was totally weird—it was too soon to send one.

CANDACE
Merry Christmas.

MITCHELL
Happy New Year.
Want to see a movie?

Yes.

CANDACE
What should I wear?

TRACEY
Jeans and a nice top.

LORETTA
Dungarees and a twin set.

What's a twin set?

TRACEY
A nice top and matching cardigan.

LORETTA
Lord, what do they teach in school these days.

Sounds kinda formal.

LORETTA
Is this a date or a monster truck rally?

TRACEY
Or a date AT a monster truck rally?

Oof. Don't think I have a twin set, tho.

LORETTA

Ask your mother.

TRACEY

Jeans and a nice top.

"Mom, do you have a twin set I can borrow?" Candace stuck her head into the living room.

"Do I look like a Southern deb?" her mother said.

"What's a deb?" Candace asked, dropping onto the couch, where her mother was reading reports.

"A debutante. A young lady of means on the hunt for a man. Your grandmother used to talk about it. Every white girl in Louisiana had her picture taken in a twin set and pearls when she came out or got engaged. It's very proper. Or it makes you look like an Evanston mom."

"Oh." Candace didn't want to look like an Evanston mom. "Sounds like the wrong look."

"For what?"

"For the movies. With Mitchell." She mumbled the last couple of words. Her parents had given her grief for her new "friend who is a boy."

"Who cares what you wear to the movies? Oh . . . don't tell me—you need fashion advice because this 'friend who is a boy' is maybe cuter than you mentioned . . ." She gave Candace a piercing look. "And your new friends just gave you the matronly makeover. The mature coiffure. The sixties experience."

Candace shook her head and laughed. "That's rough."

"I'm surprised Loretta didn't tell you to wear a dress."

"She's more practical than that."

"Well, what did Tracey say?"

"Jeans and a nice top."

"The battle cry of the modern woman. And what did *you* decide?" Her mother shuffled her papers and stacked them on the coffee table, far more interested in the conversation than in her work.

"I was going to do jeans and a twin set until I found out what a twin set was. Who knew it had such a history of patriarchal oppression? I guess I'll just wear a shirt."

The sucky part was that Deen would have helped her pick a decent top. The really sucky part was that Becca would have picked the perfect top.

Candace settled on jeans and a scoop-neck sweater in sea green that made her look like a mermaid.

"You look nice," her father said when she was ready to go.

"Thanks, Dad."

She and her mom grabbed their coats.

"Tell Deenie I said hi," he said, heading into the kitchen. Candace's mother caught her eye and shook her head.

"He's not ready for you to have a 'friend who is a boy' that he hasn't met," her mom whispered. "Especially not one you dress up for."

"But it's not like it's a date," Candace whispered back.

It was like a date. When her mom dropped her off in front of the theater, Mitchell came over to say hello. And then they stood in line for popcorn. Close together. Like a date. And he kept sort of bouncing, like he was nervous.

"Did you have a nice Christmas?" she asked.

"Yep. You?"

"It was pretty to really good."

He stopped bouncing. "'Pretty to really'?"

Candace smiled slowly. "Yeah. I mean, parts were pretty good, and parts were great."

"What was the best part?"

"Dinner, Christmas Eve." And she told him about the birding app and the Christmas crackers, and Hamageddon.

"That's gonna be the name of my new band," Mitchell said.

"You play an instrument?" Candace had always wanted to play guitar. Without all the lessons.

"Only in video games," he replied. Which led to a list of bands and individual songs they liked, and the promise of a playlist. At which point Candace got a funny feeling in her stomach. This was totally a date.

And then Deen and Sergio walked into the lobby.

"Oh no . . ."

"What?"

"It's . . . nothing. Just someone I used to know. *Two* someones I used to know, two lines over."

Mitchell looked around.

"Don't look!" Candace hissed. But it was too late. Deen and Sergio had spotted her.

"Hey, Candace! Mitchell, what's up?" Sergio said. He actually looked happy to see her. Clearly, he wasn't following the drama.

"Hey, Serge. Nadine." Candace tried to look Deen in the eye, but couldn't seem to make it stick.

"Hey, guys," Mitchell said. Wait. Was Mitchell holding Candace's hand? When had he started holding her hand?

"What are you here to see?" Sergio asked.

Deen glanced up at Mitchell, down at his hand holding Candace's, and up at Candace. In the before times, this would have been followed by some intense eye conversation—"OMG!" "I know!" "You too!" "Right?" all orchestrated with varying degrees of eyebrow raises and dilating pupils—and a rushed conference in the ladies' room.

These were not the before times.

Candace decided to keep a smile on her face and look at the wall over everyone's head.

"Yeah, man!" Mitchell dropped Candace's hand to return Sergio's high five, then turned it into a complicated handshake that Sergio clearly did not know.

Candace had missed something. "What just happened?"

"We're seeing the same movie!" Mitchell said. "Let's sit together!"

Candace, who had nearly choked on her tongue, managed to say, "It's assigned seating."

"You guys want any popcorn? We'll see you guys in there!"

"All right, man," Sergio said. Deen was already dragging him away. "What? He's cool," Candace heard him say.

It took a moment for her to be able to look at Mitchell. When she did, his arms were full of candy.

"What are you doing?"

"You didn't say what you wanted."

She refused to laugh. She wanted to, though. "I mean with Deen and Sergio!"

"What? They're friends of yours."

"No— Never mind. Let's find our seats."

She took some of the candy from his arms, uncovering a massive bucket of popcorn and two drinks.

"We are never going to eat all of this," Candace said.

"Yeah, we will."

They made it into their theater just as the trailers were beginning. Mitchell pulled his phone out of his pocket to find their designated seats.

They were sitting right next to Sergio and Deen.

"Seriously?" Candace said. It wasn't even a full theater.

They slid down the aisle to hear Deen saying, "That's okay. I don't need popcorn. This is great." She pulled a jelly bean from a box in her lap. "See, this one is popcorn flavored."

Mitchell dropped down into his seat, popcorn flying. Candace tried to sit on his far side, but he said, "Sorry, your seat's right here."

Candace sat next to Deen. "Hey," she said.

"Hey," Deen replied. The longest conversation they'd had since Thanksgiving.

"Dude, are those Milk Duds?" Sergio asked. He grabbed the box, then hesitated—probably because Deen kicked him in the ankle—"I mean, if you're sharing."

"Sure, man," Mitchell said. "They don't take returns."

It seemed natural halfway through the movie when Candace offered Deen the vat of popcorn, and Deen offered her a handful of jelly beans, but only the green ones that she liked. Like they were making up for their lost Thanksgiving. It felt a little less natural when the lights came up and the boys both had tears in their eyes that they tried to hide, but Candace and Deen didn't hide theirs. They burst out laughing. And it felt pretty okay, after all. Maybe they weren't besties anymore. But that didn't mean they couldn't still be friends.

Only later that night, getting ready for bed and replaying the day in her head, did the jelly beans stand out in a non–*Charlie Brown Thanksgiving* way. Deen had sorted them just for her, the way they used to sort M&M'S and fruit snacks together when they were little. The way Loretta's magpies shuffled through time collecting things like Tracey's purple notebook or purple pom-pom pens.

Candace's toothbrushing slowed to a stop. A thought trickled slowly into her brain. She froze, afraid to even spit in case she chased it away.

Purple notebooks. Purple pens. Purple.

That was it! That was the answer!

Candace spat and rinsed excitedly. She'd buy some ribbon tomorrow and test her theory back at school.

33

CERISE WAS STANDING BY THEIR LOCKERS ON THE FIRST day after winter break. Candace tromped across the hallway in her snow boots. The skies had opened up the night before, but not enough to allow for an actual snow day.

"Hey, Cerise. Happy New Year!" she said.

Cerise turned slowly, a puzzled look on her face.

"Hey, Candace, same to you. Have you seen a highlighter? I thought I left one in here."

Candace made a mental note to look for magpies carrying highlighters. "Nope, but I can lend you one. They dry out pretty fast," she said, and slung her backpack down to hunt for a marker.

"Thanks, man," Cerise said. "I'll get it back to you later."

"Yep."

Cerise was swallowed by a wave of kids kicking snow off their boots, shrieking hellos, or grumbling about having to get up early again. Candace was feeling that herself.

She hung up her coat and rewrapped her scarf the way Tracey had taught her. Scarves really did an amazing job of keeping you warm, even though they only covered a small part of the body. She threw her backpack on the hook in her locker and fished out a little paper bag.

Inside the bag was a handful of velvet ribbons, half an inch wide, cut into nine-inch pieces. And as close to the same shade as Tracey's purple notebook and the pens as she could get. She grabbed them like a handful of worms and thrust them into the top of the locker, the landing pad, she imagined, for the knot. Birds of all sorts, not just magpies, had uses for string. In elementary school, one class project had been to cut up bits of fat yarn in the springtime for birds to use in building their nests. She wasn't sure it was something birders would comment on, but it might help her prove the magpies had been here.

She wished she could tie a purple ribbon around Mitchell's and her hands to prove he'd really been holding hers. But after the movie, he'd just acted like a friend again. They'd waved from their parents' cars and gone their separate ways. He texted "Happy New Year" on New Year's Day, and that was it.

The warning bell rang before she saw him in the hallway, but there was Deen, smiling at her, and Becca, smiling at her phone.

"Hey, guys," she said. Were they back to normal? Deen linked arms with Candace. It was a relief, like warm water on cold hands. Belatedly, Becca looked up and linked with Deen's other arm. It was a New Year's miracle. Both of her friends were back.

February was as cold as a witch's teat in a brass bra in Nebraska, as Candace's father liked to say. Candace cringed every time her dad used the word "teat," but she got his point. It was freaking cold. But that didn't stop folks on eBird from commenting about the magpie with the purple ribbon in its beak near Waukegan, Illinois. After spending ages driving to the most popular birding spots in the area, it was a relief to have an actual lead rather than just shooting in the dark. Candace had sent the alert to Loretta and Tracey, and the following Saturday found her and Tracey huddled in Tracey's car for warmth on the edge of a park. Unfortunately, Loretta had caught a cold, and Lotte wasn't letting her out of the house. She wasn't missing anything, though. There were no bruise-colored cabbage roses in the sky.

"I know a cool bookstore in an alleyway in Evanston," Tracey said. "Want to check it out?"

Candace did.

The bookstore was like something out of Harry Potter or Dickens. Off the main street, down a little alleyway, it looked like it had once been a craftsman's workshop or something, cobbled out of stone. Candace found the books on birds and art.

Tracey looked like she belonged here.

"This is my retirement dream. Run a store like this. Have a writing desk in the back. It's like a hobbit house for book lovers."

"Right! You wanted to be a writer when you were my age," Candace recalled. "What happened? Did you do it?"

Tracey's face seemed to age a couple of years. "No. Not really. I mean, I wrote, but I never published, aside from a few academic papers."

"Well, that's something!" Candace said. "Cool. I don't know anyone who's ever published anything, except for you."

"And Loretta," Tracey pointed out.

"And Loretta." They had wandered into the children's section. One shelf held a whole section of picture books from around the world. Stepping past the floor cushions in the reading-time space, Candace dragged her finger along the spines on a higher shelf until she found *Window in the Sky* by G. Edward Macey.

"Hey, they have the whole series here," she said. "And they're used, so they're pretty affordable."

Tracey had grown quiet. She ran her hand across the rainbow-colored spines, and she turned away. Was she sad?

"It's funny," Candace burbled into the weird silence. "Loretta wanted to be a scientist, but had to become a writer to share her science. You wanted to be a writer, but now you're like a scientist."

Tracey looked like she was waiting for the L in a lonely station. "Yeah," she said quietly. "Funny how that is."

Candace straightened up, her arms full of books. "What's wrong?"

"Nothing."

"Looks like *something*."

Tracey shook her head. "Just how we dream of things we never do."

"But isn't that what most dreams are?" Candace asked. "I mean, last night I dreamt I was riding a whale down the Chicago River. Don't think I'm ever gonna do that. And then there are dreams we have for ourselves. Like, I wanted friends, and I want to do art. And now I have that. It's not that dreams don't come true, it's that we stop showing up for them, I think. You've just got to show up and see what happens."

Mitchell flashed through her mind.

He had finally shown up over the holidays, and it was great. And even if he'd taken a step back since then, at least it had happened.

"So," Candace asked, "why don't you write a book?"

Tracey's whole face blinked.

34

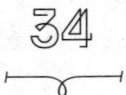

IN A CLOSET IN A BOX ON A SHELF BEHIND THE DARK hanging things sat a stack of pages littered with words. Typewritten, handwritten, dot-matrix printed, laser printed, yellow college ruled, wide ruled, laid, linen, scraps of napkins, cobbled together over days and weeks and years. It sat and it waited, haunted by so many voices:

"You can do anything!"

"After your mother died..."

"Don't be such a child."

"I just worry what will happen to you if I'm gone..."

"You read fantasy? You write fantasy?"

"Be careful!"

"How's that scribbling gonna pay the bill?"

"Is it finished? Can I read it?"

"You've got student loans. You need a real job."

"Summers off is plenty of time to write."

"You know, I could probably write a book, too."

"You still working on that thing?"

"I read it, but I... well, I don't get it."

"Will you move in with me?"

"We could really use you for summer school."

"What's for dinner?"

"Don't you want kids? A family?"

"Just a light heart attack. I'll be fine."

"You look tired."

"Where does the time go?"

And so the thing in the back of the closet would never live and never die. And always it waited for daylight to come.

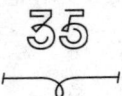

"ARE YOU OKAY? TRACEY? YOU LOOK LIKE YOU'VE GOT cartoony spiral eyes," Candace said.

Tracey shook her head again. "Yeah, I'm fine. We should probably get going."

"Okay. Let me just pay for these." Candace hoisted her collection of Loretta's stories and a book on drawing wildlife, and hauled them to the front cash register. Thank goodness for Christmas money and generous grandparents.

The sky was deepening into twilight when they reached the car.

"You can put your books in the back."

Candace opened the door. "There's stuff on the back seat."

"Oh, let me get that." Tracey dragged a folder and a couple of papers her way.

"What's it for?" Candace asked.

"Oh, nothing. Well, not nothing. A promotion, I guess you'd say. I'm up for a tenured position at another college."

"What's tenured?"

"Like a permanent position with more benefits and better pay, in theory."

"Don't you work permanently now?"

"Yes and no. Think of it as job security. If you're *not* tenured, like me, and they need to lay people off for whatever reason, I'm one of the first to go."

"Oh, like a red shirt in *Star Trek*. My dad always says they're only there to feed the monster."

"Yeah. I'm a red shirt right now. But I finish this paperwork, and I'm in the running for command gold."

"Okay, I don't know what that is exactly, but I get it. It's a better job. Cool! I hope you get it."

"Yeah. It would be good for my résumé and my bank account. But it's also more administrative work. Longer hours. And it means moving to Wisconsin."

"Wisconsin? You can't move to Wisconsin!"

"I've got to take care of myself, kid, go where the opportunity is."

"But you *live* here! Your stuff . . . us . . . everything is here!"

Tracey shrugged. "That's what moving vans are for. I'd sell my condo, and maybe my car. They have a good public transportation system—"

"This car? You can't sell this car! It's the car we do stuff in. We'd have to stop doing stuff together," Candace wailed.

"Which is what would happen if I moved out of the city either way," Tracey said. "I know, it stinks. We were just starting to have fun. But I'd only be a phone call away. Now, get in, it's freezing."

"It's not the same," Candace said, not moving. The thought of losing Tracey made her realize how much of a Band-Aid their friendship had been after losing Deen and the others. But it was more than a Band-Aid. It was real. And it could be gone just like that.

"But what about my birthday party?" Candace asked. Candace always had a pizza party on her birthday, followed by movies at home. This year would be the first time she'd get to introduce Tracey and Loretta to Deen and her other friends. Lotte was invited, too. It was super important. And a little nerve-racking. It was also a week away. "You'll be here for that, won't you?"

Tracey looked at Candace across the roof of her car.

"Of course, kid. I wouldn't—"

And a nine-inch length of bright purple velvet ribbon fell from the sky to land on the car roof.

"What the—" Tracey said.

Candace gasped. They both looked up and—

Bloop!

A bird of unordinary colour swooped down to retrieve its ribbon before disappearing through a window in the starry night sky.

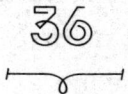

"WE'VE BEEN LOOKING AT IT ALL WRONG," TRACEY SAID. "We've been thinking about normal birds instead of birds of unordinary colour."

Loretta looked at the blurry photo Candace had taken with her cell phone of the sky above their parking spot in Evanston.

"Candace and I spent nearly two hours parked in the woodland preserve near here and saw nothing birdwise—"

"Not true, we saw two Cooper's hawks, a blue jay, and a nuthatch. And a very loud starling."

"In terms of what we are looking for," Tracey concluded, cutting Candace a look. It had been a decent day for birds, just not Jordan magpies. And even the terrible news of Tracey possibly moving to Wisconsin had been pushed aside by the discovery of the Evanston knot.

They had driven to McHenry the next day to show Loretta their findings and look at her map of knots. Being Sunday, Lotte had the day off, which seemed to mean spending it in the kitchen baking for fun, instead of for company. But Candace had gotten two hot cross buns out of it, so she wasn't complaining.

"We've been looking in bird preserves and woodland areas," Candace said, picking up the narrative. "But think about it. The Chicago knot is in a locker in the middle of an elementary school in the middle of the city. The Batavia knot is above a meadow now, but twenty years from now, that might be a shopping mall or something."

"Heaven forbid," Loretta said. "But I see your point. I've been following birds and birders all these years, and unintentionally limiting my scope. We need to look for unordinary birds in unordinary places."

She sat back in her seat and studied the map of Illinois hanging from the ceiling. Over two dozen locations were marked. All of them in rural areas with the exception of the original knot. The cities and suburban areas sprawled like a desert across the rest of the map. Unexplored territory.

A sigh escaped her. "That's a lot. A lot." She turned a gleaming eye on Candace and Tracey. "All right, youngbloods, how do you propose we do this?"

Candace grinned.

"Hashtag BasicBird."

"What?"

Candace held up her iPad, which she'd brought with her for its bigger screen. "See? Hashtag BasicBird. People use it on social media when they see a bird somewhere it shouldn't be. It's like, 'Look, this ostrich in a strip mall is basically being a bird.' Or actually more like, 'This bird is basically just like us.' See?"

She scrolled through some posts. An ostrich indeed was spotted in a strip mall, mesmerized by its own reflection in a storefront mirror. A penguin racing through an aquarium hallway. And dozens of less-exotic birds soaring through office buildings, nesting in parking garages, or sitting at café tables as if reading the menu.

"Jordan magpies are weird birds. Maybe knot locations are weird, too. This might help us find them."

Loretta took the iPad and swiped through a few more photos. "Lucky for us, folks don't have anything better to do with their time, I guess." She handed it back to Candace. "So, have you found any hashtag-basic Jordans out there?"

Candace, who had been feeling particularly shiny, deflated a little at this. "Not yet. But I've set some notifications, so if there are new pictures, we'll know. And if anyone uses the words *magpie*, *purple ribbon*, or just *ribbon*, too."

Candace had already explained her ribbon idea. Loretta had reached into the knot in her office and held up a tangle of dirty velvet strips. "That explains this," she'd said with her coughing laugh. "Lord, I thought it was some new kind of hair tie or something."

"So the good news is no more sitting out in the cold looking for a needle in a haystack," Tracey said. "Unless this comes up empty, in which case we can go back to plan A."

"At least when the weather is warmer," Candace added.

Loretta looked at the table for a long moment. Candace was suddenly hit with the realization that she had her whole life ahead of her. But Loretta had nearly a century under her belt. Months, for her, might seem short, but they were a long time to wait.

Candace's stomach soured into its own bruise-colored knot. But when Loretta looked up, she was smiling.

"Thank the Lord for that. Lotte!" she called down the hallway. Lotte appeared a moment later, hands covered in flour. "We can cancel the heated tent. At least for now. Looks like these two have saved us from more cold mornings in the woods."

Lotte clapped her hands together in a puff of white dust. "Wonderful! Wonderful! Well done!" And she bustled down the hallway again, singing "Oh Happy Day" in a fluttery voice.

37

YESTERDAY, CANDACE WAS THIRTEEN. TODAY, SHE WAS fourteen. Yesterday, she was a girl. Today, she was . . . well, still a girl, but an older one. She looked in the mirror. Was she a little taller? A little curvier? Her hair was a bit springier, but that was probably the new moisturizing leave-in conditioner she was using to keep her colored hair from getting too fried. So maybe she hadn't grown much after all.

School was the same, too, except folks wished her a happy birthday if they knew about it. Deen and Becca had decorated the front of her locker with a sparkly poster and balloons, so it wasn't exactly a secret.

"Thank yooou!" Candace sang when she saw it. And none of it was purple, thank goodness, or who knew what kind of magpie storm would appear when she opened her locker. There were hugs all around and a promise to eat lunch together in the cafeteria. Mitchell said happy birthday, and so did Sergio and Nate.

"See you tomorrow," Mitchell said.

"Great!" Candace grinned. It wasn't like a big, raging party, just the usual pizza at Giordano's and movies in her living room, but this year was different because there would be boys—well, Sergio, Nate, and Mitchell, who had lit up when she invited him. And Cerise was coming to pizza, too.

"Sorry I can't stay for the movies, but I promised my parents I'd watch my little brother later," she'd explained. That Candace's birthday came so close to Valentine's Day made it understandable. And also very pink and red, like her locker decorations.

It would also be the first time her school friends were meeting Tracey and Loretta.

Candace got nervous bubbles in her stomach when she thought of it, so she tried not to, and the day went pretty well. Mr. Jones even made the class sing "Happy Birthday" to her, which some people grumbled about, but they did it for every birthday, so everyone actually joined in. It was terrible and off-key and great.

Saturday night, Candace settled on jeans and a pink sweater with a red heart in the center. "You look like a Care Bear," Becca announced when she and Deen showed up together at Candace's house. Everyone else was being dropped off at the restaurant by their parents except for, obviously, Tracey and Loretta. Candace's dad would make the rounds, bringing the kids home later on.

On the drive to Giordano's Pizza, Becca stayed on her phone while Deen whispered questions about Mitchell.

"Are you guys, like, a thing?"

"Yeah, a friend thing," Candace whispered back.

"'Cuz at the theater it seemed like you were a thing, maybe."

Candace remembered the hand-holding moment and shrugged. "Maybe. I don't know. At school it's like nothing happened."

"Oh my God!" Deen inhaled, and almost choked. "So something happened?"

"No! Just when he held my hand." Candace dropped her voice to subvocal levels, knowing full well her parents were in the front seat and had ears like bats. But then she and Deen started giggling, which was a surefire way of confusing her parents' radar. Becca was pretty quiet, though.

At the restaurant they got a long table that could fit everyone. For some reason, it turned into kids at one end, adults at the other. But Candace sat in the center.

"And your grandma will be right here," the waiter said, holding the chair on her right for Loretta.

"She's not my grandmother," Candace said.

"Oh, sorry. Great-grandmother. My mistake," he quipped, and pushed her chair in. Loretta guffawed.

Deen sat to Candace's left. Becca squeezed in between Nate and Sergio on the end. Mitchell sat across from Candace, flanked on either side by Tracey and Cerise. It looked a little bit like a game of dodgeball with sides taken.

"Where's Lotte?" Candace asked.

"Oh, she sends her regrets," Loretta said. "She had some business in town, but she'll swing by tonight to pick me up."

"Oh. Okay." Candace felt a little bad. Lotte was more than a chauffeur, or should be.

"Who wants spinach? Who wants sausage?" Candace's dad called down the table. Orders were taken, and they settled in over garlic breadsticks and salad while Candace made introductions.

"Hey, guys, this is my friend Loretta, and this is my friend Tracey," Candace said.

"Your friends?" Becca said. "Not your aunt and granny?"

Nate laughed. Sergio coughed. Clearly, she hadn't heard the waiter's mistake earlier.

Loretta smiled down the table at Becca.

"Well, you must be Becca," she said in a way that made Becca frown and Candace stifle a snort. "Well, let me tell you, Becca, I'm no one's granny. I'm what you call a 'bestie.'"

All the kids laughed at that, even Becca.

"Oh, Loretta lives in a house designed by Mies van der Rohe!" Candace said.

"That's cool," Mitchell replied. But Deen just looked apologetically blank, and Sergio shrugged.

"And Tracey is an English literature professor!"

They nodded. The boys pulled out their phones and waited for the pizzas to show up.

For the first time in her life, Candace wished she hadn't ordered deep-dish pizzas. They took forever.

But then the pies came, and it was all eating and no talking, and then Cerise's dad picked her up, and it was time to go back to Candace's place for movies.

"I got you a little something," Loretta said as they all bustled into the living room.

"Oh, but I said no presents. You didn't have to do that," Candace said.

"I wanted to," Loretta assured her, and shoved an envelope into her lap.

"I bet it's money," she heard Nate whisper to Sergio.

"Go on and open it," Loretta said, and handed her coat to Candace's dad. "Thank you, son."

Candace glanced at her mom for the okay. "Usually we

open gifts after the party's over," her mom said. "But I think we can make an exception."

It was a gift certificate to an art store. "You've got talent, youngblood. Invest in it," Loretta said. Candace gave her a hug, and soon all of the other presents were being handed her way.

Candace sat on the floor with the other kids, beaming from ear to ear. Becca gave her lip gloss in the same shade she wore, which probably would look good on Candace. "Thanks, Becca!"

Nate and Sergio went in on a can of disinfectant wipes.

"In case another bird gets into your locker," Nate explained.

Deen swatted him for that, but Candace thought it was funny.

Mitchell gave her a book on birds. Tracey gave her a little set of binoculars. Her mother told her their gifts were clothes and could be opened later. And then Deen's gift was the last one left. Candace smiled at Deen, who smiled back weakly.

It was an envelope. Inside was a gift card to an art supply store.

"Surprise," Deen said.

"Great minds think alike," Loretta crowed, and clapped. She even tried to fist-bump Deen, but it was kind of awkward.

"Thank you so much, Deenie." Candace walked over on her knees and hugged her friend. "This is amazing. You guys are all so great!"

"All right." Candace's mom rose and started gathering wrapping paper. "Tracey, Loretta, would you care to join us for adult beverages and conversation in the kitchen?" she asked. "Unless you want to watch movies."

"What are we watching?" Nate wanted to know.

"*Skylark*," Candace said.

Tracey rolled her eyes. "Have fun." She gave Candace a keep-your-mouth-shut look before joining Candace's parents for wine in the kitchen.

"Cupcakes in an hour," her mom called over her shoulder.

"It's so weird," Becca said when the adults were all gone.

"What?"

"That those people are your 'friends.'" She made air quotes with her fingers. "That lady's, like, a hundred years old, and the other one's not far behind. What kind of old weirdo wants to hang out with a fourteen-year-old girl?"

"They're not weirdos. They're cool! And I like them," Candace said.

"Okay. Weirdo." Becca sank into the cushions on the floor and back into her phone.

"I think it's sweet," Deen said, coming to her defense, the awkward same gifting apparently forgotten. "I'd totally hang with my lola if she was here. And they did seem to get you."

Candace smiled at her gratefully.

"But she's your grandmother," Becca said without looking up.

"Maybe multigenerational friendships are just a Black thing," Mitchell said.

"What? I'm part Black," Becca replied.

"So you only think it's part cool," Mitchell said.

Candace laughed, then caught herself. "Let's just watch the movies."

"*Skylark* sucks," Nate said.

"So do you," Sergio replied. "It's her birthday. You want to watch some talking-dog movie instead?"

The movie started, and it wasn't very good. The CGI looked awful, and the story was kind of confusing, but there were birds and windows in the sky and some whole other angle that Mitchell said wasn't in the original story, about a little blond boy saving the kingdom.

"You've read the books?" Candace said. "I just got them."

"My parents used to read them to us when we were little," he said. "My sister and me. We have the whole set at home."

"So you knew the movie stank and still watched it?"

Mitchell shrugged. "Sometimes even bad movies make for good times."

Candace passed him the bowl of popcorn. "That's great." She and Deen shared a secret smile.

Lotte showed up after cupcakes but before they could start the second movie, and everyone used it as an excuse to leave. Candace's dad stretched and yawned like a bear coming out of hibernation, and grabbed his keys.

"Everyone who needs a ride, downstairs in five," he said.

Candace hugged Tracey and Loretta good night. She hugged Lotte, too, who had brought a bag of fresh-baked cookies for the birthday girl.

"Mom, can I ride with Dad?" Candace asked.

"Honey, let's call it a night. He won't be long."

So Candace waved goodbye at the door to everyone. And the door swung shut on her fourteenth birthday and her weird, amazing groups of friends.

38

"INTERESTING."

Ms. Parker loomed over Candace's work, ten portraits of birds seen in the Chicago area.

"Still working on birds, I see," she said, making Candace's palms sweat. "What are these numbers?" Ms. Parker pointed past the drab colors of a female house finch to the data Candace had worked into the feathers of one wing.

Candace's mouth had gone dry. It was like the science fair all over again. "Um . . . Those are annual population estimates in the Chicago area, one feather for each year, with the year next to it."

"Hmm," Ms. Parker said. "The numbers are going down?"

"Yeah, for a bunch of reasons. Cats. People. Traffic. I haven't figured out how to work that in, or if I should. I think it will get messy. I was trying to blend the numbers in with the bird's coloring so you wouldn't see it right away, but you would if you knew to look for it. Kind of like actually birding, you know?"

Whether Ms. Parker did or did not know, Candace couldn't tell. The woman merely repeated, "Interesting."

So maybe Candace wasn't much of an artist after all. Which would be terrible, since she'd just decided that was what she wanted to be. Maybe not for museums and fancy people's houses, but she could illustrate books. Or at least she thought she could, one day, with more training.

Ms. Parker picked up a T-square from her desk and laid it across the page. "Lovely work," Ms. Parker said suddenly. "Your use of the golden ratio for the spiral of the wingspan is well done." She turned her keen eye onto Candace, who had frozen like a deer. "What do you plan on doing with this? The science fair is over, but this could have a life outside of school. It's worth considering."

"Really? Thank you! Yeah, I don't know. There's this whole resurgence, or maybe it's just a surgence, of Black people going birding? You know Audubon is rumored to have been half Black? But also kind of a racist slaveholder, so it's this whole equality thing? Maybe . . ." She stopped, realizing how self-important it sounded.

"Don't bury your light under a bushel," Ms. Parker said. She sounded so much like Loretta that Candace did a double take. "My granddad used to say that. The world's ready to cut bright young women off at the knees, Candace. Don't do it for them." She smiled.

"Okay . . . Well, I was thinking maybe I could turn it into a little booklet to give to kids at school, like, in biology classes? Or maybe even the Audubon Society could use it? The Chicago branch, not, like, the whole world or anything."

"Why not the whole world?" Ms. Parker said.

Candace shrugged. "I guess it could go online."

"That's a wonderful idea. And then you could include the information on cats and people, and ways we can help reverse the trend." Ms. Parker gazed off into the distance, like she was seeing the future. Then she shook herself. "Let's see where things are at the end of the semester. This could be the makings of a worthy piece of environmental art. People have been known to get college scholarships for work like this."

"Wow," Candace said. "You really think ahead."

"Think ahead to get ahead," Ms. Parker said, and closed the portfolio. "Well done."

Candace bopped down the hallway feeling pretty darn good about herself. She was an artist! She and Deen were speaking to each other again, and even Becca was coming around a bit more without coming around too much. Life was sweet.

"Candace!" Deen came out of the crowd at a jog. "Hey, I was talking to Sergio and Becca. We're thinking about getting a limo for the Spring Fling."

"Aren't limos more like high school prom territory? And expensive?"

"If you and Mitchell join us, then it's only, like, fifty dollars a couple."

"Spring Fling's in the gym, Deen, not like a fancy hotel or something."

"So? We can party on the ride, too. Think of the photos. Oh . . ." Deen paused. "I guess Mitchell hasn't asked you yet."

"What? He's not, like, my boyfriend," Candace said.

"Seriously?" Deen said. "He hasn't *asked* you yet?"

"No, he hasn't asked me. And I haven't asked him to Spring Fling either." Spring Fling was a whole three weeks away, after spring break and Easter, thanks to some funky calendar changes. Last year it had been the Friday before vacation.

"Okay, don't get mad at me."

"I'm not mad," Candace said. She wasn't.

"Well, I hope he asks you. And I hope you ask him so we can get a limo. And because it would be fun. And it won't be the same without you, 'kay?" Deen squeezed Candace's arm, and they headed into class.

Candace felt a funny lump in her gut. It was still there at lunch. She texted Mitchell on the way to the cafeteria.

CANDACE
Hey. Want to go to the Spring Fling dance with me?

MITCHELL
Can I wear a powder blue tux?

I don't know, can you?

I guess we'll find out. 😊

Oh, Deen and them want to share a limo. Can we join in?

A limo? For the gym?

I know.

I guess so. The pictures will be cool.

Great! See you at Hamageddon!

Candace grinned. It was a date! Two dates! Easter was officially Hamageddon, when Tracey and Candace's dad were going to have their ham-off. Candace and her mom were responsible for the side dishes. Mitchell had offered to make T-shirts, which was weird but also hilarious.

Great. Now all Candace had to do was get her parents to cover the limo.

Today was a good day.

—⚡—

"What? No!"

Hamageddon was canceled. On the other end of the line, Tracey apologized.

"Remember when I told you about that job possibility in Wisconsin? Well, they want me to come visit the campus. I fly out on Easter Sunday and meet them first thing Monday morning."

Candace dropped down onto her bed and went boneless.

"But who does that? Flies on Easter?"

"Lots of people, Candace."

"But my dad! He's so looking forward to this!"

Tracey sighed. "And not just your dad, from the sound of it. I'm sorry, kid, but business is business."

Candace did not want to be understanding. But she did understand. "We made you a T-shirt," she said.

"What now?"

"A T-sh— You just have to see it to get it."

"Maybe we can do the ham-off when I get back," Tracey said.

"Yeah. Maybe. Well, good luck with the interview. I hope it goes"—*terrible,* she wanted to say, *I hope they turn you away at the door and you have to stay in Chicago for at least four more years until I graduate*—"well."

"Thanks, kid. I'll bring you some cheese or something."

"Ha. Fly safe."

Candace hung up and went to break the news to her dad.

As a result, Easter was a lot quieter than expected. Mitchell and Deen both came over for lunch, but Deen came late because of a family church thing, and Mitchell was understandably nervous under Candace's dad's stare. Even with the gift of hand-drawn "Hamageddon" T-shirts for everyone. Also, her dad had made a lot of ham. A lot. Candace's mom was caught up in some work drama that had her fielding phone calls, even on a Sunday. Candace didn't want to live in a world where Easter was also a work day. Mitchell left shortly after lunch, with a promise to amaze her with his tux for Spring Fling. Candace did some lackluster online shopping for a dress to wear to the dance. Some start to spring break.

With her dad packing away the rest of the ham, Candace turned to her alerts for #BasicBird. And found a lead. She forwarded it to Loretta and to Tracey, who was on a plane and did not respond.

Loretta wrote back: **Happy Easter, youngblood. We'll be in the city tomorrow for some shopping. You and I can check it out.**

Lotte was planning a trip back home to Denmark. "I have all of these people I need presents for," she explained, holding up a scroll of paper like Santa Claus. "It will take me two, three hours at least. Have fun. I'll meet you back here by dinnertime."

"We're having ham," Candace said.

"Wonderful!" Lotte said, and left.

"Dial up a car service, youngblood," Loretta said. Candace pulled out her phone.

The #BasicBird sighting was a weird one. Someone had posted a blurry photo of a black-and-white bird flying out of what looked like the drive-thru-ordering menu of a fried chicken restaurant in the suburbs south of the Loop. The post read *Chicken attack!* Although it was clearly not a chicken.

It was kind of a long drive.

"Man, has this city changed," Loretta said, gazing out the window. "When I was your age, State Street was all the rage. All the big department stores were down this way—Marshall Field's, Carson Pirie Scott. There were theaters! Oh, Field's had its own ice cream parlor, a beautiful place decorated like a Victorian tearoom. Not that I was allowed to eat in it, of course, but some friends washed dishes in the back. It was luxurious. And then, when I was older and the world had changed enough so that I *could* eat there, I found I didn't want to. The one time I went, the ice cream tasted bitter to me."

She pointed out the sights—things she remembered, things she'd read about, what had changed and what little had stayed the same. Until at last they were pulling into the drive-thru of a small family-owned fast food chicken joint.

"Are we seriously just here to order food?" their driver asked.

"Pull up, and you'll find out," Loretta said. The guy sighed and inched the car forward until Loretta was at the ordering speaker.

"How may I help you?" a voice crackled over the intercom.

"Two chicken wings and two small Sprites," Loretta said through her window. They had planned the order with tonight's leftover ham feast in mind. "You want something, son?" she asked the driver.

"Could I get a Coke and a chicken sandwich?" Loretta added it on. "With pickles."

"That'll be eighteen dollars and ninety-five cents. Pull on up."

"Eighteen ninety-five!" Loretta said. "For wings and a sandwich?" She shook her head and reached for her purse.

"I've got this, Miss Loretta," Candace said. Her parents were determined to stop her from freeloading. "But I don't see anything unusual about the menu. Do you see a knot?"

They pulled forward, and Candace paid with her bank card. Then they found a spot in the parking lot with a view of the ordering board and the takeout window and waited. They ate their wings, which were really good, and drank their pop, which was pop. The sky was darkening, Candace noticed nervously. April showers were more like thunderstorms in Chicago. It might be pouring by the time they got home.

"Ladies, I appreciate the sandwich, but I can't stay here all day. I've got a living to make," their driver said.

"Can't you keep the meter running?" Loretta asked.

"It doesn't work that way, ma'am," he said.

"I think we should go," Candace said.

"I need to use the bathroom," Loretta replied. So that was a whole thing. They got out, their driver left. They went in, they peed, they washed up. They came out again, and it felt like hours had passed at the speed Loretta was moving.

Passing the kitchen, they heard a shout.

"Damn! It's that bird again!"

Candace and Loretta looked at each other. Candace raced to the counter and craned her neck for a view of the takeout window. There, swooping back and forth, was a little black-and-white warbler with a fat pink hair scrunchy in its mouth. Not bright purple velvet. Not a Jordan magpie. Just a common local bird with a vendetta against fried chicken and ponytails.

"My hair!" the cashier cried. "Again!"

"Well, I guess that's that," Candace said.

She turned around to see Loretta holding on to the counter, her mouth a tight line.

"Loretta! Are you okay?"

Loretta's mouth worked, like she was chewing something hard. Candace rushed to take her by the elbow, an arm around her back.

"Just a bit tired, youngblood," Loretta finally said. "Get me a chair. And some water. I forgot to take my pills."

Candace did as she was told, hands sweating. She lowered Loretta into a nearby seat and grabbed a little plastic water cup at the soda machine.

"Here. Where are your pills?" She took Loretta's purse

from the older woman's trembling hands. "What pills? What am I looking for?" Nothing looked like a pill bottle. She started dumping things on the table. Outside, the sky ripped open in a burst of lightning and thunder.

"Oh, just . . . there." Loretta pointed a shaking finger at a tiny silver rabbit. It looked like a bean.

"The rabbit?" Candace struggled to figure out the latch. It popped open. There were tiny pills inside. She shook one out into Loretta's hand. Loretta had gone ashen beneath her warm brown skin.

"Should I call Lotte?" she asked. "I'll call Lotte." Loretta washed the pill down with a sip of water and shook her head.

"Just wait, youngblood. I need a minute. Get us a car back to your house. That's all. I'll be fine."

Candace fumbled with her phone and opened the app. The wind was blowing rain against the restaurant windows. The thunderclaps kept making her jump. But somehow she hit the right buttons. By the time the car was arranged, Loretta was looking better.

"Now," she said, "wipe your eyes." She handed Candace a tissue from her purse. "We're all right. I was just excited. Need to remember to take better care of myself. And you, young lady, you need to work on your nerves. We've got no business exploring the universe if we're both a mess."

She laughed her horsey laugh, and something twisted in Candace's gut. On the one hand, Loretta did sound much better. On the other, Candace was indeed a mess.

"I love you, Loretta," Candace said. She'd always been glad it was the last thing she told her grandfather before he died. She'd visited him one summer, with plans for a second, Christmas visit. And then he was just gone. Candace had been a kid, and even though she'd understood death, it didn't make it easy. When you love someone, her mother told her, you're still connected, no matter where they go.

Candace looked at her shoes, unable to push away the realization that Loretta was much older than her grandfather had been. That no one lived forever.

Her phone bleeped the arrival of their driver.

"Ha! There we go," Loretta stood up, as nimble as if nothing had happened. When Candace didn't move, Loretta patted her hand.

"Come on, youngblood, let's get out of here." She pulled a tiny folding umbrella from her bag. And as they reached the restaurant door, Loretta added, "I love you, too."

39

"SOUNDS LIKE A CRAPPY DAY," DEEN SAID, REACHING for the cinnamon. She and Candace were making cookies—something they used to do all the time before this year. It was super comforting to be in Deen's kitchen with the oven on and her best friend acting like a best friend for real. The kind who'd be around for years and years.

"Yeah. It was like I was suddenly responsible for Loretta's safety, and I was totally failing at it."

"But you weren't responsible," Deen said. "She's the adult, right? Should we add chips or M&M'S?"

"Chips *and* M&M'S." Candace measured out a double dose of chocolate goodness and added it to the dough. "And yeah, you're right. But she's usually got Lotte around, and I don't know, it just felt too real."

"Like worse than when we got lost at Old Orchard mall out in the 'burbs and we thought Becca's parents were going to leave without us because there were so many girls crammed into their car?"

"Don't remind me!" They'd just turned eleven, and Becca's party was a shopping spree. Candace had gotten left behind in a dressing room, Deen in the ladies' restroom. They'd been terrified. And then they'd found each other.

"At least we didn't have to face it alone," Candace said. She nudged Deen, smiling at the memory. But Deen was frowning.

"Yeah," she said. "We had each other."

"And we made it home," Candace added. Her smile faltered. "Deenie, what is it?"

"Oh . . . nothing." Deen focused on scooping out cookie dough balls like it was the cookie dough Olympics. It was suspicious.

"Seriously, what's up?" Candace asked. "Something to do with Becca?"

Something to do with why Becca was always over at Deen's, except not today? Or why Becca's sweater was hanging in the hallway, and her bookbag was by the door, even though she wasn't here? But Candace didn't ask that part out loud. She didn't want anyone to know she had noticed it. Instead, she just gave Deen her best Loretta look, and Deen crumbled.

"I wasn't supposed to say anything! But Becca's parents split up, and she's been staying here while they work it out, but today they're all meeting with a lawyer or something to figure out who she's going to live with, and she's been really unhappy about it but doesn't want anyone to know, so don't tell her I told you, okay?"

It took Candace's brain an extra second or two to decipher everything Deen had just said. Divorce. Custody. Unhappy.

She took a deep breath and let it out. Suddenly, it all made sense. Becca taking over Deen as her bestie. Becca being snippy. She wasn't snippy. She was sad! And Deen was her anchor, just like she used to be Candace's anchor.

"I'm so sorry to hear it, Deenie," she said, and pulled her

friend into a hug. They had to hold their cookie dough hands awkwardly away from each other, balled into fists, but it was a hug, one they both needed.

"I wish I could have told you, but my parents said it was Becca's business, not mine. But it's been so weird with us lately, and I just don't want it to keep going like this."

"Me either," Candace said.

They washed their hands and dried their faces, which had somehow gotten wet. The cookies went in the oven, and Candace made tea using Mrs. De La Cruz's old beaten-up kettle. She added honey and two bags of chamomile to their mugs.

"Smells good," Deen's brother said, passing through on his way from the living room to his bedroom in the basement.

"Stop buttering us up, Mac," Deen said. "You know we always make enough cookies for everyone."

Mac grinned and disappeared down the stairs.

Candace laughed. She could never decide if she had a crush on Mac or thought he was an old man. He was in his first year of community college, studying hiking or forestry—Candace never really understood which. But it meant he was super outdoorsy, when he wasn't super indoorsy playing video games.

He'd been in outdoorsy mode for that end-of-summer camping trip with Deen and Becca. The one without Canda—

Candace stopped herself. She and Deen were in a better place, finally. Bygones could be bygones.

"Hey, tomorrow will be fun," Candace said. "Maybe we can take Becca's mind off of things."

"Yes!" Deen agreed, plopping down on the banquette that lined the back of the kitchen table. Candace slid in beside her.

"We can get mini makeovers to match our dresses and then come back here to figure out how to do it on our own. I'm going to wear all black."

"I thought you wanted to wear pink," Candace said. Deen shrugged.

"Black is Sergio's favorite color."

"Your hair is black. That should be enough for him."

Deen laughed, touching her shiny hair. "Yeah, it was too hard to keep up the purple highlights. Especially since they were more like lowlights. I'm surprised you didn't say anything."

"What? No, I could see it in the sun. It was cute."

Deen rested her head on Candace's shoulder. "Ugh. I feel like I've been holding in my stomach all year and I'm finally letting it out." She pooched out her gut. Candace did the same.

"Much better," Candace said.

"Much."

Later, beached out on the sofa watching anime, with enough cookies in their stomachs to make them pooch out for real, Candace was just nodding off when her phone buzzed.

"Is that Mitchell?" Deen sang in a loopy voice.

"Nope. Tracey. Just a sec."

TRACEY
Candace, check your phone.

LORETTA
Candace, check your phone. Loretta.

TRACEY

Are you there? All okay?

LORETTA

I'm fine, thank you.

TRACEY

No, I meant Candace.
She's usually on
top of this stuff.

Candace rolled her eyes. Like she didn't have a life, too. Maybe she wasn't retired or traveling around interviewing for jobs in other states, but she had stuff. She wasn't *always* glued to her phone.

She checked her other notifications. "Holy cow."

#BasicBird was blowing up. It was spring, so bird sightings weren't uncommon. Swallows and warblers and all sorts of ducks and geese were winging their way home to nest and mate. But not all of them brought streamers to the party.

What's up with the ribbons?

Birds be upgrading.

Mating season and the ladies are strutting it!

Magpies?

Post after post of sightings of birds with purple ribbons. Sure, some had string, others had yarn, and every shade of purple was mentioned.

But in the southern tip of Illinois, near the Shawnee National Forest, the birds appeared to be magpies. And the ribbons were notebook-purple velvet, nine inches long. (Some birders were *very* specific about their sightings.)

"What's up?" Deen asked.

"Just a sec." Candace's fingers flew across her screen.

CANDACE

I'm seeing it! Amazing!

TRACEY

This week is my spring break. What about you, C?

Mine too!

Field trip!

"What do you mean you're leaving?" Deen asked. She had pillow creases on her right cheek from the sofa.

"Something's come up with Loretta and Tracey, you know, for our . . . birding stuff?"

"Birds? You're ditching me and Becca for birds?"

"I'm not ditching you. *You* ditched *me* to go camping with Mac and Becca last year." The words were out of her mouth before she could stop them. So much for bygones.

"You're still mad about that? I explained—"

"It's fine! I'm not mad!" Candace sounded mad. "It's just . . . there's some sightings down south, some place called the Shawnee Forest. We're going to go scout it out."

"But does it have to be tomorrow?" Deen asked, sitting up.

"Yeah," Candace said. "Tracey and I both have school next week. And it's kind of a long drive, so we're going to stay a night or two. We drive down tomorrow, go birding Friday, and maybe Saturday depending, and I'll be back Sunday night."

"Sunday night! When the malls are closed and there's no time to shop? Sunday's a school night!"

Candace's stomach sank. "I know. I'm so sorry," she said. "I feel awful."

"You don't look like you feel awful. You look . . . *excited*," Deen said accusingly. "Becca was right. You'd rather hang out with your grannies than us."

"Well, maybe I would," Candace snapped. "They're, like, totally mature, and they don't make me feel bad just because *they* feel bad. And they don't keep secrets, and they don't—"

"Don't what?" Deen shouted. They were both kind of shouting now, and standing up, and this was really happening, and Candace didn't know how to stop it.

"They're my friends!" Candace said.

"Then what am I?"

"It's about the freaking universe!" Candace cried.

"What?"

"My locker is a wormhole! That bird was a space-time magpie! We're not exploring Shawnee, we're exploring the entire flipping universe!"

"What?" Deen screamed.

"Whoa."

Mac had entered the room, munching on a cookie.

"Lighten up, Deen. She's got nerd friends, and you're more like a girly girl. Been there, done that, but, like, manly man instead. It's cool. There's some sick hiking in Shawnee," he said approvingly. "You can both go your own way."

"I don't *want* to go my own way!" Deen shouted at the same time Candace shouted, "Is that what's happening?"

The air left the room then. They stared each other down, panting.

"I don't know," Deen said.

"Well, neither do I," Candace said.

She thought of the birds and their knots and the way the weirdness of it was starting to make more sense than the normal things in her life. She thought of Loretta, whose time was running out. And Deen, who was still young like Candace. They had all the time in the world to work this out.

"You don't believe me," Candace realized out loud. "About the locker, I mean. The birds?"

Deen stalked off to the kitchen. "It doesn't matter, Candace. We still need you for the limo. See you at the dance."

"And at school next week, right? Deenie? We have time..."

I assumed you were here because you are ready, Loretta had said that first day at her house. And it turned out Candace *had* been. But Deen wasn't. And maybe she never would be.

"That was intense," Mac said. He was still standing there, still holding his cookie.

"Yeah. Thanks, Mac." She pulled on her shoes. Grabbed her coat. Texted her mom for a pickup. "I'll just... wait outside."

O'HARE WAS KIND OF A NIGHTMARE. CANDACE STOOD by the trunk of Tracey's car avoiding eye contact with the cop who was giving them the stink eye for not moving on. But Loretta would not be rushed. Lotte was headed home to Denmark, so the two had shared a ride to the airport. Tracey and Candace had come to pick Loretta up from there.

"Have fun! There are cookies in the small basket," Lotte said, trundling Loretta's suitcase toward them.

Loretta held the basket in the crook of her arm like a second purse. Like Candace ever wanted to see a cookie again. They just reminded her of how terrible she felt.

"Now, Candace, I also told Tracey, but don't let Loretta get so excited that she doesn't take her pills. It's just iron to keep her strength up. She will be okay," Lotte said. "Being prepared is the best defense." She patted Candace's arm.

"Okay," Candace said. Lotte had explained it all before. Loretta was as healthy as a lady her age could be. "Bye, Lotte. Have a good trip."

Lotte waved to them and wheeled her massive bags into the terminal. Tracey ran after her for a quick conversation. Loretta opened the back door and transferred the cookie basket to the car.

"Those bags won't lift themselves, youngblood," she said.

"I know." Candace opened the trunk and moved her duffel bag to one side, Tracey's carry-on to the other. Which left almost enough room for Loretta's own massive suitcase.

"Lift with your knees," Loretta said helpfully, waving her cane.

Candace squatted down and hefted the big green softside over the lip of the trunk. With a bit of wiggling, she managed to slide it into place.

"Good job," Loretta said. "I call shotgun."

Candace climbed into the back and jostled into the cookie basket.

"I'll take one if you do." Loretta was watching from the rearview mirror. Tracey opened the driver's side door.

"All in? Ooh, can I have one, too?"

Candace passed a snickerdoodle to each woman, stared at the huge chocolate chip cookie lying on top of the rest, and sighed. As they pulled out of O'Hare and onto the expressway, Candace snuggled into her fleecy hoodie and pulled out her phone for Talking to Deen, attempt number six.

She had tried the love letter of her voice, and texting.

Then she had called Mitchell, because Deen had Becca but Candace didn't have any other friends. She'd hoped Mitchell would have some insight, but he had only said, "That sucks."

Candace didn't even try to explain the knot and the birds to him. Maybe if she had just lied to Deen, things would be easier.

"Is it lying to not tell someone something?" she asked her real friends. Loretta was trying to give directions, but Tracey was following her phone's navigation app. They both glanced back at her.

"It's called a lie of omission," Loretta said. "Like when someone says, 'Does this outfit look good?' And you say, 'Pretty colors,' because it's an attractive outfit, even if it looks awful on them."

"Depends on the situation," Tracey said, giving Loretta a look. "If you didn't like that pantsuit, you could have just said so." She glanced at Candace in the rearview mirror. "Loretta helped me choose an outfit for my interview last month. Or maybe she just sabotaged me, I don't know."

Loretta guffawed her horsey laugh, but otherwise kept quiet.

"Did you hear that?" Tracey pointed out. "That silence there, after a laugh that was all but a confession? That is a lie of omission."

Loretta swatted Tracey's arm as if to say, *I wouldn't lie to you.*

Tracey shook her head and looked at Candace in the mirror again. "Why?" she asked. "Is this about your parents and the knots?"

"No," Candace said. "Although it could be. And probably *should* be. But it's about Deen. We were supposed to spend the whole week together shopping for the spring dance."

"I thought she dumped you for Becca," Loretta said.

"So did I. But it turns out Becca's parents are getting a divorce and Deen's been trying to be supportive of Becca but also keep it a secret because that's what Becca wanted for some reason. Which was totally a lie of omission that made this whole year so awful. And I'd just found out the truth when you guys texted, and Deen was so upset when I said I had to leave that I . . . I told her about the knot."

The car wobbled.

"You what?" Tracey exclaimed.

Loretta shook her head and patted Tracey's arm. "It's all right," she said. "And how did it go?" She sounded curious, not mad.

"Not well. She didn't believe me. And her brother thinks I'm talking about a video game or something, and now Deen's not answering my calls or texts."

"Her brother? You told her brother, too! I thought we were keeping this between ourselves," Tracey said tightly.

"And we are," Loretta said. "Calm down. Youngblood, you've just learned what we all know as children. It's easier to be disbelieved than believed. How many wonders and insights have been dismissed as the product of an overactive imagination? As a lie of *invention*? Now, you can cry about it, and Lord knows Lotte gave us enough cookies for you to drown your sorrows in sugar, if you'd like. Or you can see it for what it is—protection.

"The failure of imagination in others allows us to operate in broad daylight. We'll go to the forest, see what there is to see, and when you come back, you can talk to your little friend and tell her the real truth, that you're indulging an old lady in her final years."

"Final years?"

"Don't deny it, Candace. I am older than either of you are ever likely to be, quite frankly. If this was a trip to Disney World instead of bird-watching, who would complain? God gave Black women invisibility, and we've spent years—decades, generations—being unseen. We might as well use it to our advantage now.

"Besides," she added, "I, for one, think your friend cares about you, or she wouldn't be so upset. Just like you care about Tracey, or her new job wouldn't bother you so much. Or me."

"What? What just happened?" Tracey said. "This is about Deen and Candace, not me."

"It's about friendship," Loretta said. "I'm just drawing a parallel example."

"A good one," Candace added.

"Hey, I'm not the bad guy here," Tracey said. "If I didn't have such amazing 'invisibility,' as Loretta just put it, I might not need to leave my job in order to be seen. We don't always get to do things the way we want to, Candace. But if we're lucky, we get to choose something. Do I want to leave Chicago for Wisconsin? Not really. But I do want a tenured job, real security, a retirement plan, and if I'm honest, the prestige that goes with it."

"Fine," Candace said.

"None of that means anything to you right now, kid. I get that. But one day you'll understand."

Candace pulled a piece of cookie from the basket and broke it into tiny crumbs in the palm of her hand. "Does 'real security' mean you'll get to write your novel?"

"Novel?" Loretta's ears perked up.

"Yeah, Tracey wanted to be a writer when she was my age. Someone told her she couldn't do it. And I guess she believed them."

"Candace!" Tracey's voice had tightened again.

"What? It's true!" Candace didn't know why she had said it. To help or to hurt? She angled toward help. "Maybe Loretta can give you some pointers or something," she mumbled. "I mean, if you still want to write. Maybe you don't."

Geez. Maybe she *was* mean after all.

Loretta said nothing. Which was surprising, Candace thought. But then, seeing the veins popping out in Tracey's neck, maybe it was the smart thing to do, since Tracey was driving.

"Please don't have a stroke!" Candace said. Which was the wrong thing to say. The tires actually screeched as Tracey pulled to the side of the road. Trucks and cars went whizzing by, but she got out of the car anyway and walked away.

"You pushed her too far, youngblood," Loretta said.

"I didn't do anything," Candace replied, which was a lie of omission. Or just a lie. She sat up. Cookie crumbs fell into her lap and down her shirt. "Crap."

She opened her own door and got out to dust the cookie bits off of her clothes. Tracey hadn't gone far, but her back was turned.

Candace swept out the back seat of the car with her hands. Tracey was already pissed. She didn't need to find chocolate chip stains, too. Then she might as well move all the way to China. She'd never want to see Candace again.

"It isn't safe out here." Tracey's voice carried over the whiz of traffic. "Get back in the car."

Candace straightened up and squared her chest.

"You first."

Tracey did not look happy. "You're a pest, you know that?"

"Of course I know it. I'm one of your pest friends."

Which made Tracey laugh. And Candace unclench enough to smile. And then they both looked angry again, but they both got back in the car and on the road.

They didn't talk for a long time after that. Sergio texted to say the limo for next week was squared away. Candace sent him a thumbs-up. But it just made her miss Deen all the more.

So far it seemed like (1) Deen might be done with her, (2) Loretta might die soon, (3) Tracey was probably moving away, and (4) Candace was . . . well, feeling sorry for herself. The people she liked were all going away, one way or another.

At least Mitchell was still around. She took a picture of the passing scenery and texted it to him. He sent back a picture of his legs on the sofa in front of a video game. Which actually made her feel better. She could be at the mall right now, or loafing in front of the TV. But instead, she was off to unravel the secrets of the universe. And that was still pretty freaking cool.

UNPACKING THE CAR WAS A BIT OF A PRODUCTION. THE hotel was unsurprisingly busy for spring break. Candace had to make a dash to grab one of the rolling luggage trolleys near the front door the minute one was returned. Tracey helped her unpack the trunk while Loretta went to check in.

"I cannot wait for a hot meal and a soft bed," Tracey said as they wheeled their way through the front doors and up the little rampway to the carpeted area. Suddenly, Loretta's voice rang out across the lobby.

"Young man, you will not sass me!"

"Oh, Lord," Tracey said. Candace couldn't see through the crowded lobby beyond the luggage piled in front of her.

"What's happening?" she asked.

"I'll see." Tracey disappeared.

Candace parked the cart to the side of the doors in time to see Loretta hoist her wizard staff and point it at the pimply-faced white guy behind the counter.

"Young man," she repeated, then peered at his name tag. "Gene. You're a hard worker, and I want to see you prosper. But if you continue to ignore me and help all these fine people instead"—she waved her staff at a sunburnt white family and a line of other folks behind them—"then I am going to scream. I have been standing here at your counter waiting my turn. It's my turn now. Don't look away. We are here to check in. The name is Spencer."

"What's wrong?" Tracey asked.

"Gene, do you want to tell her?" Loretta asked in a voice that was not like asking.

Gene's eyes darted from Loretta to Tracey to Candace and back again. They settled on the knob at the end of Loretta's staff.

"I'm sorry. I didn't see her there. Mrs. . . . Spencer. I, uh . . ." Gene pounded his keyboard frantically. Candace kind of felt bad for him. "I thought she was with—"

"The last Black family that just left?" Loretta waved her staff toward the front doors, where an African American couple was bundling their luggage outside.

"I'm so, so sorry," he said. "It's been super busy. Spring break . . ." He shrugged and kept typing. "Did you say Spencer?"

Loretta's face hardened. "Now, I know you didn't give away our rooms. We have a reservation right here." She waved a printout in the air.

Gene seemed to shrink into his collar. He looked around the crowded lobby. "We have . . . one room. I'm sorry. It's, uh, got one bed." He brightened. "I can give you two cots! Or maybe Mom and Grandma can share?"

He looked hopefully at Tracey and Loretta.

Loretta laughed, and it wasn't her usual horsey guffaw. It was sharp as a knife.

"I don't mind a cot," Candace piped in.

"No. We'll go somewhere else," Loretta replied. "After I speak to your manager."

"Loretta, I think—" Tracey began.

"You think, but I *know*," Loretta said.

Gene lunged for the phone.

―※―

The rooms were really nice. A king suite with a balcony overlooking trees for Loretta, and an adjoining room with two queen beds for Tracey and Candace, just like the reservation had promised. Gene himself wheeled in the luggage trolley. Loretta gave him a ten-dollar tip and asked for a restaurant recommendation.

Gene fell over himself trying to leave afterward. "Watch yourself, now," Loretta said as he picked himself up off the hallway floor. She shut the door behind him. "Now, this is more like it."

Candace was leaning against the wall by the window, looking out at the twilight sky. "What was that?" she asked.

Tracey had taken a seat on the edge of the sofa, hugging her purse and looking uncomfortable.

"That was good old-fashioned Southern hospitality," Loretta said.

"We're not in the South," Candace said.

"We're not in Chicago anymore, either, youngblood. And as open as the world can be, it isn't always just that. Lotte and I booked these rooms. They are paid for. And I was not going to give them up because some little pimple-faced white boy was redlining for his boss."

"He probably couldn't see you over the counter, Loretta," Tracey said.

"What's redlining?" Candace asked.

Tracey sighed. "It's an old practice of keeping people of color out of certain neighborhoods by refusing to sell or rent houses. I'm not sure if applies to hotel rooms . . ." She looked at Loretta and whispered, "Or old people," then resumed her normal volume. "But the principle is the same."

"If it looks like a duck," Loretta said. She dropped down onto the bed. "Well, we're here now, and we've got work to do. I suggest we get a good dinner and plan for an early day tomorrow."

"Yes, ma'am," Tracey said, and wheeled her suitcase into the other room. Candace lingered by the window. Three flights down, there was a swimming pool. Some kids were actually using it, despite the chilly day. She felt a little chilly herself. Should they be staying here if they weren't wanted?

"Go on, now," Loretta said. "Give me some privacy. I want to wash up a bit."

Candace hesitated, then headed for the adjoining doorway.

"What's on your mind, youngblood?"

Candace turned around. "It's just, the older I get, the harder things turn out to be."

Loretta nodded, and used her wizard staff to slip off one shoe, and then the other. "Folks in power like to ignore four things—women, people of color, and anyone older or younger than they are. You get used to it, Candace. Even if you don't want to. And you change it when you can."

"Did we change anything tonight by staying here?"

Loretta shrugged again. "Well, Gene won't forget us anytime soon. But change doesn't often last. That's why we keep at it. Now, go pull yourself together. I could eat enough for the both of us."

⁓*⁓*

Between the meat loaf, the redlining conversation, and the weirdness of maybe losing Deen and maybe starting to be okay with it, Candace did not sleep well. Given their five a.m. wake-up time, she was surprised that she was still excited for the trip to the park. The sooner they found Jordan magpies, the sooner she could get home to see if her friendship with Deen was really over. That was an in-person sort of thing, she figured.

"This place is really big." Candace had a map up on her phone, but she had switched it out for a paper map from the information center. It was now spread awkwardly across the backs of the front seats. Shawnee National Forest was ten, no, twenty times the size of the Magic Hedge. It was like its own mini city, bordered by the Mississippi River to the west and the Ohio River to the east and along the southern border, with all kinds of named areas and four different geological regions in one place. Fortunately, eBird gave them an idea of where to start. "Someplace called . . . 'Garden of the Gods'?" Candace read. Loretta started to laugh.

Tracey drove them into the park as far as they were able to go. The area was crisscrossed by hiking trails. They decided to visit the Observation Trail, figuring it would have the best view. It was downright spooky at six in the morning. The sky was still dim, a sort of colorless wash that was hard to see by, but not so hard to see that Candace didn't notice the people on horseback.

"We could've gotten horses?" she said.

"Not this time of morning. See? They have to wait until it's bright enough for the horses to travel safely," Tracey pointed out.

"Do you know how to ride?" Loretta asked.

"Do pony rides count?" Candace asked.

"No, youngblood, they do not."

The sun was just hinting at rising when they set Loretta up in her folding chair at the trailhead, with her eyes on the sky.

"It's just a quarter mile there and back," Tracey said, looking at the signs. "We shouldn't be long."

"Do you think there are snakes?" Candace asked as they made their way into the trees. The rocks made weird shapes against the sky. "Do you think there are werewolves?"

Tracey snorted. "It is kind of spooky. And that name! Gives me the shivers."

"Where did it come from?" Candace asked.

"No idea, but it sounds like a B movie. If we see any gods, be polite, but run."

They didn't see any gods. Just a few other birders, easily identified by their telescopic camera lenses and binocular necklaces. Candace and Tracey fell silent but for the sound of their breathing and the rising wind that seemed to come up with the sun. And the snatch of sudden birdsong.

"Look." Candace pointed. A sparrow had launched from the trees just overhead. Through her binoculars, Candace spotted its nest. And then the sun burst above the tree-and-rock line, illuminating the nest. It was festooned with purple ribbons.

"Well, somebody's been here," Tracey murmured, her own binoculars pressed to her eyes.

They scanned the trees. A few hints of purple here and there, but the risen sun made it hard to see in the shadow of the understory. Instead, they turned to face the Garden of the Gods.

It was wild. The cliff face looked like stacks of humongous rounded river stones built into cairns, emerging from the deep greenery like the Zen garden of a bonsai-loving giant. The stones ran along a ridge like a spine. And the view!

Candace caught her breath. Surrounding the cliff, there was nothing but rolling green hills as far as the eye could see.

"Like broccoli," she whispered.

Tracey's laugh started low and built steadily. "You have a way with words, Candace."

"What? It does look like broccoli." It really did.

The bad news was, there was an awful lot of sky. They chose a hill at the midpoint to divide the view and each took a side of the landscape, scanning up and down the way a search party might walk a field looking for clues. There were birds in the sky, but none of them were blooping. And none of them seemed to be magpies.

"I could've done a whole science project just from here," Candace said to Loretta when they reached the car again. "Must have been, like, twenty different species up there."

"Wasn't your project on Chicago?" Loretta asked.

"Yeah, but still," Candace replied.

"So, purple ribbons, but no Jordan magpies," Tracey said. "Clearly they've been here, but they're coming from somewhere else. We're looking in the wrong place."

They consulted eBird again and drove to a new section of the forest. By lunchtime, they were getting discouraged. Fortified by burgers and Cokes, they tried again. It was beautiful, but none of it appeared to be a knot.

"Let's try again tomorrow," Loretta said.

Tracey looked like she was about to protest. Instead, she said, "Okay. One more day."

Candace woke up from an unintentional nap to the smell of pizza coming from Loretta's room. It was nine p.m.

"There she is," Tracey said. "There's a microwave by the mini fridge. Help yourself." She and Loretta were watching an old movie on TV.

Candace snagged a slice of pizza with the works, ate the mushrooms off of it, and put the rest in the microwave for a few seconds. She sat at the little dinette table/desk and pulled out her phone.

CANDACE
Hey, Mitchell.

MITCHELL
Candace! How's it going?

Okay. Lots of birds.
Amazing landscape.

She texted Mitchell a picture taken from the ridge of Garden of the Gods. Mitchell gave the picture a heart.

CANDACE
How's spring break?

MITCHELL
Meh.

Too bad. Maybe you should go on an adventure.

Maybe you can share yours?

Her phone buzzed. It wasn't a text, but an actual phone call. Candace's heart did a little flip. Finishing her slice, she took a bottle of water back into the room she shared with Tracey and quietly shut the connecting door.

"Hello?"

"Hey, Candace." It was weird hearing his voice miles from home. Like Mitchell was right there in the room with her. "What's up?"

"Tracey, Loretta, and I went to the Shawnee Forest today. There's a place called the Garden of the Gods—"

"Sounds like a B movie."

"That's what Tracey said! And it's really cool. Such weird rock formations and tons of trees. You'd like it."

"Draw a picture for me?"

Candace's heart fluttered. She'd already sent him a picture, but he wanted her art.

She lay back on the bed, and smiled.

SATURDAY MORNING, CANDACE, TRACEY, AND LORETTA put their heads together over Candace's phone and the big paper map of the Shawnee National Forest. Last night, the two older women had marked the areas with the most sightings of purple ribbons and magpies on the better map they'd picked up at the information center. The little X marks were thick in some places, thin in others. They had visited most of the thick spots yesterday and found nothing. Loretta wasn't interested in "traipsing over hill and dale" today without a plan.

"Maybe we're looking at this the wrong way," Candace said. "I mean, my knot is in a locker. And while maybe that drive-thru wasn't actually a knot, it doesn't mean the idea was wrong. We keep looking up. Maybe we should look, I don't know . . . down?"

Loretta sighed. "Meemaw described windows in the sky, so I've always looked to where birds fly. And since I found so many places, I thought I was right. But maybe . . ." She shrugged.

Tracey studied the map. "Okay, so today we look 'down.' What's that give us? Caves? Look here. Sand Cave, Cave-in-Rock, and something called Iron Furnace. And it looks like there are a lot of birds at Bell Smith Springs, which is nearby."

"Well, how come there aren't a lot of birds near my locker?

Or Loretta's house?" Candace asked. "In biology class, my teacher said animals try to stay away from their dens so predators can't track them. Maybe the birds are trying to hide their knots?"

Tracey's eyes had widened. "Are there knot predators?"

Loretta shook her head. "Not that I've seen. No birds have come through with a chunk taken out of them. But anything's possible."

"Shoot," Tracey said, reading the guide. "There are other caves, too. Whiskey Cave, Fern Cave . . ." She pulled out a highlighter and marked them on the map. "Would you look at that?"

One of the caves marked with Tracey's yellow circle stood out. The X's radiated from it, first thick, then thin. It looked like a sun.

"Wow," Candace said. "That's got to be it, right?"

Sand Cave. Candace pulled it up on her phone.

"This says Sand Cave might have been important to the local Illiniwek tribe. There's a stone ring and a rock in the center that gives you a view of the whole cave. And, hey! It used to be a stop on the Underground Railroad! Listen. 'In the 1840s, the Dabbs, Singleton, and Miller families escaped to the North, bought property, and created Miller Grove, a Black community made up of freed slaves. They created a safe haven to shelter those on their way to "Canaan Land," a phrase for Canada, where those who escaped could reach freedom.' So cool!"

"What do you think, Miss Loretta?" Tracey asked. "Looks like about a mile or so of easy walking, if we park close enough."

Loretta rose to her feet. "Then we best get going. And if this isn't the spot, we can check out the others. And try again tomorrow."

Tracey opened her mouth, and closed it again with a nod. "Well, let's see how the day goes."

An hour later, they were parked on the side of a gravel road. The trail to Sand Cave was rutted by tire marks, from park service trucks apparently, as signs said no horses or vehicles were allowed. It made for a lumpy but walkable path, which Loretta had no trouble following, boots stomping alongside her wizard staff through the moldy leaves and hardened mud. It would be a nightmare in the rain, Candace thought, wishing she had her own wizard staff.

Through the trees on her right, a bluff rose out of the earth in a moss-covered stack, like the layers of a Butterfinger candy bar, but gray and green instead of orangey-brown. The trail rose along with the bluff, but the rocks climbed higher, and suddenly they were looking at it. Sand Cave. It gaped like a big dark archway in the rock. Candace could smell the breath of the cave. Cool. Damp. Green and mineral. There were people there already, milling around in their windbreakers and hiking boots. At a nod from Loretta, Candace unhooked the folding chair from her back and found an even piece of ground to set it on. She helped Loretta into her seat.

"Now," Loretta said, accepting a bottle of water from Tracey, "I'm going to bird sit out here for a breath or two. Go on in and see what you can see. I'll follow presently."

"No, you won't," Tracey said. She sounded a little worried. Candace had to admit Loretta looked winded. She was probably more fragile than she liked to pretend. "We'll come back and get you if there's something to see, okay? Promise me you won't try to navigate the rocks without us?"

"Fine, fine, youngblood. Go make yourselves useful. Like I said, I'll be out here."

"I want to make a quick sketch," Candace said. She pulled her sketch pad out of her backpack and found a good vantage point. The cave really did look like a giant mouth, like a stone man caught in mid-yawn. When she finished the first sketch, she did another one, this time defining the cheeks and nose. She went and checked on Loretta when she was done. "See anything?" Candace asked. The trees were pretty barren, even though it was April.

"Not yet," Loretta said, pulling the binoculars from her eyes. Tracey was making her way back toward them.

"Loretta, it's pretty even inside. I think we can move your chair in there, if you want. Maybe the change of view will help?"

By the time they got her settled inside the cave, most of the other hikers had moved on, talking of hidey holes in the bluff above and something called the Devil's Backbone.

"Look at this!" Loretta exclaimed. The cave was really more of a hollow in the rock, like someone had scooped out a high, deep mouth. But the cave didn't have a throat. The ceiling soared and then sloped down the sides and to the back like a dome. Under the "eaves," there was a circle of stones on one side. And in the middle of the cave, there was the large boulder the guide had mentioned. Candace went and climbed onto the rock. She could see everything from here—the mouth of the cave, the back, the sides. But there was no bruise-colored cabbage rose that she could see.

"Maybe it's just too dark to tell."

"Those other hikers mentioned some hidey holes up the bluff," Tracey said. "Loretta, mind if we check those out?"

The older woman shook her head. "I'll be here. But don't be too long. It's a bit chilly without sunlight."

In the end, they moved her to the mouth of the cave so she could have the best view of both spots. Then Tracey and Candace followed the trail up the side of the bluff. Sure enough, there were plenty of crevices and dark holes where birds could easily fly out. Or bats, Candace realized with a little shudder. But they didn't find a knot.

Climbing back down the path, they heard whistling. Not just whistling, but a high, warbling note that echoed off the rocks. Coming around the side, they saw Loretta, still in her chair, half in the sun, whistling into the cavern. Sand Cave seemed to whistle back, echoing the sound of her birdcalls. The same call she had used to summon the Jordan magpie back at her house.

As they got closer, Loretta smiled. She tilted her head slightly to the right. "Look who found us." Sitting on her shoulder, half hidden in the shadows, was a Jordan magpie.

Tracey stopped in her tracks. Candace pulled out her phone. She'd left her sketch pad with Loretta, but she could draw this later. As her camera snapped, the shadows triggered the flash, and the magpie took off. Ten feet above the entrance of the cave, it went *bloop!* and was gone.

"Oh my God," Tracey said. Candace tilted her head. She walked under the spot where the bird had disappeared. The knot was here, above them, nearly impossible to see in the shifting light and shadow. And it was huge.

43

"I'VE NEVER BEEN ABLE TO FIGURE OUT ALL THE connections," Loretta said at lunch. They'd driven into the nearby town of Equality to warm themselves up after the morning chill. Candace was nomming on a bowl of chili mac, Tracey had a veggie burger, and Loretta had opted for chicken and dumplings. "Or why the time shifts occur. The best I can figure is it's like a revolving door or maybe an elevator. Birds go in, the door turns, and they exit."

"Where do you think it goes?" Candace asked.

"Maybe like the old folks said, all the way to Canaan Land." She smiled at the thought.

"But then, how come some of the 'floors,' I guess, seem to be connected, like our locker and your house?" Candace asked, reeling a string of melted cheese around her spoon.

"Maybe it's more like a pinball machine," Tracey said. "With flaps that open and close, and springs that shuttle the ball—the birds—to different outcomes. They might get to know those routes. Maybe . . ." She hesitated. "This is all probably wrong, because scientists aren't supposed to speculate, right?" She looked at Loretta.

"We can hypothesize. Most science starts as speculation and ends up as observation."

"Well, you described them as knots where these pathways cross. We met through a forty-year knot. What if it's only forty years to us?"

Loretta nodded. "It could be it's some sort of generational knot, where Jordan bird number one goes in, and its great-great-descendant, Jordan four hundred, comes out the other end, but I don't think so."

"The Jordan in your living room seemed to know you," Tracey said. "It came right to you."

Loretta nodded. "That's how it seems to me. Like I've been seeing some of the same birds over and over again."

"So what's your . . ." Candace searched for the science word. "Hypothesis?"

Loretta smiled. "I've got a lot of thoughts, but not enough to hypothesize just yet."

"For all we know, it really is like your books, and there's a whole world on the other side of these knots," Tracey said. "Like a parallel universe."

"Well, there's only one way to find out," Loretta replied.

"Send a bird through with a beacon or something?" Candace said. Loretta cut her a look.

"Child, do you think I haven't tried? I've marked them with leg bands, but even a crow can remove a leg band, and these Jordans, they're smart. I have yet to see one come back with it still on."

"But maybe a chip, like a lost dog or something?"

"And wait who knows how long for it to come out who knows where?" Loretta countered. "And then hope someone takes it to a vet to check for the chip?"

"Well..." Candace said. "So, what was your idea?"

"We go through it ourselves."

The silence that followed was so profound, Candace could hear the cheese melting on her chili. *Go through it.* A hole opened up in her chest. The words—the possibility behind the words—punched a gaping portal through her, full of stars.

Her spoon trembled. "Uh..." she said.

Tracey folded the map, tucked it away, and said, "With respect, that's ludicrous. Actual skylarking? Wandering off into a...a...black hole—"

"Wormhole," Loretta said.

"Without a clue as to what's on the other side? I thought you said only birds could go through."

"I may have been mistaken," Loretta replied. "To date, the knots have been in the sky—or a locker—and too small for humans. That's no longer the case. The Sand Cave knot looked to be a good eight feet in diameter."

"Um, and, like, fifteen feet over our heads," Candace pointed out. She could breathe again. Loretta cut her another one of those looks.

"They do make ladders, youngblood."

Candace almost laughed. "But you can't just, like, climb into the sky and—"

"'On Thursdays, the sky windows opened and the birds of unordinary colouring escaped their invisible world. Dorianna placed a ladder in the woods, climbed to the sixty-first rung, and pressed her eye to the peephole there. What wonders she saw,'" Tracey recited like it was scripture from the Bible or something.

"What?" Candace said.

"*Window in the Sky*. The opening lines of the first Skylark book? Seriously, Candace? We've been chasing down knots for months, and you still haven't read the books?" Tracey said.

"They're bulky! And I'm busy. With school and other books and things. And I did watch the movie." She turned to Loretta and reached out a comforting hand. "It was kind of terrible. But I'll get to the books. I promise. Maybe over summer break."

Tracey exhaled. "That's beside the point. We aren't Dorianna. We aren't imaginary people peeking through holes in the sky anymore. You're talking about walking *through* one."

Loretta simply said, "'But she was very brave to see them. Are you? If so, come back on Thursday....'"

"That was in the movie," Candace said.

But Tracey was no longer worried about Candace's *Skylark* knowledge. She and Loretta were locked in some kind of telepathy battle, a staring contest of wills.

Tracey broke first. She deliberately turned to her purse, pulled out her wallet, and put a credit card on the table. She signaled for the bill. Candace began to double time her chili mac. She was still hungry, and things were wrapping up faster than expected.

"Loretta. Like I said, I respect you," Tracey said. "And I think this is all fascinating. But it's not worth your life. Or mine. And especially not Candace's."

"Why especially me?" Candace asked through a mouthful of meat and beans.

"Because you're a child. Okay, a young woman," she corrected. "What if we go in and never come back? What will your parents think? Or worse, what if we *do* come back, forty years later, and everyone you know is my age, and everyone *we* know is dead?"

"Oh," Candace said. That sounded bad. More than bad. Besides... "I have a dance next week, so... Sorry, Loretta."

"Don't apologize, child. I asked if you were ready, but the answer's been made clear. I don't expect you to want this. You still have our own world to explore, and Tracey has some living to do, too. But I have been on this earth for nearly ten decades. While I'm not quite ready to shuffle off this mortal coil, I am ready to be an othernaut."

"Othernaut?" Candace said. Loretta smiled softly.

"You like that? I've been thinking on it. Might write another book when I get back."

"You've been *thinking on it*?" Tracey said. "You mean, you thought this might happen?"

Candace's chili-filled stomach churned. "Have you been lying to us by omission? Were you always planning—"

"Not planning, hoping," Loretta cut her off. "Nothing wrong with that, child. A little hope. Even old people need that from time to time."

Loretta's eyes had shut down somehow, like a shade over a window. She wasn't really looking at Candace anymore. It was like she'd moved on.

Oh no. Had Candace done it? Had she been a False Alarm Clock, like in Tracey's notebook, waking Loretta up from her dreams? Or was she a real alarm clock? Was it time to wake up?

"Loretta, I'm sorry—"

"Don't," Tracey broke in. "Don't let her guilt you. Miss

Loretta Spencer is nobody's fool. This was fun while it lasted. But the line has to be drawn somewhere, for safety's sake. Right, Loretta?"

Loretta avoided their eyes, staring out the window, like she could see something they could not. She rested her chin on one hand. It was trembling.

"Did you remember to take your pill?" Candace asked.

Loretta cut her a sharp look that turned to embarrassment. She fumbled through her purse. Candace called the waiter for more water.

Loretta took her pill in silence.

The waiter brought the bill, slipped away with their credit cards, and returned before anyone spoke again.

"Take me back," Loretta said, breaking the silence. "I don't want to be here anymore."

They picked up their bags from the hotel and hit the road, this time with Loretta sitting silent in the back seat.

44

CANDACE WOKE UP WHEN THEY REACHED THE CITY limits. Loretta had declined Tracey's offer to stay at her place until the trains were running in the morning. Instead, they drove to a hotel on Michigan Avenue. A really nice hotel, Candace decided. The bellman raced to get Loretta's bags. It sounded like he knew her.

"Bye, Loretta," Candace said, and gave the old woman a hug.

Loretta wrapped a stiff, cane-wielding arm around one of Candace's shoulders and said, "All right now. Enough of that. Get some rest, youngblood. Back to school on Monday for you, isn't it?"

"Yeah." Candace stretched, stifling a yawn. "Sorry we couldn't do everything," she said. And she meant it. Loretta looked a little smaller to her tonight, standing in the curved hotel driveway off the busy avenue.

"Well, I suppose I've got enough for a new story at any rate," Loretta said. "Who knows, maybe that one will tackle writing again, too." She smirked and pointed her cane at Tracey, who had come around the side of the car and was leaning against it, arms folded against the surprisingly warm night.

"You never know," Tracey said. "Take care, Loretta. Order up some dinner, and let me know when you get home tomorrow."

"Me too," Candace chimed, holding up her phone.

"Don't worry about me," Loretta said, waving them off. She shuffled toward the big glass doors and the lobby beyond. "I've been at this longer than you two have been alive."

And with that, Loretta and her bags disappeared into the glow of the hotel.

Tracey pulled out into traffic. After a few lights, Candace sat up straighter. "Do you think you'll do it?" she asked.

"Do what?" Tracey sounded far away, probably already thinking about Wisconsin.

"Start writing again. Like, a whole book."

"I don't know. Why?"

"It just seems like something you wanted to do, so you should probably do it. Just to say you did. And you could use my locker to tell yourself that it's possible. I wish older me would send me a note telling me what was possible."

"Kid, you've just had me and Methuselah and the universe telling you what was possible. You need something more than that?" Tracey laughed.

"But that's not about *me*," Candace said. "That's like saying 'hurricanes are real.' Good to know, but what's it got to do with me or my friends, or where I go to college, or what I do with my life?"

The light in front of them turned green and Tracey pulled onto the expressway.

"You've got a point. I've seen a wonder of the universe, and I still don't know if I'm going to Wisconsin."

Ha, Candace thought. She *was* thinking about Wisconsin.

"The most amazing thing that's ever happened to me—to

us," Tracey continued, "and in some ways it almost doesn't even matter."

"But it could," Candace said. "If you wrote a book."

"And said what? Loretta was right, no one would believe it."

"But they can still listen and learn from stories. She was also right about that."

"And what about you? If I write a book, what are you going to get out of all of this?"

"I still have my science project. And I made some art. I suppose I'll keep drawing."

"You really like it, huh?"

"Yeah."

"And you're good at it, from what I've seen."

"Thanks."

"So maybe that's something for your future."

Candace felt a little shock go through her. "How do you mean?"

"Well, Chicago is known for its world-famous Art Institute. And my school has a few fine art degrees."

"You can go to college to be an artist?"

"You can go to college to *learn* about art—art history, art preservation, art techniques. But I think you're born an artist. Or you become one."

"Huh. Am I a born artist?"

"I don't know. But if it looks like a duck . . ." she said, sounding like Loretta.

Candace smiled. "Thanks, Tracey."

"Sure, kid."

Tracey declined the invitation to eat dinner at Candace's,

claiming exhaustion, which was the truth, considering how Candace felt.

"Thanks for driving," she said at the door.

"Let's have lunch soon," Tracey said.

"You bet." Candace waved from the front steps.

Somehow it felt final, like the end of a good movie, the last day of school. The adventure was over. Candace hugged herself as if she could hold on to what was already past.

"Oh, good," Candace's mom said when she saw Tracey wasn't staying. "Now I don't need to cook to impress."

After grilled cheese sandwiches, a description of all the sights they had seen (minus the knot), and a long, hot shower, Candace sat in her favorite fleece sweatpants and hoodie and texted Deen. It was only nine thirty. Not too late for a Saturday night.

CANDACE

I'm home!

But Deen did not reply.

45

PROFESSOR TRACEY AUBURN SAT AT THE DESK IN THE second-bedroom-turned-office of her two-bedroom apartment, staring at her computer screen. An email had arrived from Wisconsin. There it was, the job offer in black and white. Hers for the taking. All she had to do was e-sign it.

On her desk, blocking her view, was a thick pile of paper, made colorful by Post-its and margin notes. It looked like a clown manifesto. It might read like one too, she realized. It was her first novel. Or at least her attempt at it.

Six more months! read the top sticky note. When had she written that? Back when she believed she was six months away from a finished book. Judging from the dust on the note and the loss of stickiness on the back, it had been quite some time ago.

She could take a sabbatical, finish the book, and return to the job she currently had. She could take the new job, move to Wisconsin, and be too busy to write.

Tracey sat staring at her options. Her phone bleeped. More alerts on the bird app. Of all the knots in the universe, the biggest one seemed to be right here, inside of her. Which way to go? And where would she be when she arrived?

With a sigh, Tracey put the manuscript back into its drawer, pulled her laptop closer, and hit reply.

※

Loretta Spencer sat in the cream-on-cream living room in the isolated house that her writing had paid for, with its forty-year knot, its quiet hush. Light refracted through the window, casting soft shadows. Every stone in the gravel driveway stood out, etched against its own darkness. She had bought this house after her second husband had died. They'd had no children. And yet there had been a child here, laughing over her phone. There had been a holiday dinner here, and gifts, and joy. There had been friends.

But Tracey and Candace had dropped her at the hotel on Michigan Avenue like an old sweater at the lost and found and driven away, out of her life and back into their own. Loretta had been here before. She knew what to do: wish them the best, and get back to work.

※

Candace had stayed up late, burned by the long nap in the car, but had been too tired to do much other than moon over her phone and her incomplete album of This Is Us drawings. She kept trying to draw a new one for the year. But Deen looked angry, Becca was too big, and Tracey and Loretta ended up in the background like two cartoon birds on a branch. Then Candace realized she'd forgotten to draw herself. What was wrong with her?

※

On Sunday, she woke up late and won the world championship of moping.

"You've got a happiness hangover," her father declared, pouring her a tall glass of orange juice.

"That's not a thing."

"Sure it is." He shoved a plate of eggs toward her. "You spent last week thinking about spring break, you spent this week doing all the things you planned, and now it's over and you are crashing. Spring break done broke you. It's a natural fact."

He refolded the newspaper he was reading and crossed an ankle over one knee. Her father had declared Sundays all-day mornings. Breakfast was served until dinnertime, when he preferred a slow roast of pork or beef, or a roast chicken. Proper attire was an old robe, slippers, socks, and whatever he'd slept in. He and Candace were good at it. Her mother was not.

Candace's mom came in with two baskets full of vegetables from the farmers market down the street. "Candace, come help me wash these. Carl, preheat the oven. If I roast some of these now, we can eat off them all week." It was a fantasy that never worked. By day three, no one could identify the vegetables she'd roasted, and they got blended into Something Soup—made up of bits of roast something—or, if truly tragic, simply thrown into the compost.

Candace rolled up her sleeves.

"Loretta make it back home?" her mom asked as she scrubbed potatoes.

"I guess. Haven't heard yet. But she wouldn't be there yet if she slept in."

"Miss Loretta Spencer does not strike me as a woman who sleeps in," her father said, stretching sideways to turn on the oven without letting go of his newspaper.

"I'll check in after this," Candace said.

"And no Deen, I see," her mom commented. What was her deal? Did she have a checklist of everyone Candace knew?

"Nope."

"Everything all right there?"

"I guess. Why?"

"No reason," her mother said.

"Why, did she come by or something after I left?"

"No, baby. I'd have told you that. I was just hoping you'd work things out."

"Me too."

After all of the root vegetables had been tossed with olive oil and shoved into the oven, Candace retreated to the living room. She sent a text to Loretta. She almost called her, but she didn't really know what to say. She felt bad about the othernaut thing. It was too risky, though, wasn't it, to step into the unknown?

CANDACE
Hey Mitchell, I'm back.

MITCHELL
Cool.

They texted for a while and Candace felt better after that. Still, there was something sad about being home again. Especially because Loretta had seemed so excited and determined, and Candace and Tracey had brought her back to reality. Like reality was so great anyway. Especially when it looked like a week's worth of laundry.

She hauled her basket down into the basement, where they shared a tiny laundry room with the upstairs unit of her little building. With her first loads in, she called Tracey.

"We weren't wrong, were we?" she asked. "It's too dangerous, going through a knot, right?"

"Exceedingly," Tracey said. "It could be deadly, for all we know. Birds are not people, and those birds might not even be normal birds. It's just not safe."

"Right!" Candace said. But why didn't she feel any better? "Do you think we let Loretta down?"

Tracey was quiet for a long time. Candace wondered if she was packing for Wisconsin or sitting at her desk to write.

"I don't know, kid. On the one hand, even she would say this has been the best time she's had in a long time. Think of how much further she's gotten in her research because of you, eBird, the three of us together. And I guess if she'd told us her plans from the start, we might have said no."

"Definitely," Candace said.

"So the journey was a good one, even if it didn't go where any of us expected. That's the way life is sometimes. Some risks are just not worth taking, so you have to appreciate how far you did get."

"That's kind of crappy," Candace said.

"Life can be crappy. But I don't think this is a bad thing. I mean, I don't know about you, but what I got out of all of this that I cherish the most is the two of you. That still exists. We might not go knot hunting again, but that doesn't mean we can't do a proper Hamageddon or see each other soon."

"Yeah," Candace said. "It just feels like . . . like graduation. Elementary school's going to be over soon, and who knows what comes next?"

"Trust me, I've seen a million graduations by now. Change is always hard, but also rewarding. It's not something to fear."

Candace wasn't sure if she believed that. Or, more precisely, if Tracey believed that. Because if that was true, why not write her book? Was going to Wisconsin running away, or was it accepting change?

"I gotta go, kid. Talk to you soon."

"Okay. Thanks, Tracey." She hung up and tried Loretta, but the phone just rang and rang.

And then it was time to swap her laundry for the dryer.

While she waited for the clothes to dry, she pulled up her This Is Us album on her phone. Drawing after drawing of her and Deen together, hair in different lengths and styles, dresses, jeans, leggings, and tees. The flip-book of her life. And then there were the Christmas pictures she'd drawn of Loretta and Tracey. These were better. They might have been her best.

And now it was over.

Candace didn't bother to fold her laundry. Let it wrinkle. She carried it back upstairs and dumped it on her bed. Her dad was right. She did have a happiness hangover. And she thought she might know the cure.

Monday dawned on a new hair color. Pale blue roots, plum-colored ends. Bruised-cabbage-rose-colored hair.

"Cool," Cerise said.

"Nice," said Mitchell. Although neither of them knew what it was a reference to, and never would.

Deen and Becca pretended not to notice, so Sergio and Nate followed their lead. Or maybe they really didn't notice, because Becca and Deen had both showed up with blond hair, which was weird to see.

Candace's happiness hangover turned into a grousing week. Nothing felt right. She tried to draw but kept breaking her pencil tips. She ate lunch with Mitchell and Cerise, which was actually kind of nice, but they laughed when she dipped her fries in ranch dressing. Deen never laughed. She dipped hers, too.

Her mother chalked her attitude up to growing pains. Her father just called it "groaning up."

Candace missed her friends.

And she still hadn't heard from Loretta.

That just made her feel guilty all over again.

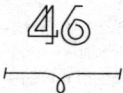

46

FRIDAY ARRIVED, ALONG WITH SPRING FLING AND A rainstorm. Everyone was too grumpy for face-to-face discussion, so they sorted out the limo situation by text. It was apparently too expensive to have the guy drive around and pick everybody up. Instead they would all meet at Becca's house and go to the dance from there.

Great. Fine, Candace texted. She just wanted to go home.

It was weird to see Mitchell in a good mood at lunchtime. Like he existed completely outside of space and time. He was an interdimensional magpie. No, a bluebird of happiness.

"How about I meet you at your house and we go to Becca's together?"

"Perfect," Candace said, and she smiled at him, feeling a little less alone.

Candace posed in front of the limo for a selfie at six thirty on the dot. The rain had let up just in time for the sun to slip behind the buildings. Still, she grinned up at the camera, checking to make sure the black bike shorts she had on weren't showing beneath the pink dress her mother helped her order online. They were not. Mitchell actually was sporting a powder-blue tuxedo jacket, complete with ruffled shirt and bow tie, over black jeans. Together, they looked like the poster children for gender color norms.

She and Mitchell took a few pics, making peace signs, sticking out their tongues. She'd send some to Tracey and Loretta later on. She wanted them to know coming home had been the right choice. She was a regular teen having a good time.

Becca emerged from her house in a slinky red number. Deen wore a black maxi that looked like an evening gown. Which was overkill, but definitely chic. The girls posed together. Becca's dad took a group shot with Mitchell, Sergio, and Nate flanking them. Candace was squeezed in the middle. Her smile was a little squeezed, too. And so the night began.

The limo driver took the long way to the school, down Lake Shore Drive to Michigan Avenue, where he opened the sunroof and let Sergio live out his dream of sticking his head out and howling like a wolf. Then they doubled back up to the school. Where it became very apparent that renting a limo had been overkill. And that even buying dresses had been overkill. A group of skaters hanging out by the front steps all turned to gawk at them. Becca strutted on by. Nate jogged to catch up to her. When the skaters also came inside, Candace realized they didn't have skateboards. And, for like half of the people here, baggy pants and T-shirts were the dress code.

Across the gym, the other half of the people—some in bow ties and lots in strapless dresses with too-high-to-walk-in heels—huddled together for warmth. All together, the student body looked like rival street gangs. Slobs versus snobs. That should have been the theme of the dance instead of Spring Fling.

"This blows," Becca said, slumping onto the bleachers.

Music played. A disco ball spangled light around the gym. But it still smelled like socks and disinfectant. And the only people dancing were two of the chaperones. Sergio and Deen sat on the bench next to Becca, each staring off into the distance.

The funny thing about dances, Candace noticed, was that mostly people just stood around not dancing. They could just call them "stands," and it would be more accurate. Then Nate got up in front of the group and spun on his toes. He started to dance, something from a video game. And Becca actually laughed. And joined him. It was like an alternate reality where Nate was the cool trendsetter. The King Bee.

Mitchell grabbed her hand. "Let's do this," he said.

And they danced. And danced. And it was actually kind of fun. Like a sweaty, ridiculous good time. Deen melted away, and so did Becca and the others. It was just Candace and Mitchell, and he was cute and a good dancer. And really cute.

So it took a while for her to notice her cell phone was buzzing. Like, a lot.

WHEN THEY FINALLY STOPPED FOR DRINKS, CANDACE realized her phone wasn't getting texts. They were actual phone calls, from a number she didn't know.

She stepped into the hallway, where the thump of music was a little lower.

"Hello?"

"Candace?" a sweet, grandmotherly voice said.

"Yes?"

"Oh, good. This is Lotte, Miss Loretta's caregiver."

A jolt of fear shocked her. She moved farther down the hallway.

"Lotte! Is Loretta okay? Did she die?"

"Oh, no, dear! But that answers my question. I am home now from Denmark and was wondering, is Loretta with you?"

"No. I haven't seen her since we got back from the forest, like, a week ago. Tracey and I dropped her off at a hotel."

"The one on Michigan Avenue?"

"I think so, yeah." Candace was on pins and needles.

"I called. They say she checked out on Sunday."

"But she didn't go home? She was supposed to take the train in the morning."

"Well, she might have, dear. I can't yet tell if anything is missing. But she isn't here now. You haven't heard from her?"

"No. I mean, I sent a couple of texts, but she didn't respond."

"Oh. All right, then. Miss Tracey said as much. It's possible . . . Well, one doesn't like to call the police without making sure first."

"The police?" Candace yelped. "Maybe she's still in the city, at a different hotel. We almost switched hotels down south because of 'red linen' or something—"

But Lotte simply made calming noises, said she would be in touch, and hung up.

Candace ran through her texts. Nothing from Tracey or Loretta.

She texted Tracey. No response.

She tried Loretta again. Nothing.

She texted her mom.

Her phone rang.

"Mom! Loretta's missing!" She repeated everything Lotte had said, her heart racing. Mitchell appeared in the hallway. Candace waved him away.

"Candace, calm down," her mother said. "You said Lotte called the police. They'll put a Silver Alert out for Loretta. And they'll be looking for her, too."

"But that's not enough! I have to help. I'm going to go to the hotel where she stayed. Maybe somebody knows something." Candace felt like she was going to fly into a million pieces.

"But you said Lotte already called the—"

"Yeah, but what if she talked to some racist idiot who didn't give a crap about an old lady?" Candace shrilled.

Mitchell was suddenly in front of her. "What's going on?" he asked, just as she heard her father come onto the call.

"Whoa," her dad said. "Calm down. Loretta is a smart, capable old lady. Even if she's a little . . . lost right now, I don't imagine her taking any guff."

Lost. The way he'd said it made it sound like Loretta had dementia—which she most certainly did not. Did she? Candace had to admit she'd wondered it herself when Loretta had said she wanted to go through the Shawnee knot. But Loretta was the most rational person Candace knew.

"Listen," her dad said. "You said the place was on Michigan? We're passing there on the way home. We'll check it out."

"You will?"

"We were just finishing dessert. I'll call when I know something."

"Okay," Candace said. "What can I do? Call the hospitals around there? And . . ." She didn't want to say it. "The morgue? Where's the morgue?"

She could hear her mother's sigh as she took back the phone. "Honey, you don't need to put yourself through that. Lotte has informed the police. They'll do the legwork."

"But what if they miss something? Something only I'd know?"

"Fair enough," her mother conceded.

"Let's go talk to them! I can take a cab!"

She looked around, but now Mitchell was gone. Fine, she would do this on her own.

"Candace! I know you love Loretta. We do too. But it's most likely she's just gone away for a few days and forgotten to tell Lotte. Busting into a police station in a panic isn't going to help her, or you, for that matter. Now, take a pause. Maybe Mitchell or someone can get you some water. Your dad and I can pick you up in an hour."

"An hour? I can't wait an hour!"

Mitchell reappeared and took Candace's phone gently from her hand. "Mrs. Wells, we'll get Candace home. Okay. Yes. Bye."

He hung up and handed her a can of soda. "Your mom says they'll meet us at your house."

"Okay," Candace said gratefully. She wiped her cheeks, aware now that she was crying.

"What happened?" Nate asked. Mitchell had summoned the troops.

"Loretta's gone missing and she's, like, a hundred years old and no one knows where she is."

"Old people go missing all the time," Becca said. "It's not a big deal. The cops will find her."

"What if they don't?" Candace said. "She wasn't . . . she wasn't very happy the last time I saw her."

"Hey, don't think like that," Mitchell said, and handed her back her phone. "I'll get us a car."

Deen, who had been silent this whole time, suddenly said, "Take the limo. We'll come with you."

"Really?" Candace asked.

"Yes, really," Deen said.

Becca bit her lip, then nodded. "This dance was kind of whatever anyway."

⁓H⌒

"What are you looking for?" Mitchell asked. He was squeezed in next to Candace, even though the limo was huge. It was kind of nice to feel his warmth against her side.

"eBird. We use it for bird spotting. People post when they see something unusual in their area."

"You think she's gone bird-watching?" Deen asked.

"In the middle of the night?" Becca added.

"I don't know. It's possible. But it doesn't make much sense. We get these app alerts. I cut them off, but there were a bunch of them this week. Maybe she went to check them out?" Candace scrolled through her phone, dashing through the alerts and accompanying photos. A few ribbons, none of them purple. Even a stray magpie—but not a Jordan. And some of them didn't show birds at all.

#SandCaveSurrealism, one of them read. The photo stopped her breath. It had posted on Thursday.

"Oh no," she breathed.

"We're here," Mitchell said.

They piled out of the limo. Candace dashed up the front steps to her apartment while someone thanked the driver and let him go on his way.

She jammed the doorbell. Her parents were home. She could hear them rushing to the door. But it wasn't just her mom. Tracey was with her, holding up her phone.

"I know where she went," Tracey said.

Candace held up own screen. The photos matched: the Sand Cave in Shawnee National Forest, early morning. A ladder stood before the entrance of the cave, ten feet tall. **Like a ladder to nowhere**, a second post read.

#SandCaveSurrealism.

"I DON'T UNDERSTAND," CANDACE'S MOTHER SAID, looking at photo after photo of the ladder to nowhere. It had apparently stayed there for a full day before the rangers took it down. There were daytime shots and spooky evening shots lit with a reddish glow from the flashlights of night hikers. It gave Candace the chills. "What does a ladder in the forest have to do with Loretta?" her mom asked.

"Weird," Nate said, passing Candace's phone around.

Candace and Tracey exchanged a look.

"'On Thursdays, the sky windows opened . . .'" Tracey quoted softly. Loretta had gone missing on a Thursday. She'd placed a ladder in the woods. How much could they tell everyone? Not the truth—no one would believe them, and that would just slow things down.

"Hey, isn't that from the Skylark books?" Mitchell said.

"Oh yeah." Tracey gave him a stiff smile. "Loretta loves those books . . ."

"Totally," Candace said, recalling the audience watching them. Expectant faces and a few heads over cell phones greeted her.

"You think the ladder thing is like in the book?" Mitchell asked.

"Oh, you've actually read them?" Tracey cut Candace a look. Candace cut one back—she'd seen the movie! Then she noticed Tracey's outfit. The professor was in sweats, with a trench coat thrown on top. Her hair was windblown. And there was a suitcase in the corner by the door.

"What are we talking about?" Candace's mother asked.

"Were you going somewhere?" Candace asked Tracey.

"Coming back. From the airport. Yes, there's stuff to talk about. Later." She turned to Candace's exasperated mom. "Cheryl, any chance for a glass of water? Or some coffee?"

"Airport?" Candace said. Tracey grimaced.

Candace's mother narrowed her eyes for a moment, and then her hospitality mode took over. She offered drinks to all of the kids crammed on the sofa, and moved off into the kitchen with Candace's dad. But that didn't get rid of the five other sets of eyes.

"You don't think she actually went through, do you?" Candace whispered.

"No. I don't think that's possible. But she might have tried," Tracey whispered back.

"Why are you whispering?" Sergio asked.

"I'm pretty sure that ladder is just fan art," Mitchell offered. "It'd be wild if Miss Loretta thought the Skylark books were real . . . Did I say something wrong?"

"Sorry, guys," Tracey stepped in. "It's just, Loretta was in a . . . weird place the last time we saw her. We need to get ahold of her caregiver. She might have gone back to the last place we went bird-watching. It's not exactly safe for a lady her age, all alone."

She faltered on the last word as if finally letting it sink in.

"It's our fault," Candace said.

Tracey shook her head and dialed Lotte.

Lotte answered on the first ring. Tracey put her on speakerphone.

"Lotte, we have an idea. Can you please, please go into Loretta's office and take a picture of her birding map?"

"Her birding map? You think she is off to see the birds again, without you?"

"We think she might have gone to the Sand Cave in Shawnee," Tracey said.

Lotte swore something in Danish. "Hold on. I will call you with the video phone."

She hung up. The room fell silent. Everyone was holding their breath. And then the phone beeped. Tracey tapped the screen. There was Loretta's pristine office, all soft creams and teak.

"Okay. It's a mess in here. Do either of you know what to make of this?" Lotte asked, and turned the camera around to show them Loretta's office floor.

It was a shambles. Or, more precisely, it looked like Christmas night at a sporting goods store. Piles of colorful rope lay next to multiple backpacks, hats, coats, hiking boots—all in different shades of purple. Except for one.

"What the hell?" Tracey said.

"She's matching purples!" Candace exclaimed. "Oh! It's something she said about colors. When we realized the birds were drawn to purple . . . I just read that birds see ultraviolet wavelengths, colors we can't see! And the notebook, the ribbons, are maybe more visible? Like, shinier than other things."

"And magpies like shiny things," Tracey murmured.

"Yes! So she was looking for the right shade to attract the birds. But why would she want to attract a bunch of birds?"

"You really think she's gone bird-watching?" Lotte said, turning the phone back around. Candace had almost forgotten she was there.

"Um . . . sort of?" Candace said at the same time Tracey replied, "Yep. That's what it looks like."

"Then I will send you a picture of the map." The phone wobbled. "Hold on. I am getting a call on the other line—" Lotte hung up mid-sentence.

"Tracey, you look dead on your feet," Candace's mother said, coming back in with the drinks. "Sit down. Carl, take everyone home, please. This is going to be a while. Thank you guys for getting Candace back here. I'm sorry about the dance."

"This is way more interesting," Sergio said, earning a look from Deen. But everyone got off the couch and was headed for the door when Lotte called again.

"I am just off the phone with the police in Carbondale. It seems you are right. Loretta's credit card was used to stay at your hotel down there. I'm driving down now."

"Tell them to search around the Sand Cave in the Shawnee National Forest. Candace is sending you a picture now."

Candace forwarded the #SandCaveSurrealism photo to Lotte's number.

"This is terrible news," Lotte said. "I will share this with the police. She must be lost. She will break a hip or worse!"

Candace clenched her fists and prayed for it to not be worse.

"Let us know how it goes, Lotte," Tracey said. "We'll keep looking up here. We'll find her somehow."

"Yes," Lotte said determinedly, "one way or another. She's lucky to have such friends. I must go now. Bye-bye." Lotte hung up. A moment later, Tracey's phone dinged with a photo of the knot map.

"Okay, kids, that's all we can do for now. Time to head home," her father announced. Nate and Sergio followed him out the door. But Deen and Becca lingered.

"Do you need us to stay?" Deen asked.

"No. Thanks, though," Candace said.

"Let us know what happens, okay?" Deen gave Candace a hug. She'd missed Deen's hugs. Then, after seeing the look on Becca's face, Candace hugged her, too.

She walked them both to the door. Mitchell was waiting on the landing. Deen and Becca exchanged glances with Candace, who was too wrung out to notice them noticing him noticing her.

"See you later, Mitchell. Sorry about this."

"I'm sorry about your friend," he said. Then he gave her a lopsided little smile. "But I had fun tonight. Sounds kind of weird. But, you know, thanks for coming to the dance."

Candace couldn't think of what to say. Instead, she reached up and kissed him on the cheek, blushing furiously, then waved him down the stairs.

HER MOTHER AND TRACEY WERE WATCHING. OF COURSE.

Tracey smiled. It turned into a yawn.

Her mom cleared her throat. "All right," she said. "That's it for tonight. Tracey, you're welcome to stay over."

"I don't want to impose."

"I think we're imposing on you. It's just a sofa bed, but it's not too bad."

Tracey accepted gratefully. "Half my apartment is in boxes. A sofa sounds great right about now."

"I'll get you some towels and sheets. Miss Kissyface here can make up the bed for you."

Candace started to protest, but then Tracey yawned again, and it was contagious.

"Tomorrow will look better, I promise," her mother said. She came back a few moments later with the linens. "I'll leave you to it." And with that, she headed off to bed.

Candace pulled the cushions off the sofa. As soon as she heard her parents' bedroom door shut, she said, "We need to go after Loretta. We need to go to Shawnee."

Tracey was carefully folding her coat over one arm of the sofa. "The police and Lotte are on it, kid. This isn't a swoop-in-and-save situation."

"But they aren't on it, are they? They're looking in the woods! We know she's not there."

"We know nothing of the sort," Tracey said. "It's a ladder by a cave. Loretta's a smart lady. She wouldn't go it alone. Never mind she's ancient. She *couldn't* do it on her own, I don't think."

"Well, I do. I think that cane was a put-on. I think she wanted us to think she couldn't do it so that we'd help her. And we didn't. But she needed us to. Needs us to."

Candace moved the coffee table out of the way, and Tracey unfolded the sofa. They started making the bed in silence.

"Are you willing to die for this?" Tracey suddenly asked. She was kind of quivering when she said it, like a squirrel about to bolt.

"No! We're not talking about dying," Candace said. "We're talking about saving Loretta!"

"Kid, you can't save someone from themselves. She made a choice. And it's Loretta, so we know it was a calculated one. She's ninety-three! Even the oldest of us makes it to maybe a hundred ten? But you, you've got your whole entire life ahead of you. Don't rob the world of Candace Wells for ten more years of Loretta Spencer *maybe*."

"Rob the world?" You had to be valuable to be stolen. Was Candace that valuable? She'd never thought of it that way before. But Tracey obviously had.

"Look at it another way," Tracey was saying. "What if you do go into the knot, you find her, you haul yourselves back out somewhere—God knows where. For all we know, you'd be gone for forty years. Forty years! Your parents—who will have spent those forty years looking for you, mourning you—will be in their eighties. All of your friends—Deen, Becca, Mitchell—will be middle-aged empty nesters who only remember you as the girl who went missing. Assuming you don't age, you'd be too young to live on your own, but have no home to go back to!"

"I could live with you," Candace said. She made a face. "In Wisconsin."

"Candace, I'll probably be dead. Not everyone lives as long as Miss Loretta."

Candace's face crumpled into tears. It was awful, too awful, to imagine a future like a postapocalyptic wasteland. Her parents, her friends, her whole life erased because she wasn't in it. Even if the world beyond the knot was a full world, and not some sort of trap that would hold her and kill her, would she trade her life for it? For Loretta?

"Aw, kid, I told you, it's a losing proposition. I'm so very sorry. It's just not worth the risk."

The risk. Candace sat up, wiping her eyes. Risks were very Loretta. And very *not* Tracey.

"You're so afraid to try anything," Candace said. "Anything new and uncertain, I mean. What do you miss out on because of that?"

A storm cloud passed over Tracey's face. "This isn't about me."

"Of course not. You've already packed up your apartment. You're not leaving. You've already left!"

"Candace, I've explained this to you. I don't have a choice."

"No, you *had* a choice, and you've already made it."

She punched one of the flat pillows her mother had left out for them. She punched it again, making it fluffier. And fluffier.

Tracey said, "You know, you kept on and on about me being

a writer. So, Saturday night, I did something I haven't done in years. I pulled out my old manuscript. The novel I started when I was a kid. I rewrote most of it in college and kept going for a few years. Hundreds of pages covered in notes, with labels and flags sticking out the sides. I've been hauling it around with me for the past forty years. Like Jacob Marley's ghost."

"And?"

"And I read it. It's different from what I remember."

"Like how?"

"Well, for one thing, I thought it was longer. And finished. I could have sworn it was a finished draft. But it's only a hundred or so pages. For another, it was terrible. Really terrible. I mean, it got better in places. But . . ." She shook her head. "I don't know why I ever thought I could be a writer."

Candace grasped for something to say. "Well, I never thought I was an artist. But then you framed that bird attack picture like it was art. And Loretta never became a physicist, but she knows things those people can't even imagine. Doesn't that make her a scientist? So maybe you weren't a writer yet. Maybe you're still on your way to becoming one. But it'll never happen if you don't try. And we have to, don't we? Try?"

Tracey said nothing. But her jaw tightened and worked up and down a bit. Then she wiped her watery eyes. "I swear, I don't know if kids are getting smarter these days or just louder about it," she mumbled.

"Probably both," Candace replied.

"We're still not going through the knot," Tracey said.

"Fine. Then what about plan B?"

"What plan B?"

"Just think! Loretta said the knots had entrances and exits, like stations on the L. If I miss your train, I can try to catch it at the next station. So where does the Sand Cave knot come out? We need to be there. Now! And in forty years, too, just in case. I can do that. I'll put it in my calendar every year for the next forty years. Save Loretta Day."

Tracey shook her head, but Candace could see she was starting to think about it. "Loretta figured out the way the locker knot connected to the one in her house by sheer luck. We can't replicate that."

"Sure we can. By following the birds. We just need to look at a map. *The* map. It's like a math problem where you only know one side of the equation. If we can look at the map and figure out that connection, we can do it for the other knots. Come on. I know where to start."

CANDACE SENT LOTTE'S PHOTO OF THE BIRDING MAP TO her mother's big plotting printer. The sheet that came out was the size of a real map. She retrieved a white grease pencil from her art supplies and a magnifying glass from her mom's desk. She spread the map out on the kitchen table, stood back, and let her eyes go soft.

"What are you doing?" Tracey asked.

"Looking for a pattern," Candace explained. "Oh. Oh!"

She could see it suddenly, as if the puzzle had shifted and come together. The dots were kind of like constellations. What if you could connect them?

She pulled out her ruler and drew a line with the grease pencil from Walden Elementary up to McHenry, connecting the two dots. But there were other dots, and not in a straight line at all. She scanned the page. It looked more like a curve that curled in on itself tighter and tighter. Like an ear swirl. Or . . .

Candace stepped back and held the map up again. A tingle ran through her entire body.

"Oh!" she said. "It's the golden ratio."

Tracey yawned. "The what?"

"The golden ratio. It's a thing, a rule in art that intersects with science. It's called a . . . ." What was the word? "It's a Fibonacci sequence! See how it looks like a nautilus shell? It's, like, made of little boxes, but they form a spiral because this Italian guy noticed these ratios repeating in nature—" Candace gasped. "I was just following the lines, but holy crap! The knots are in a Fibonacci spiral." She clutched her head. It was going to explode.

"Look! The start of the spiral," she said, pressing a finger to the dot on the map that said BATAVIA, ILLINOIS. She sketched the shape of a spiral, with its intersecting tangents, along the map.

"My locker is here, and Loretta's house is here . . ."

The front door opened. Candace's father was home.

"What are you two still doing up?"

"Hey, Dad. We think Loretta might be following . . . bird migrations," Candace said.

He came over and peered at the map. "These swirls are flight paths? Fine, but how does this help us find Loretta?"

"The furthest south we've been is Shawnee. What if she's following the . . . spring migrations . . . back north?" Candace stumbled over the fib.

"And?" her dad said.

"Well, look where this spiral goes."

Tracey came over with the magnifying glass Candace had dug up.

"So, this is our Illinois spiral, but birds don't just stop at the state line, do they?" Candace traced a second spiral on the map, centered in the same spot, but flipped so that it spiraled sideways. She could see the pattern so clearly, but it was hard to explain.

"Looks like a hurricane," her dad said. "You know the symbol they use, like two commas connected in the center? Makes sense. Birds following wind patterns."

"Yes!" Candace said. "So what if it's not just one sequence? What if it shares a center with *another* spiral that swings out over Indiana, Ohio, and up into . . ."

"Michigan," Tracey said. "Detroit?"

"No, look closer. That little spit of land isn't in the United States. It's in Canada," Candace said, but the word turned into a yawn.

"Sounds like a lot of what-ifs and maybes, honey," Candace's father said.

"He's right, kid," Tracey said.

Candace clenched her fists in frustration. The pattern was so clear! To her, at any rate. She couldn't explain how or why, but she knew she was right. Probably . . . Which wasn't going to convince anyone.

"Now, *I* may not know much," her dad said, "but I promise you ninety-three-year-old Loretta Spencer did not just hop, skip, and jump her way to Canada. And you need to hop, skip, and jump to bed. We all do. Lotte will call when she has news."

"Good night, Dad." Candace kissed his scruffy cheek.

"Good night, Carl," Tracey said. Once the master bedroom door swung shut, she added, "He's got the right idea. I can barely keep my eyes open." She riffled through her suitcase and pulled out a toiletry kit. "Candace, we can unravel the universe in the morning."

"Okay." She'd try to keep her worry down.

"Loretta packed for an expedition," Tracey reminded her. "She'll be okay for one more night." She patted Candace on the shoulder and shuffled toward the bathroom.

Candace's protest turned into another yawn. "But . . ." was all she managed to say.

And Tracey turned around. "Canada. Wasn't there something about Canada when we were in Shawnee?"

"The Sand Cave." Candace yawned. "It was a stop . . . on the Underground . . . Railroad and . . ."

"And it took people to Canada," Tracey finished.

"Uh-huh." Candace yawned again.

"You mean to tell me the knot, or spiral, or whatever, is part of the Underground Railroad? Come on, Candace. How is that even possible? Who would know about it? And what, all these Black people just popped out of the sky over Canada one day? In the middle of nowhere?"

Candace yawned mightily and shook herself awake. She fumbled for her phone and pulled up the article. "Right here. It says the code for Canada was Canaan. Like in the Bible."

"Canaan was the promised land," Tracey said. "The land of milk and honey."

"Tracey," Candace said. She placed the ruler on the X marking the Shawnee National Forest.

"Candace, this is a lot. I don't know what it means. I just . . . How does it help us find Loretta?"

She tilted the ruler so that it ran through Batavia and the particle accelerator, then pivoted it across her second, backward spiral, to the point on the map where it ended. In Canada. Candace tapped a query into her phone.

"Check it out."

"Essex?" Tracey said. "What about it?"

"Not just Essex," Candace said. "This spot in Essex. It used to be called New Canaan."

Loretta had gone skylarking, headed for the promised land.

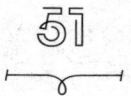

51

CANDACE'S PARENTS WOULD NOT LET HER GO TO Canada. She and Tracey had explained everything at breakfast, but it was like talking to a wall. A great big frowning wall that kept checking your forehead for a fever.

"But I have a passport!"

"And school! And there are police to handle these things," her mother said.

"Lotte's got it covered," her dad added. "Even if she is in Canada, which I seriously doubt."

"You never believe me," Candace said. And Tracey said nothing to back her up.

"Correction: You've never spoken nonsense before, not like this," her mother said. "If Loretta's on a bird-watching tour, she's fine. If she somehow got lost, the tour group would call the police. If she's on her own—well, I don't know how a ninety-three-year-old woman would do any of this all alone, so I'm sure someone is helping her."

"And if she's . . . you know," her dad said, waving his hand around his temple, "wandering in her mind somewhere, again, the police and Lotte have it handled."

As if to confirm it, everyone's phone blared an alarm. A

Silver Alert had been posted for a woman fitting Loretta's description.

"See?" her dad said. "It's as handled as it can be, baby."

"No, it's not," Candace said, and stormed off to her room. She threw herself facedown onto her bed and screamed into the mattress.

Tracey entered without knocking.

"They won't listen. You have to go get her," Candace said.

"Candace, your parents are right. I'm not driving to Canada on a hunch. Let the police handle it. Look, we can call Lotte and tell her about New Canaan. Maybe they'll send the Mounties out to look for her. Assuming she even makes it through the knot. Have you thought of that? What if it's a vacuum?"

"Birds can't fly in a vacuum."

"Or, I don't know, she falls out of the sky. Children's books are not the same as reality."

Candace sat up. "I know that. I'm not a little kid. Those are your favorite books, not mine. If you won't get her, then I will."

"And how are you going to do that?" Tracey asked.

"Like I'd tell you," Candace said.

Tracey laughed. "You don't know, do you? Look, I'll call Lotte. I'll even send her a picture of the map. Loretta will be fine."

"You keep saying that. But you don't actually believe it," Candace realized out loud.

"Of course I believe it," Tracey said.

"Liar." Candace turned her back on Tracey. A moment later, the door closed and she was alone.

Candace flopped back onto her bed. On the floor, sticking out from under the bed skirt, was her last pathetic attempt at a This Is Us drawing. Tracey and Loretta in a tree. Big Becca and Angry Deenie in the foreground.

Only, Deen hadn't been angry last night. She'd been . . . well, Deenie. Her kind best friend. The one who'd helped Candace even though Candace had hurt her feelings. The one who'd bent over backward because Becca needed her support. Even Becca had been kind of Deenie-ish last night. They all had, racing back to the limo because Candace needed help.

Candace picked up the drawing and smoothed it out on the bedspread. She grabbed a pencil and drew herself, arms reaching out to everyone. But she wasn't the one missing from the picture. Loretta was. She dragged an eraser over the Loretta bird until only the outline was left.

Loretta needed a Deenie-level friend right now.

It was time for plan C: Plan Candace.

But she couldn't do it alone.

52

                  <u>CANDACE</u>
              I need a favor. A
                  huge favor.

<u>DEEN</u>
. . .

              Life or death or I
                  wouldn't ask.

What?

        Will you call the house and
          invite me for a sleepover?

Becca's going to be
here. And my folks are
gone. Mac's in charge. 🤢

                Don't worry. I'm
                not staying.

. . .
Fine.

The invitation worked. Candace's parents were all too happy to see her go off and be normal with her friends.

"When you say camping . . ." her father said, as if it didn't make sense to him.

"Oh! You're really making up!" her mother exclaimed. She told Candace's dad about the camping slight at the beginning of the school year. "It's a do-over."

Her father sighed. "I wish I could have a do-over. Okay, be safe. A distraction is a good idea right now," he said. "Worry will eat you up if you let it."

Candace packed carefully, raiding the garage and her dad's old camping equipment under the guise of sleeping out under the stars. On the way to Deen's, she told her dad she needed to pick up some "lady products" at the mega mart where they sold all kinds of rope, as well as lady stuff.

But when she was dropped off at Deen's, both Deen and Becca were waiting for an explanation.

"I can show you," Candace said. "But I need to get to Shawnee."

"Shawnee? Like six-hour-drive Shawnee?"

"Don't worry, I'm taking the train."

"No, you aren't," Deen said. "Your dad thinks you're staying here, so if something happens to you, he's coming after me."

"My parents won't 'come after' you!" Candace said.

"Of course they will," Becca chimed in. "Your mom is hella scary when she wants to be."

It was true. Even if it came from a place of love.

"Fine. I'll get three train tickets."

"I'm not going!" Becca said.

Deen scowled. "We're *all* going. You can't stay here alone."

"Mac's here," Becca protested.

"Not for long. I've got an idea," Deen said. She ran down to Mac's room in the basement, where he was playing video games. "Mackie, are you busy?"

"Yes."

"Too busy to go camping again?"

Those were the magic words. Candace's brother paused his game.

"What? Awesome," Mac said. "I know a place in Wisconsin where—"

"Shawnee," Candace cut in from the stairwell.

Mac grinned. "Garden of the Gods! I'll book a campsite."

Deen gave Candace a conspiratorial grin. "Oh! And we're going to need—"

"A ladder. And some flashlights," Candace finished.

Mac leapt to his feet. "A ladder? I've got a folding one. I guess you don't rock climb like I do." He scratched the back of his head and stretched. "Okay. Let's do it! But you gotta pay for gas."

Six hours is a long time to sit in a carful of people with complicated feelings. The three girls sat in the back, with Deen in the middle. The front passenger seat was full of gear that didn't fit in the trunk. Mac drove with the radio on low, singing to himself.

The first hour, the back seat was silent, with everyone on their phones. Candace skimmed through eBird postings, trying not to overthink her decision.

She was going through the knot.

It was scary. And a tiny bit thrilling.

And then there were the details. Loretta disappeared on a Thursday, like in the book. It was Saturday today. If Candace went through today, would the knot be the same? There was so much they didn't know. But one way or another, she would find out.

The second hour was filled with sightseeing. While their phones took turns charging, they gawked at billboards and cornfields. The third hour, they talked about the dance. Then they stopped for food and gas, and when their stomachs were full and they were crammed into the back seat again, Candace decided to ask:

"So, Becca, how are your parents?"

"Oh my God, you told her?" Becca snapped at Deen.

"Thanks a lot, Candace," Deen snapped in turn. "We're literally going out of our way to help you, and you narc on me?"

"It's not like that," Candace said. "Becca, Deen didn't want to tell me, but we got into a fight and it came out and I felt like a jerk and I still do. But also, you guys have been really mean to me lately, and I don't like it, and I just want to figure it out or whatever."

"Great, you go and figure it out," Becca huffed, and folded her arms across her chest.

Deen turned her hands up in exasperation. Candace exhaled.

"Well, it sounds like a hard time," Candace said. "And I'm sorry to hear it. That's all."

The car hummed down the road. A billboard for a fruit stand rolled past.

"Yeah. Well. Thanks," Becca said. "Sorry about your old lady friend."

"Thanks."

And that was that.

Candace must have nodded off, because the next thing she knew, they were driving away from Carbondale and down the road toward the Shawnee Forest and the pathway to the promised land.

⁓H⁓

Candace pulled on Mac's headlamp and tightened her backpack. Mac had driven them to a campground to the east of the Sand Cave. They'd unloaded their gear, occupied a rental cabin—since Becca insisted on indoor plumbing—then begged Mac for an evening hike. Now the ladder was set up, just like in the photos. The day was getting gloomy. Mac was exploring the Sand Cave. They could hear the echo of his shouts and giggles as he played with the acoustics inside.

"We call them knots," Candace explained. "But it's better if I show you because they're kind of hard to see. Otherwise, you won't believe me, but I need you to trust me. I'm going into this thing, and I might not come back. I need you to call Tracey Auburn. Tell her, and my parents, that I went to find Loretta. And if I don't return, then I need you to go to Canada in forty years and find me at this place, okay?" She handed them the knot map, with New Canaan circled in red.

"This is—" Deen shook her head. "Why are you doing this?"

Candace shook her purple-haired head. "Because she's my friend."

Deen made a little noise, but didn't say anything else.

"And, not to feed into your delusion, but if you disappear

and turn up, like, forty years later, how will we know it's you?" Becca asked.

"You'll just know. I might still look this, or . . ." Candace swallowed hard. "Or, I don't know. Maybe I'll be fifty-four and totally different. Time changes people, right?"

It had changed them, after all. Best friends. Virtual strangers. And now this.

Deen shook her head.

"I'll recognize you," she said. "No matter what."

Candace choked a little, unable to speak. Instead, she threw her arms around her oldest, dearest friend.

"Thank you." She stepped away to pull out her phone. "I'm texting you Tracey's number. Mac's going to want to know where I went. She can cover for us. And, if things go . . . weird—"

"Ha!" Becca scoffed, and crossed her arms.

"Weird*er*," Candace said, "she can talk to my parents, I guess. You'll be fine." She looked up at the ladder. "This is fine."

Deen squeezed her hand. "Just don't die, or I'll kill you."

"And I'll haunt you," Candace said.

And then Candace was climbing the ladder with the rope on her shoulder and a copy of the map in her jacket pocket. Her backpack was full of food and water and more copies of the map. She turned on the headlamp at the top of the ladder.

"Aren't you just going to, like, fall?" Becca asked. "Should we spread a blanket or something to catch you?"

"Nope. Watch this," Candace said, and hoped she didn't just fall. She'd never live that down.

And then she could see it in front of her, like a window in

the sky, a blooming bruise-colored cabbage rose unfolding and unfolding in front of her. A pot boiling over with a tiny universe inside. She climbed to the top of the ladder, to the platform that said DO NOT STAND ON THIS STEP. And she stepped through.

53

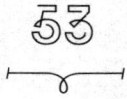

BLOOP!

"What the—" Becca was too stunned to finish swearing. Deen gasped and clapped her hand over her own mouth.

"She's gone," she said in a choked voice.

Inside the Sand Cave, Mac was still yodeling, but his voice was getting closer.

"Quick." Deen moved into action, collapsing the ladder. "Becca! Help me!"

Together, they had the ladder deconstructed and folded up by the time her brother emerged from the cave.

"Should be a killer view from the clifftop. Wanna come before it gets too dark? Then we should head back—" He looked around. "Where's Candace?"

Becca wiped sweaty hands on her pants. Deen used her teary eyes to her advantage.

"Gone! I mean . . . can you believe it? We . . . we had another fight, and she went off with those weird old friends of hers."

Mac's eyes went round. He scanned the woods. "You let her leave? With weirdos?"

Becca sighed hugely. "It's fine. It's that old professor lady she hangs out with. We ran into her, and it got . . . dramatic. Can we just, like, forget about it? She's with adults. It's not like we abandoned her in the woods or anything."

"Jesus, guys. You are so freaking melodramatic," Mac said. "I'm responsible for you." He pulled out his phone. "What's Candace's number?"

Deen's and Becca's eyes widened. "Wait. Here." Deen pulled out her own phone and dialed Tracey's number. Her heart pounded as it rang, once, twice—

"Tracey Auburn," a woman's voice said on the other end.

"Hi . . . Ms. Auburn? This is Nadine De La Cruz, Candace's friend? We're camping in Shawnee, and my brother, Mac, just wants to make sure Candace is okay. She followed Loretta out of here. You know? So she's . . . like . . . with you now . . . ?"

The shriek on the other end of the line was kind of hard to hide. Deen yanked her phone from her ear and grinned at her brother. "Ha ha. She's driving. Just . . . hold on . . ."

Mac held out his hand for the phone. Deen gave it to him reluctantly.

Whatever Tracey said to him, he nodded. "Cool, thanks. Drive safe." And that was that. "Next time," he said to Deen, "tell me before you let something like this happen. Now it's too dark to stick around. Car's this way."

The girls watched him trek down the path to the parking lot.

"Oh my God, I thought I was going to barf," Becca said.

"You and me both."

"I can't believe she went through like that. Like some sort of . . . door in the sky or something," Becca said.

Simultaneously, they looked back at the knot. It was impossible to see in the gloom. Becca bit her lip.

"I wish I had a friend who'd do that for me."

Deen took her hand. "You do, silly. Two of them. Obviously."

Becca looked emotional. She pulled her hand away. "To be clear, I wouldn't do it for you."

Deen threw an arm around her. "Yeah, you would."

Together, they followed Mac down the pathway. At least the worse part was over.

Or maybe it had just begun.

54

"WHAT!"

Tracey screamed into the phone. "What the— Oh, hi! Sorry. Uh . . . driving . . ." She took a breath. "You must be Mac. Yes, sure, everything is fine. Candace is fine. Sorry for the confusion. Okay. I will. Bye-bye."

Tracey hung up and dropped into her chair, the letter she'd been writing forgotten. The one in which she was telling Candace to visit her in Wisconsin. The one in which she was saying goodbye.

"No, no, no, no, no," she muttered, burying her face in her hands. Her purple fountain pen rolled to the floor.

Loretta, gone. Candace, gone.

She'd lost them both.

This was so much worse than moving to Wisconsin.

So much worse.

A hole opened up inside of her where her stomach used to be, and she fell through it, and kept falling and falling and falling . . .

The same hole she'd fallen through the day she'd lost her mom.

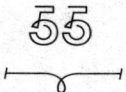

TRACEY PICKED UP THE PEN. HER UNPOSSIBLE PEN.

She stood up, looked around her half-empty apartment.

She wasn't nine years old anymore. She was an *adult*.

She had responsibilities.

She had agency.

And she had a car.

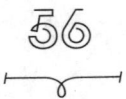

CANDACE EMERGED IN A WOOD. BUT NOT THE SAME wood as the one she'd left behind. For one, it was colder. Brighter, too, although the sky was dimming toward evening. And the trees smelled different. Less moldering leaves, more piney. She was also ten feet above the ground, standing on the limb of a winter-bare tree. She shimmied over to the trunk and eased herself into a sitting position. Behind her and above her, the knot roiled, like a boiling pot of sky.

"I can breathe," she said. So, not a vacuum at least. "And I'm alive." Which was a more obvious observation, given the first one. Still, she opened her little notebook and jotted down both facts. Then she pulled out her cell phone, which still had power, if no reception, and took some pictures of the knot and Loretta's brave new world. Then she did a quick sketch of the trees.

Despite the height of her tree limb, she couldn't see very far. The trees were mostly evergreens, hence the smell.

If it got dark, she had a flashlight, but she didn't love the idea of walking in a dark wood alone. Then again, Candace had fallen out of her own bed once or twice when she was little. Spending the night in a tree had its own hazards.

"Okay, down to the ground," she said, taking comfort from

her own voice. The only other sounds were of the wind in the trees and, distantly, the singing of birds. Interdimensional magpies, she assumed.

Candace pulled some regular yellow hiking rope from her bag and looped it over the tree limb, one side pinched in a U. She pulled the open ends through and tugged until the rope was tight on the limb. Then she used the rope to steady her descent, her father's thick winter gloves on her hands to protect them from rope burn. She had purple rope in her bag, too, but it wouldn't do to attract magpies that might want to steal it. After all, this could be the only way back home. Yes, she'd have to figure out how to climb the tree again—she should have used a rope ladder instead—but that seemed surmountable. At least the dangling yellow rope would tell her which tree to climb.

She pulled out a little compass and her map, then tried to figure out which way was north. If there *was* a north here. Whatever it was, the compass seemed to tug in one direction. She unfolded a piece of graph paper and laid it over her map, orienting it toward "North." Marking a square at the bottom corner of the page with an X for the knot, she drew a spiral. This would be her path; no matter which way Loretta had gone, she would find her. Hopefully. She set her phone's timer for ten minutes and started walking. When her phone vibrated, she marked a smaller X on the graph, a trail that would lead back to the knot in ten-minute segments. She reset the timer.

The woods were as normal as woods in her world. Not that she was an expert on woods, but the suburbs of Chicago had some pretty impressive preserves. She froze a couple of times at the sound of something scuffling in the underbrush, but nothing came out. No squirrels or birds or deer. Just a wild silence and her own thoughts.

She had kissed Mitchell. On the cheek, sure, but she had *kissed him*. He really did seem to like her. What if he was trying to reach her? She checked her phone. No bars, no nothing. Just the ten-minute vibrations. What if he was texting her right now and she was stuck in a fold in the universe and couldn't get back to him?

"You're an othernaut, Candace," she muttered, and put away her phone. Mitchell would have to wait. There were worlds to explore.

The woods went on forever. Or at least that was how it felt. Whatever passed for a sun on this side was invisible now that she was on the ground, and the sky was getting really dim. Candace did *not* want to be stuck in the woods at night alone. She debated shouting Loretta's name. But what if someone or something else heard her?

For the first time in her life, Candace realized she was completely alone. Even when they were fighting, Becca and Deen had been there when it mattered. And her mom and dad had never left her side. Roaming the city looking for magpies had been a group effort. Mr. Jones and Ms. Parker had been pretty involved in her art science project. But this . . .

Candace took a deep breath to still the butterflies in her stomach. Every adventure story had a moment like this, when the hero was left to their own devices. Every *story*, imagined or real, had this moment when the hero had to decide if they were going to forge their own path. Candace looked around her. The other side was completely new. Loretta had faced it on her own. So could she.

But then she realized she didn't have to.

Loretta had done it first!

There were footsteps to follow in. She just had to find them.

Candace kept scanning the forest floor as she walked, but it wasn't the sort of story where Loretta left breadcrumbs or anything. As it got darker, Candace turned on her flashlight and immediately turned it off. It made her feel too exposed. Instead, she moved tree to tree for what felt like hours. But it was better than attracting an animal, or walking off a cliff. Which was probably why she smelled the breadcrumb trail before she saw it. Leaning against a tree trunk, the smell of pine sap was extra sharp. Someone had cut an arrow into the bark. She reached out a hand to feel the pale edges on the dark trunk.

That was worth turning her flashlight on again. She marked the spot on her graph paper with a big arrow, then looked for another arrow. A few trees ahead, she found it. There was a path to follow after all.

Something rustled in the underbrush. Candace froze, turned off her flashlight. *Just a squirrel,* she told herself. Or whatever passed for squirrels on this side of the knot. She hoped. Maybe it was better to wait until morning, when she could see.

Candace settled against the tree trunk with its pale arrow and waited for dawn.

Dawn was actually still pretty dark. Candace wiped the sleep from her eyes and took a granola bar and bottle of water from her backpack. She was going to have to pee in the actual woods, which she hadn't really planned for. But at least she had hand sanitizer.

Once it was light enough to make sure she could find the marked tree again, she went behind some scrub brush and did her business, hoping Loretta didn't pop out of the bushes before she was done. Loretta did not.

Candace followed the arrows, no longer walking the spiral, but a straight line. She picked up her pace. The day grew brighter. And then the marks on the trees stopped.

"What?" Candace made a slow circle around the nearest trees. Nothing. Maybe Loretta hadn't been blazing a trail. Maybe she really was here all alone.

Overhead, a bird suddenly burst into song, high and sweet. Candace recognized the melody. It sounded like a Jordan magpie. It sounded like hope.

She changed direction, moving toward the birdsong.

And then up ahead the trees grew thin. She hoped it was the end of the forest. But it was just a clearing, with more trees on the other side.

Except, in the middle of the clearing, someone was sitting on a fallen log with their back to Candace.

She gasped and slowed her steps. But she wasn't exactly stealthy. The whistling stopped. And the person half turned her way.

"Is that you, youngblood?"

57

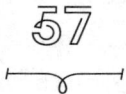

"LORETTA!" CANDACE RACED FORWARD TO SEE IF SHE was real. "Are you hurt? Are you okay?"

"Stop fussing! I'm fine. Just a little turned around."

"Turned around? Turned around! You went through the knot! We're on the other side of reality! 'Turned around.' I can't believe you did this!" Candace burst into tears.

Loretta pulled her down into a hug and patted her until her sobs became hiccups.

"And I can't believe you followed me in. That was foolish."

"I came to bring you home."

"You were supposed to wait for me, youngblood. I sent you a letter."

"Well, I didn't get it," Candace said. "What kind of letter?"

"One telling you to look for me in forty years."

They held each other on the fallen log in the woods for a long moment. Candace could feel Loretta quivering in her arms. No, not quivering. Laughing.

"You followed me! I can't believe it. Come to take me home! How will we do that, youngblood? Climb back up that tree?"

"Well, yeah. I brought a rope."

"So did I, youngblood." She pointed to the kind of emergency ladder people were supposed to keep in their houses in case of fire. Folded up next to the log, it had real metal rungs strung across bright orange nylon ribbons, with two hooks at the top. "Nearly killed me on the way down. But the real question is, is there still a ladder on the other side?"

"I thought we could use the rope again."

Loretta did not look enthusiastic about that.

"You got any food?" She gestured at her backpack. "I'm tired of nutrition bars."

"Sure." Candace slung her own pack to the ground and rummaged inside. "Water, too. And a first aid kit. What do you need?"

"A turkey sandwich and a bowl of soup," Loretta said. "But I'll settle for whatever you've got."

That turned out to be a peanut butter and jelly sandwich, which they decided to share.

"How long have you been here?" Candace looked around for the first time and realized Loretta had built a camp for herself. There was a small circle of rocks with the remains of a fire in it, and a tent the same gray-green as the trees, so that she'd missed it at first.

"Couple of days. Well, three, as of this morning. How long was I missing out there?"

"The same."

"Huh." Loretta pulled out a notepad and made a note.

"I have one of those, too," Candace said, holding hers up. "And a map. Well, of our side. And I'm making one of this side. I think I know where the Sand Cave knot lets out, if we can find the right exit point."

"So it might be more like a courtyard than a subway,"

Loretta mused as Candace unfolded the map. She spread her old hands like branches. "A place of entrances and exits."

"Like in book three, when Lilabet faces multiple options in the Library of Empty Books," Candace said. In the story, Lilabet walked down a long hallway lined with different-colored doors.

Loretta was staring at her.

"What?" Candace asked.

"You finally read the books?"

Candace's face went hot. "I read summaries of the books on the drive to the Sand Cave."

"Summaries." Loretta's mouth hardened.

"I'm sorry! I just really had a lot of reading for school!"

And then Loretta was shaking again until her mouth burst open with the biggest, horsiest laugh yet. A twig snapped in the woods. Loud as a gunshot.

"What was that?" Candace yelped.

Loretta nudged her. "Youngblood, get my gun."

"You have a gun!" Candace exclaimed.

"No, but they don't know that," Loretta hissed. She pulled a flashlight from her backpack. "I got my gun on you!" she shouted at the trees.

"No! Don't shoot! Don't shoot!" a voice cried. "It's me!"

And a figure emerged from the trees, hands in the air and a piece of paper in one hand. In the other was a purple fountain pen.

"Tracey?" Loretta exclaimed. "How on earth did *you* get here?"

"I drove. With Candace's map." Tracey waved the piece of paper and lowered her hands. "You were right, kid. We're in Canada. Welcome to New Canaan."

"Hmpf," Loretta said. "Is that my pen?"

53

"SO I GUESS I WON'T SEE YOU FOR FORTY YEARS AFTER all," Deen said. Candace's parents were allowing her one phone call to tell her friends how she was doing.

"Hardee har har," Candace said, but it wasn't far from the truth.

Tracey had followed Candace's spiral map to New Canaan and relied on eBird sightings of magpies in the area. Sighting the smoke from Loretta's fire had been sheer luck, but Loretta said that was true for most explorers. They had made it out of the woods with Tracey's help and called her parents as soon as they had a cell signal, which wasn't very long. She'd texted Deen and Becca, and Mitchell—who actually had been trying to reach her. It turned out Loretta's pen was what had been bothering Tracey the whole time. It was proof she could hold in her hands that the knots were real, which was why she hadn't told them she had it. But that day, hiking out of the forest to her car, she confessed. Loretta let her keep the pen.

"Proof that 'there are more things in heaven and earth,'" Loretta had said. Which was apparently a line from Shakespeare.

They'd piled into Tracey's car, driven past the Underground Railroad Museum, and found a motel to spend the night—

Loretta had insisted on a bath and some real food. In the morning, they'd driven home.

Candace was glad she'd brought her passport. Crossing the border was a little scary, but not a huge deal.

Back in Chicago, Lotte called off the police search and took Loretta to the doctor for a checkup, just in case, with much complaining on Loretta's end.

Candace's parents had swept her into a big hug. Lotte hailed Candace as a hero and praised both her and Tracey.

But the minute everyone had left, Candace was in the doghouse big-time.

"Running away? To Canada! My Lord, how did you even get across the border! No, I don't want to know," her mother said.

"But if you do it again, you can stay over there," her father said. "That was a foolish thing."

"I know," Candace said. It was more foolish than they would ever realize. But it was also necessary. Her mother had hugged her again, then swatted her lightly on the bottom. "Now take a bath and go to bed."

The rules after running away were strict. Her parents would drop her off at school and pick her up immediately afterward. She was not allowed to spend time with Deen or Becca or anyone—not even Tracey, who her parents considered an angel for rescuing their little girl.

Which, really, was all fine by Candace.

After all, she'd been through a window in the sky.

If she had to wait another forty years to leave her bedroom, she could.

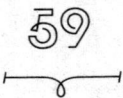

THE LAST MEETING OF THE YOUNGBLOODS CLUB DIDN'T take place until school was over. Loretta, Tracey, and Candace met at a diner in McHenry. Candace's parents joined Lotte at a booth across the room, ordering lunch. They'd been reluctant to let Candace out of their sight again.

"Those women are a bad influence," her father said.

"Those women are remarkable," her mother added. "Too remarkable for a fourteen-year-old." But they'd been willing to bring her anyway.

"So," Tracey said, after the waitress delivered their drinks—black coffee for Loretta, a latte for Tracey, and a peanut butter milkshake for Candace—"the knots are basically portals."

"To human senses, anyway," Loretta said. "It was in one side, out the other. But birds don't see things the way we do."

"Ultraviolet rays," Candace said, sketching on her art pad. She paused to squinch up the paper wrapping on her straw into a crinkled worm shape. Scooping some of the condensation off the side of her milkshake glass, she sprinkled a couple of drops on the paper and watched it writhe.

"And I've got a new hypothesis," Loretta announced. "Candace's chickasaur theory about Fermilab. Did the accelerator cause the knots across time, or are they naturally occurring? That would make the lab a coincidence, which I don't like. Or—"

"Or maybe the knots made the location more, I don't know, accelerator friendly?" Candace said. She pulled out her phone. "Whoa. There are over thirty thousand accelerators in the world. Why? If they thought it would rip apart the universe, why build so many of them?"

Tracey shook her head. "Hubris," she said. "Recklessness."

Loretta just swatted the table with her hands and said, "Science."

"So, we should set up bird alerts at all the accelerator sites?"

"For a start," Loretta agreed. "But you can narrow the list. Accelerators come in different sizes and with different capabilities. It makes sense to begin with the Hadron Collider in Switzerland. It's the biggest, and then at least we'd know if the knots were global." She grinned. "This might be so much bigger than I ever imagined."

Tracey seemed less enthused by that idea. "Maybe we should just stick to Illinois for now. I'm not flying to Switzerland to bring you back home. Besides, this knot is fascinating historically speaking, right? An instant doorway to the promised land? We should explore the entire Underground Railroad. Who knows what other entry and exit points exist."

Loretta clucked her tongue. "Somebody's been bit by the bug." Candace grinned.

"Me?" Tracey said. "You're the one who risked her life out of curiosity," she pointed out. "And curiosity killed the cat."

Loretta laughed. "That's only half the saying, youngblood."

"Oh yeah, what's the other half?"

"Curiosity killed the cat. Satisfaction brought him back."

Candace started to chuckle. Loretta joined in. Tracey shook her head at their lunacy, but it was infectious. Across the diner, Candace's parents glanced their way. And then the bell over the diner doorway rang and Deen and Becca entered with Mac. Mac sat with the other grown-ups. The girls slid into the booth next to Candace.

"What's so funny?" Becca wanted to know.

"Everything, apparently," Tracey said.

Candace finished the sketch she'd been doing and snapped a picture with her phone for her This Is Us album: Loretta, Tracey, and Candace in the woods.

Loretta slapped her palm on the table like a gavel and said, "All right now, I'm calling us to order. Last session of the Youngbloods Club is closed."

Candace flipped her sketch pad to a new page. Loretta slapped the table again.

"Let the first meeting of the Othernauts begin!"

ACKNOWLEDGMENTS

The trouble with books is that they take a long time to write, and some of the people you are writing them for grow up while they are waiting. This book took a long time. A pandemic, an election, and a lot of unknowns about this world pushed what was meant to be a contemporary story into the realm of post-apocalyptic science fiction. It grew, and grew, shifting shape until it was too unwieldy to survive outside the draft phase. And then the pandemic wound down enough to allow me to sit with a writer friend and tell her my woes. That brilliant woman had the presence of mind to tell me I had not written a bad novel. Rather, I had written two novels, and I just needed to find a way to untangle them. It was like she had revealed a dotted line. Thank you, Cecil Castellucci!

But that wasn't the end of the story. Candace changed ages and schools, with advice from my editor, Stephanie Pitts. She lost a boyfriend and gained friend who is a boy. She still lived in Chicago, where I also attended eighth grade at the nearly completely bird-free Louisa May Alcott Elementary. And her locker neighbor, Cerise, is named in honor of Cerise O'Connor, a young woman I met before the pandemic even began. She sat through a class I taught on writing comics at an author event in East Washington and shared her story with me. Cerise, I hope you're not too old to enjoy this book. Sorry for the wait.

Many thanks to my local Audubon Society for guiding me on my first bird walk and my first bird sit. Deep thanks to Hedgebrook writing retreat for a room of my own in which to wrestle with this story, and to my cohort: Catharina Coenen, Jenna van de Ruit, Lola Milholland, Emi Nietfeld, and Monique Laban. Our wish circle worked! At least on the book front. World peace and healing are pending.

To my dad, the chemist, who knew what it was like to be one of a few in his profession. And to my father-in-law, also in chemistry, who knew the same. Thanks to my agent, Kirby Kim, for getting behind this indescribable book. Special thanks to Stephanie Singleton for her gorgeous cover art. And to everyone at dinner who gasped when I summed it up as "the girl with the wormhole in her locker." To my niece and nephew for explaining middle school dating norms. To my husband for all of the title changes and suggestions along the way. And to my mother, who was my Tracey, my Loretta, and my window in the sky.

SHERRI L. SMITH is the author of numerous acclaimed fiction and nonfiction books for young people, including *Pearl: A Graphic Novel*, art by Christine Norrie; *American Wings: Chicago's Pioneering Black Aviators and the Race for Equality in the Sky*, co-authored with Elizabeth Wein; *Flygirl*, the winner of the California Book Awards' Gold Medal; *The Blossom and the Firefly*, the winner of the Golden Kite Award from the Society of Children's Book Writers and Illustrators; and *Orleans*. She teaches creative writing at Hamline University. Born in Chicago, Sherri now lives in Los Angeles.

SHERRILSMITH.COM
◉ | @RHYMESWITHCAPRI